Saving Grace

D.M. Barr

Punctuated Publishing

New York

The author grants the final approval for this literary material.

Second printing

Praise for
Saving Grace

BRONZE MEDAL WINNER, PSYCHOLOGICAL THRILLERS
— 2021 READERS FAVORITE BOOK AWARDS

FINALIST 2021 BEST BOOK AWARDS (MYSTERY/SUSPENSE)

... **Ms. Barr's storytelling** is a master class of Oooh! Whee! delight ensuring her fans, old and new, a "just-one-more-chapter" reading experience they will not soon forget! *-Tonya Mathenia, InD'tale Magazine*

... **Expert pacing**...A wild ride whose propulsive energy will keep readers turning pages. An intriguing murder mystery that readers will rush to finish." *- Kirkus Reviews*

Saving Grace **is a psychological thriller** with more than enough twists, turns, and misdirection to keep even the most jaded reader turning pages all night long. It is beautifully paced and convincingly narrated, and the suspense builds to a most satisfying conclusion. A terrific read, from start to finish. *- Lori Robbins, author of the Silver Falchion Award-winning novel, Lesson Plan for Murder*

Saving Grace **is a fun and fast-paced mystery that will have you laughing out loud,** while you're wondering if Grace will save herself and catch the bad guys. If you like Susan Isaacs, you'll love D.M. Barr. *- Cathi Stoler, author of BAR NONE A Murder on The Rocks Mystery*

Is Grace a delusional paranoid in need of psychiatric help or is she really in danger of being murdered by the husband who seems so solicitous? That's the question in *Saving Grace,* an unstoppable rollercoaster of a novel that is one part *Gaslight* and one part *Suspicion*, topped with a twist of Me-Too. Reality itself shifts, as the suspense builds and Grace fights to define who and what she is. Masterfully written and plotted with memorable characters, *Saving Grace* asks the reader to look beneath the surface to find the truth. I give this novel an enthusiastic two thumbs up. *- S. Lee Manning, author of Trojan Horse*

Saving Grace is a roller coaster ride of fun and frantic sleuthing that steadily builds to a thrilling climax. A page turner, *Saving Grace* was impossible to put down! -*Suzanne Trauth, Author, Dodie O'Dell Mystery Series*

This twist-filled mystery by D.M. Barr offers plenty of wit, a nice supporting cast, heart-stopping finale and, best of all, an underestimated, in-over-her-head hero worth rooting for. - *Deb Pines, author of the Mimi Goldman Chautauqua Murder Mystery Series.*

The latest treat for mystery lovers and a contemporary story of riveting suspense. - *June Trop, author of the Miriam bat Isaac Mystery Series*

Saving Grace **is a testament to a main character literally writing her way** out of mortal danger, with more than one dead body along the way. - *Rona Bell, author of the award-winning short story, Prey of New York.*

This book is a page-turner, with many twists and turns. The writing is well crafted, creating a fast-paced, exciting scenario. Author D. M. Barr will keep every reader on the edge of her/his seat in this compelling work. A fascinating read! - *Deborah Lloyd, Readers' Favorite*

Saving Grace **by D.M. Barr was an exciting psychological thriller.** I haven't read anything quite like it before. I would highly recommend this book to others and am excited to see what else this author has in store! - *Shannon Winings for Readers' Favorite*

I enjoyed Saving Grace because it is a complex novel that will keep you intrigued. D.M. Barr has done a great job of writing a wonderful suspense thriller that will keep you intrigued to the very last page. - *Sherri Fulmer Moorer for Readers' Favorite*

D.M. Barr weaves a yarn with strong themes and characters that are real and fascinating. I couldn't put it down. *Saving Grace: A Psychological Thriller* was a wonderful companion for the night. - *Ruffina Oserio for Readers' Favorite*

To my grandmother,
Judith Koch Ferester
You always made me proud of every word I wrote.
All the success and heartache that followed, I owe to you.

Acknowledgements

I've said it in previous books, but it's never been truer than for *Saving Grace*: no author writes a book in a vacuum. This novel exists due to the assistance and encouragement of some very special people:

Without the advice of the amazing writer and editor Elf Ahearn, the entire second half of this book, including any mention of computer hacking and Bitcoin exchange, would not exist. John Paine's edits inspired *Saving Grace's* most vibrant dramatic scenes. And developmental editor Terri Bischoff's insistence that I focus on Grace's story over all subplots was responsible for making my publishing contract a reality. So, my undying thanks to the three of you.

Thanks also to Gary Lipton, Esq. for advising me on estate law; to Michael Zaretsky for verifying the library situation at mental institutions; and to Efraim Kastel, my go-to guy for all questions Yiddish and Hasidic. To Mordechai Ekstein and everyone at Ark for inspiring me with your humor to write Zev and make him one of my favorite characters. Thanks to mortgage expert Alfie Schloss who advised me on reverse mortgages even though that entire subplot didn't make it past my first draft. To John Schneider and Betty Hirsh for your excellent beta reads and comments. And to my son Justin, who deigned to explain what today's kids say now instead of "Cool!" and ultimately relented on his demand for a quarter of my royalties in return. I warned you no lawyer would take the case.

To my NY/Tri-State Sisters in Crime chapter, my Mystery Writers of America chapter, and the Hudson Valley Romance Writers (especially my critique partners), you rock! You never fail to educate me, inspire me, and keep me sane. Thank you.

And finally, to my long-suffering husband Josh, children Justin and Julianne, my father, brother, sisters-in-law, my trivia team (Go Penguins!), social media contacts, readers and friends: I know all I do is talk about writing. I realize I'm insufferable. Thanks for your tolerance. I owe you, big time. Someday, I'll find something else to discuss. Just not any time soon.

Saving Grace

Part One

Chapter One

One felony was all it took to convince Andrea Lin she was better suited to committing crime on paper than in person. As renowned mystery author Lynn Andrews, she understood conflict equaled good drama. Like her readers, she should have expected the hiccups, even relished them. What she hadn't counted on was the accompanying agita, especially while sitting in her Bergen County kitchen, far from the action at the Bitcoin Teller Machine.

Her one job had been to place a single phone call when the money hit and tell the hacker to lift the encryption on Grace's computer. Trouble was, her dozen calls remained unanswered until a few minutes ago, throwing their meticulous plan off schedule.

Andrea stroked the blue-gray Nebulung purring on her lap and tried to ignore the churning in her stomach. "Denver, the next time I consider helping a sibling with some crazy scheme, you have my permission to use my leg as a scratching post until I come to my senses. Agreed?"

Denver looked up, his green eyes filled with innocence, and answered with a single meow before leaping onto the table toward her plate of shortbread cookies.

"I'll take that as a yes." She sipped her tea, willing the sugar to sweeten the acrid taste in her mouth. The phone interrupted her meditation. No doubt a check-in from her brother, the extorter-in-chief.

"I figured you'd have called by now. Everything on track?" Joe's strained voice conveyed his own jangled nerves. They'd agreed to be vague when communicating. In these days of Siri and Alexa, anyone could be listening.

"Finally. Took forever to get through to our friend, but she said she'd take care of 'our project' as soon as her meetings wrapped up. From here on out though, I'm sticking to fiction. Real-life intrigue is too stressful."

Andrea missed Joe's response, instead perplexed by her cats' sudden change of behavior. Denver had tilted his head and leapt from the table; Vail and Aspen sat frozen, ears perked, staring toward the foyer. Then she heard it too, the sound of papers shuffling in the living room. She leaned forward, muscles taut, hackles raised, ready to pounce.

"Joe, hold on a sec. I think someone's in the house. I'll call you back later."

.   .   .

"Wait, what? Andrea??" Silence. The connection was dead.

After twenty minutes of weaving in and out of rush-hour traffic to travel one mile, Joe "Hack" Hackford pulled up outside his sister's Ridgewood home. Adrenaline pumping on overdrive, he jumped from his car and sprinted toward the house. Door wide open—not an encouraging sign. He steeled his nerves and hastened inside. The living room looked like a hurricane's aftermath, with furniture overturned and papers littering the carpets and floor.

"Andrea? Are you here?" He rushed into the kitchen, which lacked any signs of their celebratory dinner—no spaghetti boiling on the stove, no cake rising in the oven. Only the door to the backyard ajar and a shriek emanating from the next room, piercing the eerie silence. Hair stiffening at the back of his neck, he raced into the dining room where a redheaded woman stood frozen, staring across the room.

"Who the hell are you?" he growled.

The stranger remained wide-eyed and unresponsive. He followed her gaze to the floor, where he witnessed the unthinkable. His beloved sister lay in the corner, surrounded by a pool of blood, a kitchen knife stuck in her chest. Her eyes remained fixed on the ceiling. A trio of feline guards circled her lifeless body.

Hack's knees turned to jelly, and he grabbed onto a chair for support, forcing back the remains of the snack he'd consumed only minutes earlier. Once the initial shock waned, he reverted his attention back to the intruder. At second glance, she did look somewhat familiar, though the woman he'd met a few weeks back—the missing heiress whose computer they'd just hacked—was brunette. Had she uncovered their con? With a bolt of fury, he reached forward and pulled the wig from her head. A thousand questions zigzagged in his brain, but only one forced its way past his lips:

"Oh my God. Grace. Oh my God. What the hell have you done?"

Chapter Two

Four Months Earlier

Grace Rendell tried in vain to focus on her therapist's questions, and not the excitement humming through her veins. Newfound clarity threatened her mission: to maintain her usual flat affect if she hoped to get away with this charade.

Behind and above her doctor's head, a kamikaze fly's repeated attempts to escape the room had captured her attention. It would collide with the pane facing out onto the garden, only to retreat and then again confront the glass. Grace admired the tenacity. It was either the world's most determined insect, or one brain-damaged beyond repair. If flies had brains, that is. She wasn't sure. But assuming it *had* a brain, one impaired somehow, then they were kindred spirits, and what better place to meet than her psychiatrist's office?

"Grace, you were saying?" Dr. Emma Leighmann raised her eyebrows, her blond pageboy and plump, cheerful face making her appear younger than someone in her mid-sixties. "How do you plan to handle tonight's event?"

I splurged on a 'slim cool black dress, black sandals and a pearl choker' just like Holly Golightly. Well, more chunky than slim, but I don't imagine Truman Capote will come back from the grave and say anything. Grace tucked away her sarcasm and assumed her usual, monotonous tone. "I'm not sure. So many new people..."

Leighmann would flip if she learned the truth. Over the past month, Grace had committed the ultimate offense: weaning herself off Klonopin, Topomax, Abilify and her other psychotropic meds. While her usual cocktail of pills didn't prevent her from working, driving, or mothering her kids, they dulled her outlook and caused her to doubt her perceptions. Was it so terrible to crave acuity on such a special night?

She'd been one-hundred percent "clean" for a full week now, though she'd spent part of that time in bed, attributing the nausea, tremors, sweating, and other withdrawal symptoms to a bad case of the flu. Her family had bought the story, thank God. So far, so good.

"Let's look past the strangers, keep our eyes on the prize. What are your goals for the evening?"

Despite Leighmann's urging, Grace hesitated to respond. Far safer to concentrate on the insect's dilemma than her own desire to appear more lucid than languid for just one evening. After twenty-five years of marriage, didn't Eliot deserve that? If she were present and attentive tonight, it might put an end to their sexual drought. And if so, perhaps the late nights and frequent absences would also end, the ones he always explained away as work-related.

Invitations to his company's annual holiday party usually excluded spouses, or so Eliot told her, year after year. But this Thanksgiving, he'd made a point of inviting her. It had to mean something. A détente in their cold war? She'd taken a long, hard look in the mirror that morning. At forty-five, she no longer got mistaken for Sandra Bullock. But despite the trappings of middle age—the dark under-eye circles, the few rogue silver strands that eluded her bottle of Clairol, the unwelcome bulges that homesteaded on formerly flat land—was it possible that desirability didn't have an expiration date?

"Grace? Your goals?" The therapist tapped her notebook against her thigh.

The fly's buzzing reverberated, drowning out Leighmann's question. How to help it escape without appearing too focused? An idea sprang to mind, something that would play right into her doctor's expectations.

Grace gasped for breath, slowly at first and then steadily increasing until she reached full-blown hyperventilation. She tottered toward the window, winking at the fly while waiting for Leighmann to take the hint and let in some cold November air. The doctor jumped up and hurried to her side, leaving Grace delighted at the success of her plan.

Swat.

Leighmann pulled her notebook from the window and the fly's tiny carcass fell to the floor. Then she unlatched the sashes and lifted the bottom pane, urging Grace to suck in the lungfuls of oxygen she craved.

After a few deep breaths, Grace slunk back to her seat; her burgeoning mania tempered by what she saw as a clear omen of the night ahead. For the next thirty minutes, she sat comatose as Leighmann rambled on, certain that the doctor expected nothing more of her, and angry at herself that for once, she had.

Once Grace got out into the fresh air and put some distance between herself and her therapist, she started perking up again. No one could remain anesthetized with autumn air so crisp, the leaves' colors so vibrant, the streets teeming with activity. How sad that since childhood, her meds had blinded her to the sweetness of everyday living.

She hopped into her Volvo, wondering how to get through the next few hours without drowning in anticipation over the evening's festivities. The boys had extracurriculars and afterward, they could finish off the meatloaf she'd left in the fridge. Her boss didn't expect her back at work until the next morning. Then she remembered the three overdue books on the passenger seat and shifted into drive.

The Glen Valley Library occupied an aging Victorian on Main Street, but to Grace, it outshone the finest estate. More like a universe, with each tome promising a glimpse into a realm that existed beyond her limited confines. She'd amassed most of her life knowledge from those books and magazines.

Vivian at the Returns Desk waved as she approached. "Did you like them, Grace? Anything you'd recommend?"

Grace shrugged. "I enjoyed the mystery; Harlan Coben is always exciting to read. The contemporary romances weren't realistic, though. Married life is hard work, nothing like they portray in novels. Don't you agree?"

"I guess it depends on the marriage. And on the book. You're just in time for today's lecture. It started a few minutes ago so you haven't missed much."

"Lecture? What's the topic?"

Vivian handed Grace a flyer. "It's about teaching literacy. You read so much; volunteering would be a natural for you."

Grace reviewed the leaflet with trepidation. She'd never attended any of the library's events but today, her newfound alertness imbued everything with hope. She walked toward the large meeting room and grabbed a seat close to the exit, but soon found herself riveted by the speaker's enthusiastic account of the program's achievements. "Every day, we see the results of our tutoring. Parents cry as they describe the first time they read bedtime stories to their children. Immigrants brag about passing their citizenship tests. High school dropouts earn their GED and qualify for jobs to help support their families. We aren't reading coaches. We are life changers!"

When the speaker finished and asked if there were questions, Grace raised a shaky hand. "Are any mental assessments or qualifications required?"

"Only a desire to find direction and purpose in life." His uplifting response met with a hearty round of applause.

Grace had expected the speaker to describe the joys of literature, like sharing Tom Joad's journey from Oklahoma to California or Dagny Taggart's discovery that the thinkers of the world had gone on strike. What she heard instead transformed her. Considering her sons wouldn't even trust her to help them with their homework, she'd never imagined herself becoming a positive force in another person's education. Who knew what her students might achieve? Perhaps careers as teachers, lawyers, surgeons. She signed up for the next volunteer training session. First her husband's party invitation and now this. Life without meds overflowed with possibility.

■　　　■　　　■

As the Manhattan skyline loomed in the distance, bright against the clouds cloaking the moon, Grace tried to ignore the Uber driver's erratic weaving and instead, smoothed her new dress. Expensive for Macy's, but why not splurge for once? Between their two salaries, she and Eliot lived a comfortable-enough lifestyle, though they earmarked every penny for monthly expenses and savings. Almost no discretionary income remained. A far cry from the servants, the frills, the luxurious lifestyle she'd known in her youth.

Grace's entire body quivered with anticipation. When had she ever felt this alive? So much for the repercussions of discontinuing her prescriptions. Dr. Leighmann's doomsday warnings had yet to materialize: the return of the voices, the hallucinations, the violent outbursts. All scare tactics, designed to ensure the therapist's most precious commodity—an incurable patient—translated into revenue everlasting.

Grace's confidence flagged as she searched for Eliot in the Pierre Hotel's ornate gold ballroom. As she squeezed past each cluster of martini-sipping, preened trophy wives adorned in their silks, satins, and diamond accoutrements, she felt like a Rorschach inkblot accidently dripped onto a Botticelli canvas. But if her husband was embarrassed by her *Breakfast at Tiffany's* look, his effusive greeting masked any discomfort.

"There she is, my better half." Eliot exuded what looked like authentic admiration and introduced her to his co-workers: the girls from the secretarial pool, his fellow account execs and their wives, the team from Creative. Even his slip-of-a-secretary Sheryl, all doe-eyed and reverent, interrupted her Eliot-fawning long enough to kiss Grace on the cheek. Grace clenched her teeth, recalling all Sheryl's past visits to the house, claiming some "weekend work emergency." Flirtatious interference that no doubt contributed to her marriage's persistent lack of intimacy, a truth she tried not to dwell on, though it gnawed at her every night they slept in the same bed.

As the room filled, the swirl of new names became too extensive to keep straight. Eliot kept his arm around her as they mingled, reminding her with every drink of the dangers of mixing antidepressants with alcohol. She waved him off as she downed a few glasses of the free-flowing Pinot Noir. It was a non-issue, but if she admitted to being unmedicated, the ensuing argument would ruin their entire evening.

Grace laughed more than she had in years. For once, the elusive gods of small talk were smiling down on her. A cadre of tuxedo-clad waiters tempted her with elegant canapes. Diet be damned, she indulged in decadent mini-lobster rolls, filet mignon bites and chilled green pea soup served in shot glasses. She passed only on the skewers of chicken sate, dripping in peanut sauce. The smell alone had her checking her purse for her EpiPen.

How sharp Eliot looked in his Armani suit, his jet-black hair and gold-rimmed glasses accentuating green eyes speckled with gold. All reminiscent of what had initially attracted her. Charming, attentive, and driven. He had worked hard to escape the food stamps, the welfare checks, the Section 8 housing of his youth—a million miles from her world of butlers and beach bungalows. Success looked good on him. Grace leaned closer, even more confident that tonight would resuscitate the ardor in their marriage.

After about an hour, the wine got the best of her. She excused herself and tried to walk a straight line to the Ladies Room. Even in her tipsy state, she noted the bathroom's elegance surpassed many living rooms in *House & Garden*. As she stumbled into the stall, she overheard two women gossiping to her left.

"That's what's passing for hors d'oeuvres these days?"

"The Four Seasons does it so much better. The waiters are half-asleep, did you notice?"

"What do you expect for minimum wage? Speaking of which, did you catch a look at Eliot's wife?"

Grace strained to slow her pulse, eager to hear the strangers' impressions of her hair and dress. God knows she had worked hard to pull off a decent look tonight and make her husband proud.

The other voice laughed. "When there's that big a discrepancy in looks, it means one of two things. She's either kinky or she's rich. And apparently blind as well. I've heard that he and that doting little secretary of his are an item. Ambitious, that Sheryl. Rumor is, Eliot's the first rung on her five-year climb to VP."

"Well, my guess is she's one of many. He takes a lot of *extended* lunches." The two collapsed into titters.

Open-jawed and stunned, Grace's stomach plummeted. She struggled to hold back tears as the women splashed some water into the sink, ran the hand blower and left.

She lingered in her stall, waiting for a wave of nausea to pass. When she emerged, she found the bathroom empty. The mirror reflected a face apparition-pale, yet she lacked the motivation to redden her cheeks. She reached for the faucet and then froze. *How odd*. Grace checked the other three basins. All were bone-dry. She pursed her lips, rinsed her hands, and pulled a paper towel from the dispenser. The women *had* been there, hadn't they?

She staggered through the throng of guests to Eliot's side, trying to ignore the laughter no doubt directed at her expense, the poor, naïve simpleton who didn't have a clue. Every time her husband whispered into another guest's ear, she imagined him apologizing for her, or propositioning a future conquest. It took every ounce of self-control to hold herself together until exhausted, she feigned a migraine and begged him to take her home. Other than the labored smile he pasted across his lips while paying the coat check and valet, he kept his disappointment over their early departure to himself.

On the drive back to Glen Valley, Grace pulled at her cuticles, lost in contemplation. *How many others had there been? Or was it all just a malicious rumor, spread by jealous co-workers?*

It wasn't as if she hadn't suspected something all along. But when you spend a lifetime being drugged into lethargy, your every perception corrected, you begin to accept the viewpoints of others over your own. Why attempt to decipher the truth, when speaking up will only lead to more recrimination? Veer too close to reality, and you'll earn yourself a week or two in a mental hospital to recalibrate. Far safer to keep downing your pills and sticking your head in the sand like a mama ostrich, unwilling to disturb her chicks' lives with something as disruptive as divorce. The boys' welfare had to come first. Always.

Eliot was oblivious to her introspection, crossing the George Washington Bridge with ESPN blaring over the speakers. Only after he'd heard the results of the evening's hockey and basketball skirmishes did he attempt to broach the topic of their own.

"Well, other than your migraine, I believe the evening went rather well."

"For whom, exactly?" The words tumbled out, surprising even Grace. She recognized the prudence of keeping unmedicated suspicions to herself, but her now-palpable resentment, fueled by his neglect and rumored infidelity, overpowered her instinct to suppress it.

"Honey, what's wrong?"

She gritted her teeth and said nothing more, determined to return to the status quo of emotional oblivion, where apprehensions remained safely dormant. But Eliot pursued the point, pulling off onto a Fort Lee side street and killing the engine.

"Well?"

"It's nothing." She stared out at the last vestiges of autumn, the trees' few remaining gold and red leaves illuminated by the headlights. *Don't make waves, it can't end well.*

"If it were nothing, you wouldn't have mentioned it. Grace, you have a habit of misinterpreting innocent comments. Remember the Kowalski incident? Help me understand what's bothering you, so I can set your mind at ease before anything unfortunate happens."

He's throwing the Kowalski incident in my face, again? He resurrected it whenever she dared to question another person's motives. All because early in their marriage, his friend Marie Kowalski didn't invite them to her wedding. Grace construed the slur as a reaction to her illness. Those were the early days when her dosage was weaker, and she still experienced and expressed emotion.

Outraged, she confronted Marie, accusing her of being "thoughtless" and "biased." Two days after the wedding, the dog-eared invitation arrived in the mail, misaddressed and later rerouted by the post office. Eliot called Marie to apologize, but she'd have none of it. Grace's leap to conclusion had decimated their friendship and while Eliot waved it off, she was certain he resented her for it.

Couldn't anyone make an innocent mistake, even someone neurotypical? Grace was tired of being condemned for past missteps. She yearned to reveal the true cause of her upset, but if she accused her husband of cheating, he'd cry "paranoia" and call the doctors.

"Those women...I don't want to socialize with phonies like them ever again." It sounded rational, even plausible. But when her voice cracked, it diminished some of the fury she'd attempted to convey.

His lips tightened into a frown. "You seemed to be enjoying yourself, interacting for once."

"It was an act. For your benefit. That jab about how Bergen County must be lovely this time of year, or so their maids tell them? Oh, please. They acted like they were slumming."

"Baby, I'm so sorry you misinterpreted their words. They'd never met you before, remember? They were trying to break the ice. All this agitation...have you been taking your pills?"

Grace's "fake" migraine now pounded against her temples like Judge Taylor's gavel in *To Kill a Mockingbird.* But admit he was right about her lack of meds? Never. It would undermine her entire argument.

"Why is it that whenever I try to stand up for myself, or criticize anyone for doing anything, you blame it on my issues or ask about my pills? Is there the teensiest chance that someone else might be at fault here?"

"I'm sorry, sweetheart. I didn't mean to upset you further. A quick call to Dr. Leighmann in the morning should fix everything. You may need to have your dosages checked."

"Fine." But it wasn't fine. What had started as a phony argument to mask her suspicions about his infidelity had blossomed into an indictment of her inability to see things clearly. This was a lost cause—as always. Better to swallow her upset the same way she used to swallow her medicine—daily and without question. But this night, Eliot's words had left a bitter aftertaste that his "sweethearts" and "honeys" couldn't wash away. Now they were laced with poison.

Eliot restarted the ignition and switched back to a more conversational tone.

"By the way, Old Moneybags called the house today."

"You were there?" This was unusual. Eliot spent most of his days in midtown.

"I had a client meeting in Paramus at noon, so I worked from the house."

"What did he want?"

"Nothing in particular. Wondered when you might fly down to visit."

Terrific. Grace faced out the car window again so Eliot couldn't gauge her reaction. Memories of last year's none-too-pleasant trip to her father's Palm Beach estate were enough to make her regurgitate her dinner. It wasn't that he wanted to see her, per se, but like any king, he demanded reverence and an annual tribute.

"You should go, talk about what we discussed a few months ago."

"I'll consider it." She hoped that would end the conversation. Barrington, at eighty-seven, acted as if he were immortal. He'd never informed them of his final wishes, nor the contents of his will. Grace had never found a comfortable way to raise the issue, despite Eliot's recurrent reminders that as her father's only living heir, it was her responsibility to do so.

"Book the flight. You could use the break. And the sunshine. I'd like to see you smiling again."

Not as much as you'd like to be shtupping Sheryl in my absence. She nodded and returned to her private thoughts.

∎   ∎   ∎

They arrived home to a living room in shambles, Xander lying on the couch and popcorn strewn everywhere. "We were binging on Netflix when Damian called me a doofus. So, I called him a dipwad. After that, things got out of hand." He gave her a kiss and zipped off to bed. Eliot also disappeared, leaving Grace on clean-up duty.

The best-dressed maid in Glen Valley, she sulked as she searched the utility closet for the broom and dustpan, and then realized she must have left them downstairs. She turned the corner, where she noticed the basement door ajar. Odd. She opened it further, jolted by the sound of her husband's whispers.

"More often? It might be difficult, but I'll try. Let's see how it goes."

A plan to increase the frequency of their trysts. That's the final confirmation, she decided. Everything I overheard today was true.

Broomless, she retreated in a daze, pulling a trash bag from the utility closet and then picking up every rogue kernel by hand. She gave each a woman's name before crumbling it into dust and discarding it. Daisy, Kate, Irene, Dora, each effigy disintegrated under the pressure of Grace's thumb and forefinger. She popped the one nicknamed Sheryl into her mouth, chomped on it with vigor, and then spat the pieces, one by one, across the room. *Good riddance!*

∎   ∎   ∎

Their cramped bedroom was darker than usual that evening; two of the four bulbs in the overhead fixture having burnt out that morning. Eliot was already in bed when she entered; surprising, since she had no memory of him leaving the basement while she was de-popcorning the living room. But there he lay on the mattress's left side, watching the sports highlights on his smartphone. Back turned to her, he remained oblivious to her presence as she disrobed. Another night he wouldn't attempt to see her naked, no doubt too tired from sleeping with all the girls at the office. How many evenings did that make? It was a topic she had suppressed over the years, something too humiliating to admit to herself, much less discuss with her therapist. Xander, her youngest, had recently turned fourteen. So, fourteen years plus nine months gestation equaled how many thousand nights? She didn't need a precise tabulation. She needed him to find her attractive again. Acceptable. Human.

A medicated Grace might have let the whole thing go. Clearheaded Grace was more territorial, unwilling to stand by while some bimbo shredded the marriage she'd kept cobbled together, or left her sons with an alternate-weekend father. *I got here first. I have the home field advantage, bitch.*

The challenge was, they'd lived celibate for so many years, the idea of intercourse jarred her. Despite his frequent proclamations of love, she'd read more than once that you should judge a man not by his words, but by his actions. And this bed hadn't seen action in years. Around ten years back, she'd mustered up enough courage to ask if he had someone on the side. He'd deflected, attributing her suspicions to clinical paranoia. Since then, she'd remained too embarrassed to ask again, and even more afraid to hear his response. But what she'd overheard tonight had triggered her competitive instinct. It was time to seduce him and win him back.

Grace pulled off her bra and panties. She walked over to Eliot's side of the bed, shivering and exposed, only his screen separating them. How long would it take him to notice? One minute passed, then two. No reaction. She cleared her throat. His eyes remained glued to his phone. She doubled down, determined to win this standoff and discover if anything remained between them.

"Eliot? Wanna fool around?"

His eyes strayed from the Knicks recap and took in her nakedness, blinking with chagrin.

"Grace, are you okay? The last few weeks, you haven't seemed like yourself and then tonight, so moody and erratic. Did you down too many glasses of wine?" As usual, he kept his tone measured, both his passion and anger stowed away in an emotional storage locker, no longer necessary for daily use.

Her lips parted in disbelief. She'd come on, practically thrown herself at him, and his only reaction was to chide her and accuse her of being drunk? "Two glasses of wine, and that was hours ago."

Still grasping his phone, he rolled across their sleigh bed and slid off on her side.

"You must be mistaken. I seem to remember three or four." His brow reflected concern as he rounded the bed and hugged her. Humiliation fading, she shuddered and swayed in his arms, wondering if she'd broken through. She was positive about her alcohol intake, but his embrace quelled her anger at his response. Maybe she was wrong about everything. Perhaps he really did love her...

"Please mention this excessive drinking to Dr. Leighmann when you call tomorrow. If you don't, I will. I'm worried about you and I don't want to be forced to get Grasmere involved."

Excessive drinking? She pushed him away, his accusation destroying the tenderness of the moment. But deep down, she sensed Eliot's words were less concern than veiled threat. With a whispered "Uh huh," she retreated into her reticence, her flash of bravado now a faint memory. She refused to go back to Grasmere. Ever.

"Don't move." He retrieved two tabs of Xanax and a glass of water from the bathroom. "Best take these, darling, before this agitation gets out of hand." He waited as she downed the dose and handed back the glass. "Good girl. I'll sleep in the guest room, give you a chance to settle down. Good night."

He closed the door, leaving her even more broken than before.

She lay down on the half-deserted bed, now devoid of both her husband's body and the physical affection she craved. So much for her triumph over her romantic rivals. As the pills took effect and the world hazed over, the woman's insult from the party echoed like a war chant: *"She's either kinky or she's rich...She's either kinky or she's rich...She's either kinky or she's rich."*

If the bathroom prophetess was right, it explained why Eliot had stuck around all these years, despite her mental challenges and their lack of sexual relations. As well as the countless times he'd nonchalantly inquired about her father's health, about his plans regarding the estate. It had to be her money, or what would become her money one day.

As the minutes ticked by, the notion latched on, and what started as speculation evolved into possibility and then probability. Grace jerked upright, rattled by epiphany. Even the Xanax couldn't blur the clarity of her blood-chilling revelation, the only explanation that made sense. Eliot was biding his time until Barrington died, and she inherited his billions. Then, he planned to remove the one obstacle standing between him and a life of rich bachelorhood. Namely, Grace.

Chapter Three

"Mom, are you up?"

Damian's loud and insistent banging ripped Grace from her Xanax-induced slumber at 7:30 a.m. At first, her grogginess left her unsure of where, or even who she was. Then a louder voice shook her sober: "Honey, are you going to get up and fix the boys breakfast, or do you want them to take exams on an empty stomach?"

It all came flooding back—their argument, her inevitable retreat from rebellion, an embarrassing failed seduction, and finally, the terror of realizing her husband planned to do her in. Equaled by the dread of leaving him—facing the world alone for the first time, her diagnosis ensuring she'd lose her children in a custody hearing. Followed by an asylum stay for suggesting anything as "ludicrous" as a homicidal spouse. No one was about to believe the ravings of a psychotic. She felt as trapped as Henri Charrière in *Papillon,* doomed forever to imprisonment on Devil's Island. Except unlike him, she had no ally to help her escape.

She inhaled deeply and cast off the residue of the past evening's nightmares. No need to panic—yet. He wouldn't make a move until her father died. What if her suspicions were nothing more than unmedicated paranoia, intensified by too much liquor? This was not the time for impulsive conclusions and drastic actions. Instead, she needed to remain calm and vigilant while she gathered more evidence.

She pulled off the covers and attempted to stand, but her knees refused to cooperate. She collapsed back onto the mattress, cursing Eliot for forcing last night's sedatives down her throat.

"Can't you do it this morning? I'm not all that steady."

"I'd love to, baby, but no can do. Early meetings. I'm leaving now. Don't forget to call the doctor." His footsteps receded down the hall. Why had she imagined he'd help? To him, childcare was "mother's work." God forbid she stray from her preordained agenda of meal prep, chauffeuring duties, tax returns and therapy sessions. All to be performed with nary a complaint, lest she be accused of a relapse.

Grace didn't question why her fourteen- and fifteen-year-old sons still permitted her to pour their cereal and toast their bagels. Coddling them was the one part of her daily routine she enjoyed. In a heartbeat, they'd be off to college. The future flashed before her eyes, a black chasm of emptiness. She'd embrace every morsel of connection until that melancholy moving day when the bonds of motherhood would be severed. Unlike the bonds of marriage, which had merely atrophied and disintegrated over time.

She wrapped herself in a terry cloth robe and hunted in vain for her slippers which, as usual, had disappeared. Barefoot, rickety but resolute, she lumbered down the stairs to join her family. A few aspirins and mugs of joe would surely vanquish this narcotic hangover.

The boys were already dressed and sitting at the table, preoccupied with their phones. She stumbled in, surprised to see Eliot standing by the Keurig, pouring milk into his coffee.

"Weren't you too rushed to make them breakfast?"

"Got a text saying they pushed the meeting back by a half hour so I'm grabbing a little caffeine before I head out."

Damian, her oldest, interrupted their standoff. "Mom, give him a break. Can I have French toast, please? Like now?"

"Of course. Give me one second."

"We don't have a second, Mom," her youngest chimed in. "We shouldn't have to suffer because you're late."

Grace knew Xander didn't mean to bruise her with his insolence. She'd read the saying, a fish rots from the head down. If the boys took her for granted, it was only because they were following their father's lead.

"Have any of you seen my slippers? I can't seem to find them."

Damian heaved a dramatic sigh. "This again? Mom, you are always losing stuff."

"I'm just asking if anyone moved them."

Xander didn't attempt to hide his smirk. "You got us, Mom. It's a big conspiracy. We take your slippers and trade them on the black market. Coke, meth, Mom's slippers. They're a hot seller."

"Boys, have a little respect for your mother. She had another rough night."

"Jawohl, Herr Kommandant," the two boys answered, rolling their eyes.

Grace rummaged for a frying pan and a shallow mixing bowl. Then to the fridge for milk, eggs and butter before reaching into the cabinet for four slices of bread and the cinnamon. She broke the eggs, poured in the milk and tried to indulge in some light breakfast banter, anything to break the tension.

"I had something exciting happen yesterday."

"Really, honey? Weren't you supposed to visit your therapist?"

"I did and then afterward, I stopped by the library. Literary volunteers were explaining their impact on the community. I was so impressed, I signed up."

She meant to sound casual, as if still cloaked in Lithium lassitude, but glancing at their uneasy expressions, she feared she'd come across as too animated.

Eliot's eyes narrowed. "Volunteered? Grace, is that such a good idea?"

If I hadn't thought so, I wouldn't have done it. "It's only once or twice a week. It's a way to give back, set a good example for our children."

"But, Grace…You know how you get around new people. How you worry about what they're thinking or how they're treating you. What if you forget a student's appointment and they're left sitting there, waiting—"

"And Mom, what about us? Shouldn't we be your number one priority? asked Damian.

"It's true, Grace. The boys need help with their essay writing. Charity should begin at home."

"But they never even let me peek at their homework." Exasperated, she whisked the egg mixture at triple speed, causing a dollop to escape the bowl and hit the cabinet.

"That alone should tell you something, sweetie. Now is not the right time for a step like this."

Grace turned and faced the stove, deflated as a week-old helium balloon. Without meds, she no longer had a barrier from the wounds her family's thoughtless words left in their wake. And what if Eliot and the boys were right? Could her enthusiasm have exaggerated a simple tutoring job into a Nobel Prize-winning achievement? Teaching some stranger to read hardly put her in the same category as Malala. She'd cancel when she got to work and apologize for causing any inconvenience.

"Either of you have big plans for the weekend?" Anything to change the subject.

Grunts.

"Special requests for Thanksgiving dinner? Corn pudding? Stuffed acorn squash?"

Radio silence.

She dipped the bread in the egg wash and dared ask the one question every mother since the beginning of modern time has asked their teenage children. "Everyone get their homework done?"

That did it, ushering in a second round of denigration.

"Mom, remember what Dr. Leighmann said about laying off us?" said Damian. "You're not supposed to ask those kinds of questions."

"I don't understand why. Everyone needs structure and accountability. Especially when you're juggling so many extracurriculars."

Xander was quick to back up his brother. "You don't get it, Mom. Secrets protect us. If we haven't done our homework and we tell you the truth, you'll punish us. What's the point?"

Eliot was apparently not too rushed to join the onslaught. "We spoke about this, Grace. They're practically adults. You need to trust them and their decisions.

"For God sakes, make up your mind. A minute ago, you were urging me to help them with their essays. Now you're telling me to lay off and trust them. As I recall, our trust led to some less-than-stellar report cards last term."

Grace's modulated tone masked her upset at Eliot's persistent refusal to present a united parenting front. This time, she wasn't backing down. The therapist's permissive attitude might work for some people, but not her kids. In her opinion, it had been almost malpractice for Dr. Leighmann to suggest a "Don't Ask, Don't Tell" policy regarding homework, but her co-parent hadn't seen it that way.

"That's not fair, Mom. It could be true for Xander but not me. I got B's in math and science last year." Damian pushed back from the table. "I'll grab breakfast at school." He stormed out, slamming the back door behind him.

Grace hadn't intended to embarrass them about their grades. Another family discussion gone terribly wrong. "Well, I guess that means more breakfast for you, Xander." She forced herself to sound upbeat.

"Nah, I'm not hungry anymore. Thanks, anyway." Xander planted a kiss on her cheek before exiting on his brother's heels.

"Was that necessary, Grace?" asked Eliot, once the boys were out of earshot.

"I didn't do anything." She stared at the butter sizzling in the frying pan, yearning to leave her doormat days behind.

"Nothing and yet everything. You doubted their competence. Remember what Dr. Leighmann said? If they fail, they'll learn from it. Real life consequences. We don't have to be their watchdogs and endanger our relationship with them in the process."

"Just because Dr. Leighmann says something doesn't make it gospel. I reserve the right to parent my own kids." She listened to the crackle of the soggy bread as it succumbed to the heat of the butter.

"Not gospel, eh? She's kept *you* out of the hospital the last few years. For the most part, anyway. You'll singlehandedly destroy our relationship with the kids if you don't watch your words. You don't want that, do you?"

Grace shook her head, but she was really trying to shake off his condescending attitude.

"Call her as soon as I leave, okay?" He dumped his half-drunk mug of coffee into the sink and walked toward the stove. Her body flinched as Eliot embraced her, reflecting her shock over being hugged twice in less than twenty-four hours. Then he left for work, absconding with what remained of her dignity.

She concentrated on toasting the bread evenly, refusing to allow self-doubt to reduce her to a quivering heap. *It seems like no one else sees anything clearly anymore. Am I the only sane mind in a world gone mad?*

■   ■   ■

The cell's *brrring* roused her from a maple syrup-induced stupor, her comeuppance for finishing all four pieces of French toast as she treaded the waters of self-pity. By the time she'd fished her phone out of her handbag—refusing to carry it around 24/7 like a fifth appendage—Dr. Leighmann had already begun cataloging her concerns.

"Grace, Eliot called a few minutes ago and sounded very distraught. Something about you putting strangers above your own kids, becoming confrontational, even some heavy drinking. I can squeeze you in at noon if you can make it."

Grace stifled her outrage before it could escape across the airwaves. *How dare Eliot call my psychiatrist, like I was some recalcitrant child who couldn't be trusted.* "I'm sorry, I don't think that will work. I'm heading into the office late and I've got a ton of files to review before the holiday."

"How about tomorrow morning? I'd be open to a Saturday session, seeing it's for you. The situation sounded serious."

Faced with two unpleasant alternatives, a growing sense of vindictiveness helped make Grace's decision for her. "I'd love to, but I've got to make a quick trip to Florida to see my dad. He's been calling and...well, at eighty-seven, who knows how many more Thanksgivings he's got left?"

There was silence on the other end of the line.

"Dr. Leighmann, are you still there?"

"Yes. Will you be going straight to your Dad's house?"

Grace's jaw tensed. "No, I planned to stop by the World of Reptiles exhibit at the Bronx Zoo first. Strip naked in front of the iguanas, do a little jig. I mean, if they can shed their skin, why can't I?" She imagined her psychiatrist's reaction to such a dissident yet liberating response. She'd been seeing Emma Leighmann for nearly forty years. Leighmann tolerated her occasional insubordination, partly out of friendship, and partly because it was lucrative. Revolts staged around anyone else always ended badly.

"You don't sound like your usual self, Grace. Is it that dream again?"

"No, I haven't had it for months." And that was a good thing. She hated waking up in a cold sweat.

"Well, this agitation…I can't lie, it troubles me. Fly down and see your dad. The change of pace—away from the boys, work, all your stressors—may do you good. I'm setting aside an hour on Tuesday evening at six thirty. We'll speak then, but if things start spinning out of control while you're down south, call me. There's a place you can stay until the confusion dies down."

By now, Grace was fluent in Leighmann-speak. By "things," the therapist meant reality. And by "place," she meant a sanitarium. *Subtle.* Like Grace was an emotional Chernobyl, a global threat when outside her doctor's dominion. She channeled her anger into a death grip on her cellphone, causing her tendons to ache.

Still, the vague threat of being confined to some Floridian mental hospital gave her pause. Did she need to risk a trip fraught with angst, just to spite her husband and therapist? Or, would the time and distance away sharpen her perspective? If Grace realized she had misconstrued Eliot's intentions, she'd come home less belligerent. However, if her ruminations confirmed her suspicions, at least she'd return to Glen Valley more certain of her father's health—vital information if her lifeline was now inexorably tied to his.

"Grace, are you still there?"

"I'm sorry, my mind drifted. I'm sure you're right, Dr. Leighmann. I need a breather, some time to relax. Thanks for understanding. I'll call the minute I feel like I might go off the rails."

"Sounds perfect." A verbal pat on the head to an atoning adolescent. "Any time, day or night."

"Thank you, Doctor. Have a *wonderful* weekend." Grace half-regretted the sarcasm in her delivery as she disconnected the call. Between a sudden throbbing in her head and the constriction in her throat, all her mental toxicity was spilling out from the only available exit, her lips. *Not the best time to call my dad but hey, what the hell.*

Caprice, Barrington's chippie-of-the month, answered the phone on the second ring. She was the latest in a stream of floozies in her father's life over the thirty years since Grace's mom had passed. Each was blonder than the last, both in hair color and mental acuity. In his golden years, Barrington preferred relationships free from challenge. Any vacuous set of curves would do.

"*Hola.* Pierrepoint *residencia.*"

"*Hola*? Caprice, is that you? It's Grace."

"Oh, Gracie. *Lo siento.*" A flurry of giggles followed. "I'm learning *español.* That way when I talk to the maids, they won't look at me funny. They might *comprende.*" More laughter. "Hold on, I'll get your *padre.*" What was Grace waiting for? Life sounded like a rip-roaring riot down in good ol' Palm Beach.

With every phone call and visit, there was a tiny, optimistic part of her that hoped things might improve between herself and her dad. That for once, he'd treat her with kindness and respect. Even love. If such were the case, she'd petition for divorce, claiming lack of consortium—something she'd read in a Sue Grafton novel—pack up the boys and head down there for good. Problem solved. But deep down, she suspected her father would accuse her of overdramatizing some petty remark and send them back to New Jersey on the next available flight.

One murmur-blocking, hand-over-the-receiver moment later, Barrington's deep, weathered voice boomed across the miles. "Grace? I see the moron gave you the message."

Moron. That insult, an invisible anvil crushing any miniscule hope for better times. Her dad had never liked Eliot. Perhaps that's what inspired her to marry him. That little streak of rebellion, then in its infancy, proved to be her escape route from a claustrophobic childhood.

"His name is Eliot. And yes, he told me you called, wondering when I planned to come down and visit. I can ask Keira to take over chauffeur duty while I'm gone, and then grab a flight first thing tomorrow morning, if it's convenient. But I'll need to be back at work by Monday." She pictured herself walking toward a guillotine, a modern-day Sydney Carton. *It is a far, far better thing that I do...*

"Who the hell is Keira?"

"My old sitter. Remember? You met her years ago when I visited with the boys."

"Who can think back that far? Whatever. Text Caprice with the arrival time and I'll have Javier pick you up at the airport. *Javier.* Can you believe it? I can't get anyone but Cubans to work for me down here."

She disregarded her dad's bigoted spew and asked him to put Caprice back on the line. They exchanged cell numbers. She promised to text flight details after she checked Delta's schedule from work. For which she was already an hour late. Earlier wooziness behind her, Grace dashed up the stairs to shower, dress and embark on a day she hoped would end more pleasantly than it had begun.

Chapter Four

A blast of humidity walloped Grace as she exited the airport terminal Saturday morning. The challenge of locating her father's white Bentley loomed. Even though this was West Palm, not to be confused with the more hallowed Palm Beach—heaven forbid—it was still a breeding ground for overpriced, underused luxury autos. Sweaty, polyester-clad, middle-aged women were more of a rarity. In less than a minute, her father's driver picked her out from the throng of cosset-hungry travelers seeking a transfer to more civilized ground.

"Ms. Gracie?"

"That's me."

The swarthy man who addressed her through his passenger side window smiled broadly. "I'm Javier. Your father, he sent me." Passersby stared as he jumped out to open her door. Her dad's vintage Bentley S-1 stood out, even among this army of elite, six-figure transports.

Grace handed him her carry-on, which contained a nightgown, bathing suit, two changes of clothes, and a supply of pills, just for show. She'd packed light, intending to stay only long enough to clear her head, make some contingency plans, and fulfill her daughterly duties. She hopped into the back seat, grateful for a reprieve from the heat. Javier pulled away from the terminal toward the Flagler Memorial, one of three bridges which separated the rabble of West Palm from the more dignified gentry of Palm Beach.

"It's hotter than usual today. Is the air-conditioning cool enough? You are comfortable, I hope?"

"Likely more comfortable than I'll be for the rest of the weekend." She grabbed a diet soda from the Bentley's mini bar, mulling the same questions she'd been debating throughout her cab ride to Newark and her two-hour flight: Should she confide in her father about Eliot's infidelity and his possible murder plot? Since Barrington hated her husband, would he be more inclined to trust her suspicions? And could she blame him if he didn't? She was still unsure of them herself. The answers seemed as elusive in Florida as they had in New Jersey.

Her thoughts drifted back to Eliot. If he offed her, how would he do it? Her husband's creativity was undeniable. Who else would have lured her favorite actress, Harrow Paine, from the commercial he was shooting, and convince her to show up at Grace's door, pretending to be a pizza delivery girl? Or surprised her on her fortieth birthday with an extravagant weekend trip to Paris? A celibate holiday under his ever-watchful eye, but a memorable one, nevertheless. Yes, Eliot could conjure up surprises on a dime. Which meant he could plot a homicide and make it look like an accident with very little effort. She'd need to remain cautious, think two steps ahead.

Javier pulled up to the 1.5-acre, gated oceanfront estate. The white, sundrenched façade, hidden from the street by a grove of swaying palms, contained 35,000 square feet straight out of the British West Indies. Eleven bedrooms, fifteen baths, more than enough space for her father and an entire harem of concubines. To the masses, both intimidating and ostentatious. To her, a reminder that wealth didn't always translate into happiness.

"I hope the rain holds off for you while you are here, Ms. Gracie. Mr. Pierrepoint, he put in a special order." Javier turned off the ignition and hopped out to open her door.

Her father's consort, Caprice, was waiting outside to greet the limo. Barrington had called his new girlfriend a "color consultant," something about how the right hues in home décor, clothing and hair color affected mood. *She must practice what she preaches.* Clad in beige linen shorts and a navy tee-shirt, she did look a bit more respectable than her father's usual bimbos, Grace conceded, despite the dark roots peeking out from under the platinum dye job. And slightly older. Mid-thirties to be sure.

Flanking Caprice were Barrington's brace of show dogs, two English Springer Spaniels named Dewey and Dutchess. The dogs went wild as Grace stepped onto the white-pebbled driveway, jumping up, overflowing with affection. She crouched down to embrace them, careful not to rest her knees on the hot stones. She was certain her father used the duo for nothing more than ornamentation and winning accolades in the ring. Barrington's life revolved around showing up others for his own self-enrichment. No doubt once the handlers finished Dewey and he went best in show at Westminster, her father would put him out to stud. His puppies would fetch a pretty penny.

Javier reached into the trunk and pulled out her suitcase. "Put it in the upstairs guest suite, *por favor.*" A hint of hillbilly twang tinged Caprice's newfound bilingualism. She squatted to address Grace on a level plane. "We're so happy to have you visit, hon." Then her perky expression clouded over and she lowered her voice. "Your father hasn't been all that well the past few months. He denies it, but he's forgetful and a little more, um, moody than usual. Last week, he grew so impatient to get to town, he refused to wait for the driver. He jumped behind the wheel of the Jag and backed it right through the garage door. So frightening. I mean, there were no injuries, and we got it fixed in a hurry but still, best you are aware. He's waiting for you in the library."

Grace tried to tamp down a twinge of panic. She might have mixed feelings about her father, but right now she needed him healthy. If dementia were setting in, how could she confide in him? Not only would he be less than coherent, he'd either forget everything she'd shared or would blurt out her secrets like a three-year old. She couldn't risk word getting back to Eliot.

The two women rose, much to Dewey and Dutchess's dismay, and strolled toward the house like John Coffey and his jailer in *The Green Mile*, walking toward an impending electrocution. Her father's verbal jabs were as piercing as any 2,000-amp current.

Normally, from the foyer she could see straight across the living room to the sea, diaphanous white curtains fluttering against open French doors. Not today. The servants had closed off the veranda to shut out the humidity, leaving the room absent its usual seawater bouquet. Fine with Grace, who for years had linked that aroma with her father's vitriolic attacks.

She turned left into the library, home to all the books that once graced the built-in mahogany shelves of the house where she'd grown up in Short

Hills. Those tomes had been her refuge whenever the demons would accost her in her nightmares. Afraid to fall back asleep, she'd read by flashlight under the duvet covers. Reading was comfort. Books were home.

Absent from the library, however, was Barrington Pierrepoint. "That's peculiar. He was here a minute ago. Let me go track him down."

Grace rubbed her hands together, trying to curb her growing concern and the chill of the air-conditioning. The click-click, click-click of Caprice's stilettos against the Calacatta marble floor charted her trek from room to room. "I found him," she called out after a few minutes, sounding relieved. "He'd wandered into the kitchen and was standing in the pantry."

She reappeared at the doorway, Barrington in tow. Despite having lost weight and gone silver, he still appeared as sturdy and forceful as he had in Grace's youth.

"I wasn't loitering in the pantry, you dimwit; I was scanning the shelves for some cereal. For god sakes, woman, I'm not some doddering old fool. Sometimes I'm certain you're trying to gaslight me." Her father's voice dripped disdain. He pushed Caprice aside, and stiffly embraced Grace. "Hello, Spot, how was the flight?"

"Spot?" Caprice appeared confused.

Mortified, Grace diverted her eyes and stared down at the floor. "Um, yeah. When I was a kid, I used to wear a lot of polka dots." She prayed Barrington wouldn't contradict her and explain he'd used that nickname to harass her about her acne as a teen. That's when he wasn't criticizing her for snacking, instructing the butler to prepare a trough for her in the stable, instead of a setting at the dinner table. "You have no sense of humor," he'd counter if she protested or cried. No matter what her reaction, she could never win.

He cleared his throat, leaving her statement uncorrected. Had he forgotten or had he discovered mercy in his advanced age? "I asked about the flight, Grace. How was it?"

"A little turbulent but nothing I couldn't handle."

"Did you have your Xanax with you?" Barrington took refuge behind his desk, a signal that he'd grown tired of small talk. Then again, he had always lacked the ability to engage in any substantive conversation with family that didn't involve criticism.

"Yes, but I didn't need it."

"Well, keep it handy. Eliot warned us you've been a little on edge."

"Oh, did he now?" She clenched her fists to temper an outburst, unsure of which annoyed her more, her father's condescending tone or the fact that Eliot was still handling her from 1,200 miles away.

"Grace, please lower your voice and calm down. Can't a father express concern over his daughter's welfare?" As usual, Barrington accused her of speaking too loudly, a tactic he used whenever she said something he didn't want to hear. In a move suggesting the exact opposite of concern, he shuffled through a stack of catalogs. Bored of the conversation or purposely dismissive?

"Father, I'm almost fifty. I don't need you to remind me of how my husband misinterprets my reaction to his—"

"Who wants lemonade? Marquesa makes it with a little strawberry syrup. Very refreshing."

Grace appreciated Caprice's attempt to stem the escalating tension but suspected no amount of elixir would sweeten the bitterness evoked by this visit. She needed to remove herself from the situation before she said something she'd regret. "Thanks, but I'd prefer to go soak in a tub. Traveling always makes me feel a little gritty." She shot one last look at her father, who was still rummaging through his mail, and then navigated the cavernous foyer to the winding twin staircases leading upstairs.

The warm bath soothed Grace's muscles but did little to alleviate her anxiety. Memories flooded back, drenching her in a swirl of conflicting emotions. How kindly her parents had treated her until she turned six: their princess, draped in custom-made designer dresses, silk ribbons adorning her hair. The most expensive dolls and toys crowding every inch of her pink-and-purple bedroom. Once she started seeing the visions, everything changed. Without explanation or preparation, they banished her to Grasmere, the first of many visits to similar facilities. A year of being mentally poked and prodded, far from her family and friends. When her parents did visit, her father wouldn't look her in the eye. What had she done to him? Wasn't *she* the one who was suffering?

Grace closed her eyes and willed the aromatic bath salts to quell her growing upset. Her only savior during that time had been Emma Leighmann, a young doctor nearing the end of her residency. She'd been caring and attentive where others had been brusque, and Grace responded to the hours of extra attention with gratitude and trust. When her year-long exile ended, Barrington also showed his appreciation, hiring her as Grace's private therapist. Later, after Grace married, he set Leighmann up in her own practice, with his daughter remaining a weekly patient.

Grace often questioned why her father's attitude changed once the illness struck. No matter how she idolized him and obeyed his orders, he'd withhold attention and approval, barely acknowledging her existence. She never quit trying, though—like an abandoned, starving puppy that still crawled back to its master after his week-long absence and licked his foot. The therapist would listen to her anxieties without judgment and tell her to remain strong. As Grace grew into adulthood, Leighmann convinced her she held no responsibility for the impenetrable blackness of Barrington's soul. The realization deepened their bond and solidified her faith in Leighmann as someone in whom she could always confide.

So why not this time?

Grace's eyes shot open. She'd been so rude on the phone yesterday, lashing out at the wrong party. Eliot had been the one who'd tattled about her outburst, so why take out her frustration on her therapist? She reached for the loofah and began sloughing dead skin from her legs and back, willing the friction to also remove the guilt over her recent insolence.

Grace turned the left tap to reheat the cooling bath and reclined again into the perfumed water. She wished she could open up to her therapist about her recent suspicions. But accusing her husband of continuing their marriage solely for the inheritance was exactly the kind of excuse the paranoia police would use to lock her away. She'd be sure to apologize to Leighmann when she got home. No point risking the loss of any potential allies.

That included her father. How ironic that throughout her childhood, her parents had warned her not to trust outsiders, how money had a way of turning strangers into false friends with questionable motives. Yet, look at her "trusted" family now. Barrington assailed her psyche with verbal hand grenades while Eliot, the man who had rescued her from that abusive childhood, was scheming to end her life. Paradoxically, Grace needed to protect one of them to shield her from the other. As long as her father remained alive, she was safe.

She dried off, threw on a fresh set of clothes, and prayed for strength as she headed back down for round number two. *No matter what he says, I need to be patient, remember that he's impaired. He needs a sympathetic ear, much as I did when I was younger.*

Grace found Barrington and Caprice out on the veranda; a passing shower having pierced the dome of oppressive humidity. Dewey and Dutchess lay at their feet, their wagging tails heralding her return. A plate of petit fours sat next to a flute of champagne on an end table between her father and an empty lounge chair she presumed was for her. It was a beautiful setting, looking out over the azure waves as they caressed the pearl-colored sands. The breeze blew at her hair and she smoothed it as she sat alongside her father. All three spent a few minutes staring out at the tropical tableau.

Caprice broke the silence. "I hope you enjoyed your bath, Grace. I asked Marta to leave you some of the perfumed salts we brought back from Croatia last month."

"Yes, it was lovely, thank you."

"Marta. Another Cuban. Why don't we invite all of Havana to work for us? What happened to good old American help?"

Ire rising, Grace began to address Barrington's grumbles when she saw Caprice signaling to let the biased comments stand unchallenged. She winked and changed the subject to something less emotionally charged.

"Caprice, it looks like you've redecorated since I was last here. Did you use an interior designer or choose everything yourself?"

"She hired a pair of local so-called *men* who waltzed in wearing their tutus, waved their magic wands, and made all my money disappear. Didn't you, darling?"

Grace forced a smile, fighting off every instinct to challenge her father's remarks. "I've been wondering how to redo the boys' rooms. They're in that awkward adolescent phase—not quite children, not quite adults. I'm wavering between bright and dark. Any advice?"

Caprice started discussing the psychology of teenage décor when Barrington's exasperated groan interrupted the discourse. "*I* have some advice. Why don't you both shut up so people can like you?"

Grace had endured that malicious comment throughout her childhood, whenever she'd chat with the cooks and housekeepers, anyone in her immediate vicinity who might lend a friendly ear. Hearing it again made her head explode. "Why don't *you* shut up so people can like *you*?" She grabbed the Limoges china dish holding the petit fours and smashed it to the ground for emphasis.

The rest was a blur. Her father screaming and pulling his belt from his pants to threaten her, Caprice begging him to calm down as he stormed from the veranda. A heated telephone conversation to Dr. Leighmann, spiked with adjectives like "unhinged" and "violent." The orderlies showing up shortly afterward, forcing her to the ground as if she were an escaped convict and jabbing a needle into her butt. The last thing she remembered was the tickle of Dutchess licking her nose as the room spun like a gyroscope and then faded to black.

Chapter Five

Grace shook off her Klonopin grogginess. It took a minute to reorient herself and realize she was no longer a guest at her father's estate, but an "inmate" at the latest in a series of asylums.

One lousy disagreement and he had me committed? *Unbelievable.* The barred windows showcased the hospital's grounds, already tinged pink and gold with sunset, which meant she'd been out cold for hours. Grace attributed the chill to the air-conditioning set Florida-style, ten degrees shy of comfortable, and realized they'd replaced her clothes with a light blue hospital gown. She reached for the thin, waffle-weave blanket and then thought better of it. Her rising anger would keep her plenty warm.

Wherever she was, this hovel fell far short of the standards set by Grasmere. How could a patient remain asleep on a mattress this lumpy or sheets this stiff? Or, with the nostril-ravaging scent of Eau de Clorox perfuming the air? How depressing she could discern the difference. With her experience, why not blog mental hospital reviews? *Going Postal while Staying Posh,* recommended reading for all psychos by Paranoid Publishers of America.

It was a private room, of course. Pierrepoints did not fraternize with the unwashed masses, not even the ones downgraded to middle class by marriage. They also didn't end disagreements with a handshake. Instead, they committed the weaker of the two to the nearest loony bin.

She reached behind her and hurled a pillow across the room, its impact falling well short of satisfying. Punching the mattress would only shift the lumps and make it more difficult to sleep later. Screaming would earn her another hypodermic prick of sedation. She took a deep breath and exhaled away her anger, making room for more constructive considerations. Why not reframe her "time-out" as an opportunity to plot an immediate plan of action to save herself, should her suspicions regarding Eliot prove valid? First, figure out some way to convince the doctors she was the sane but unfortunate victim of a massive misunderstanding. Next, once on "the outside," keep Daddy, and by extension herself, healthy and out of harm's way. And finally, plot how to extricate herself from her marriage before it turned uxoricidal.

Grace donned the slippers and velour robe left by the side of her bed—snaps only, no sash with which to hang herself—and tested the door's handle. To her surprise, it opened. She heard a commotion somewhere down the hall and followed the checkerboard linoleum path toward its source.

An attendant name-tagged "Derrick," laden with a pile of laundered sheets, intercepted her before she reached the core of the clamor. "Ms. Pierrepoint, welcome to Quiet Pines! Should you be up and about, so soon after your arrival?"

"You tell me, Derrick. They left my door unlocked." It felt empowering to cast off her meek, milquetoast façade. "And it's Rendell."

"What's Rendell?"

"My last name. I haven't been a Pierrepoint for over twenty-five years."

"And that's a good thing?"

Derrick's incredulity didn't surprise her. Barrington had relocated to Florida decades earlier to escape the infamy of Ponzi scheme allegations. Before he left, he made sure the district attorneys were too busy with their new yachts and Porsches to prosecute. Over the past decade, her father had donated millions to Palm Beach charities, trying to buy prestige and respectability. He'd probably contributed a wing or two to this dump.

"Jury's out."

The area behind the attendant teemed with conversation and activity. She had seen "living rooms" like this before, where patients played checkers and cards, watched "approved" television, chatted before the inevitable arguments erupted into punches. A few of the inmates waved, but interaction was not a priority right now.

She pushed past Derrick toward the back of the room where a brunette, middle-aged nurse with prune-puckered lips and a furrowed brow monitored the bustle. Her badge read "Amy."

"Ms. Pierrepoint, I see you're up. Less woozy, I trust. We set aside a tray if you'd like to have some dinner."

"It's Rendell. How long am I going to be stuck here? Was I involuntarily committed, or is this a temporary tour of duty?"

"You sound agitated. Perhaps you need another sedative."

Grace swiveled to make sure no one was barreling down on her, needle in hand. Unwilling to be doped up into oblivion for another god-knows-how-long, she adopted a more saccharine tone. "I apologize, I didn't realize how that must have sounded. I was curious what my father had decided was best for me."

Her Pollyanna act was no match for Nurse Amy's, who plastered on a patronizing smile.

"Mr. Pierrepoint asked us to watch over you in this controlled environment until your husband arranged to fly down and pick you up. I imagine that after a hearty breakfast tomorrow morning, we'll be saying our fond farewells." She looked past Grace to determine if a verbal altercation between two card players was turning volatile enough to call in the Librium artillery. She gestured to an attendant to monitor the escalation and then returned her attention to Grace. "Now, can I get you some dinner?"

The notion of Eliot swooping in to rescue her, like a parent springing his daughter from detention, caused Grace's appetite to nosedive. She noticed a bookcase and seating area on the opposite side of the room. "I'd rather take a look around, if that's okay."

"That's fine, Ms....Rendell. Make yourself at home and don't be shy if there's anything you need."

She curled up in an easy chair beside the bookcase and closed her eyes. Now that her earlier fuzziness had faded, she could concentrate on how to deal with Eliot.

The most prudent course of action: anticipate the worst-case scenario and prepare accordingly. If her accounting career had taught her anything, it was the power of patience and logic. Math lacked emotion; the numbers either added up or they didn't. The same held true in life. She would use the power of logic to save herself.

Option Number One: Make up with Daddy, play nice-nice and explain that Eliot might be planning to murder her. She visualized the entire scenario, from Barrington questioning whether she'd gone off her meds, to the moment he called Eliot and together, they checked her back into this place. Perhaps a great bonding experience for the two of them, but not the outcome she had in mind.

Option Number Two: Leave Eliot and run away, something she would have never considered during her decades of pharmaceutically induced lethargy. Problem was, such a disruptive and permanent measure would leave Damian and Xander without a mother, and her with the stigma of having abandoned her family—all based on a hunch. Plus, the logistics were awful. To rent an apartment required a down payment she didn't have, since every spare penny paid for the boys' hockey camps, their tutors, their college fund. She couldn't withdraw any large sums from their joint account without his approval and using her credit card would be like handing Eliot a GPS highlighting her location. She had one asset no one would miss: her late mother's wedding ring. But she refused to hock the last remaining connection to any kindness experienced in her youth.

Option Number Three: Prophylactic homicide. Kill him before he killed her. No way. She would not be the murderer of her sons' father, no matter how dire her situation. There had to be some way to stop Eliot that didn't involve running away or giving anyone an excuse to send her to prison or back to a mental facility. A solution that wouldn't cause irreparable damage in case she was mistaken about everything.

Grace opened her eyes and stared up at the books on the shelves. After her first hospitalization, her father insisted she be homeschooled and kept out of sight as much as possible. But her mother always snuck her out a few times a week to give her a taste of freedom. One of her favorite haunts had been the library, home to her friends: Miss Marple, Sherlock Holmes, Hercule Poirot. Here at Quiet Pines, the shelves held only children's mysteries featuring Encyclopedia Brown, Nancy Drew, and the Dana Girls—innocuous series that wouldn't put dangerous ideas into patients' heads. She walked over and ran a finger across their spines. How appalling they were stuck here, like her, with no one to love them.

"Speak to me," she urged Jean and Louise Dana as she caressed the books' covers, attempting to absorb their wisdom through touch. "You've never failed me before. Now's not the time to start."

As if possessed by the literary friends of her youth, Grace pulled out *In the Shadow of the Tower* and laid it title-side up on a nearby table. On top of it, she placed *The Secret in the Old Clock*. One by one, she pulled hardcovers from the shelves and inch by inch, stacked them to form a novel ladder reaching two feet high. "An escape route," she mused. "Is that the best you can do?"

And that's when an idea struck her.

A book. She would write a book. Something longer than the short stories she'd written in her teens to ease the loneliness of her isolation. She remembered how proud she'd been of her work, once even summoning up enough courage to show the pieces to her father. He'd sneered, proclaiming that only plebs entertained the masses. Then he tossed her pages into the fireplace and forced her to watch as the flames reduced them to cinders. That was the last time she'd ever shared anything with anyone, preferring to keep her stories hidden away in the bedroom closet, stuffed inside cardboard boxes marked "Off-Season."

This might be the perfect time to resurrect those skills. Pen a novel about a frumpy, middle-aged woman whose rich father dies and leaves her a fortune. And the philandering husband, saved from poverty by marriage, who plots to murder her for the inheritance. The husband wouldn't get away with his devious scheme, but that wasn't the point. Every copy would be a literary insurance policy, preventing Eliot from pulling the same stunt. How could he? She'd already warned everyone, her book a subtle, heroic call for help. He'd be the first person they'd investigate and arrest.

And if all her suspicions were unfounded? No harm done. She'd have concocted a fictional tale as an outlet for her creative juices. If it found an audience, even better.

It was perfect. Books had saved her from the loneliness and hopelessness of her youth. And now a book would secure her future. Poetic justice. Even Nancy Drew would agree.

Chapter Six

Eliot bore the mantle of long-suffering husband as he wordlessly signed Grace out of Quiet Pines and accompanied her back to Newark. She appreciated the silence, using the flight to formulate the logistics of her plan. And even more grateful that because the asylum's nurses, amateurs that they were, hadn't noticed she'd palmed her last dose of meds, she could concentrate with clarity and focus.

Other than thanking the flight attendant for a snack, her first words came after they disembarked, when she asked Eliot why he'd deviated from the regular route home.

"We're headed to Dr. Leighmann's office, that's why." He kept his eyes glued to the road. "It was part of the condition of your release that you meet with your local therapist upon landing." They pulled up to a red light and he deigned to stare in her direction. "Honestly, Grace. Did you have to cause trouble with your father? You were supposed to take a couple days off to visit, relax, ask a few questions. Was that so damn hard?"

The mention of the "questions"—those concerning Barrington's last will and testament—reinforced her apprehension about the man she'd married. Why not ask what set her off? Or if her father had been as nasty as always? But no, those appetizers never seemed to make it onto the interrogation menu at the Restaurant Grace.

She didn't have the strength to argue, nor the inclination to defend herself. It was a lost cause. Having the world consider her *non compos mentis* played into his plans. No one would put much stock in the paranoid rantings of a mental patient, accusing her husband of plotting her demise.

If that was, in fact, what he was doing. Infidelity with other women? That part was credible. But killing her for her inheritance? No proof, at least not yet. Ever since the party, Grace had bounced around silent allegations and hated herself for her indecision. Eliot's constant patience and support ran contrary to any homicidal intent. If only he weren't so kind and solicitous, she'd be more certain. Though, to be fair, his counsel was sometimes patronizing, and his actions, like today's silent treatment, often bordered on passive-aggressive. It skewed both ways. And while he might be an adulterer, she still leaned toward giving her husband the benefit of the doubt before accusing him of conspiracy to murder.

It was more belief than she had in their marriage. Their union had fallen short of fulfilling for more than a decade, and if *she* saw it that way, as inoculated as she'd been from emotion, Eliot had to agree. Enough to seek comfort in the arms of other women. While she'd ruled out running away, Grace had never considered an amicable split. What if she handed him back his bachelorhood? Once released from the bonds of loyalty, at liberty to pursue Sheryl and Betty and God knows who else without reproach…would he jump at the chance? He made a decent living, enough to support both boys. If she started working full time, her salary would cover a cheap studio apartment, utilities, some furnishings.

Maybe it was time to broach the topic. If it worked, she'd be home free. If not, the results would be very revealing.

She turned her gaze toward the man she'd once pledged to stay with through eternity, braced herself, and rolled the dice. "I'm nothing but a burden to you, Eliot. An albatross around your neck. The time at Quiet Pines helped me realize that. It might be better for everyone if we called it quits, divided up the assets, shared custody of the kids."

Eliot remained silent: his eyes fixed on the road; his face solemn. Grace wondered if he'd been so entrenched in his own thoughts, he hadn't heard her, but then he veered off the highway into a McDonald's parking lot and gave her his complete attention.

"Are you serious, Grace? How are you going to live on your own when every morning, you can't even remember where you left your slippers? I find the milk behind photos in the wall unit, your car keys in the laundry. You can't live without my help and you know it."

She had assumed he wouldn't give up her inheritance without a fight. She'd envisioned claims of undying love, protestations of how he couldn't bear life without her. But the cruelty of his response, a gift box of disparagement, wrapped in sweetness and tied up with a ribbon of concern, was downright Machiavellian. She fought the temptation to lash out and instead, modulated the timbre of her response to match his own. "What are you talking about? I've never misplaced the milk or car keys in my life."

"I'm sure you believe that, darling. Your pills cause you to forget half of what you do, and leave you confused about the other half. No need to become defensive or blame yourself. I'll always love you, no matter what." He leaned over and kissed her cheek.

Indignation and uncertainty rendered her slack-jawed for the remaining hour until they arrived at Dr. Leighmann's raised ranch, the lower level of which doubled as her home office. Eliot harrumphed as he pulled into the driveway. Some other patient had parked a red BMW Roadster smack in the middle of the two parking spaces allotted for patients. "Damn this inconsiderate hog and his fancy sports car. Hang out while I take care of this."

Eliot's reaction took Grace by surprise. It was out of character for him to deride strangers or lose his temper, odder still for him to act on that upset. *He's on edge. Perhaps the idea I might divorce him jarred him more than he let on.*

Unless it was frustration, flying down south to collect her right before the holiday, when airline seats were elusive and therefore, expensive as hell. Or concern over preparing Thanksgiving dinner on his own. As it was, she'd have to scramble to get something on the table by Thursday.

Eliot rang the bell three times and then pounded on the side door, which doubled as the office entrance. Grace watched as the startled doctor emerged a few seconds later, gesturing for him to take it down a notch. Behind her stood a slender person, sporting shoulder-length, wavy brown hair, jeans and a loose, green-paisley shirt. Grace couldn't make out if it was a man, dressing androgynously, or a flat-chested woman.

"Excuse me. I'm trying to bring my WIFE in for an appointment," Eliot ranted, pointing in her direction, "but it's impossible to park because of the way you carelessly positioned your car." The three fell into a low murmur.

The other patient appeared subdued, directing an apology to the asphalt. Grace recognized the signs of social anxiety. She empathized with this fellow sufferer who perhaps had been so desperate for Dr.

Leighmann's guidance, he or she hadn't taken the time to park properly. The discussion ended with the person shaking Eliot's hand and Dr. Leighmann running back into her office to fetch a parka. Now warm and hooded, the patient hurried to the Roadster and drove off without further incident.

"Some people don't have the brains they were born with." Eliot restarted the car and pulled into one of the empty spaces. "I'll hang around, make some calls until your session ends."

Whoopee, more Eliot time!

Once inside, Grace took her usual place on the brown suede sectional, determined to reveal as little as possible about her survival strategy. She couldn't risk her therapist questioning her conclusions and then snitching to her father, her spouse or worse, the men in the white jackets. Leighmann, wearing a pair of tortoise shell-rimmed glasses, sat in the overstuffed recliner opposite and looked down at her notebook, pen at the ready.

"So, what's going on?"

Grace shrugged. "As usual, he kept pushing and pushing until...I lost my temper."

"The report says you broke things. Were you off your meds?"

Yes, and I plan to stay off them. But that's my business, not yours. "A Limoges plate might have found its way onto the marble floor. He's rich. He can afford to buy more."

During their sessions, Leighmann always listened to Grace's side of any altercation with acceptance and compassion. But her advice often bordered on didactic, towing the "company" line which in this case, was the gospel of Barrington. Understandable, since her father still paid the bills. It was the only expense he'd continued to cover after cutting Grace off as punishment for defying his orders and eloping with Eliot.

"The story I heard involved more than a single piece of china. They said you became violent. Shouted out insults, threats. Tipped over the breakfront, so all the dishes inside came crashing down onto the floor."

"That's a damn lie. I never went near the breakfront. Even if I had, I wouldn't have had the strength to tip it over."

"Not what I was told."

"You weren't told the truth."

"Why would your father lie?"

"I guess because his exaggerated account justified calling the paddy wagon. I did get angry, I'll admit that. Tell me, what was I supposed to do? He was taunting me, insulting his girly-of-the month, nasty as always. He wouldn't listen when I asked him to stop. I needed to get his attention."

Leighmann wore a neutral expression, but the way she tapped her pencil against her knee made it clear she leaned on the edge of reproach. "According to Eliot, all this followed some idea you had about teaching literacy. What have I told you since the day you left Grasmere?"

She rattled off the usual spiel: "Whenever a 'crazy' idea pops into my head, I'm supposed to stop and consider if what I'm seeing is real or a fabrication. Not do anything drastic until I'm sure I'm not overreacting." She dropped the monotone. "But this idea wasn't crazy. I felt confident I could spend a few hours outside the house every week, helping someone else. Is that so wrong?" She fought to keep her lower lip from quivering.

"Grace, there's a thin line between confidence and delusions of grandeur. Coping around strangers, the stress of teaching…I'm not sure how you assumed it would end on a positive note. Eliot spoke of you confronting both him and the boys. It sounds like a recurring pattern of opposition. Do you remember all the times we spoke about how paranoia can lead to lashing out and extreme behavior?"

"I remember." Grace rolled her eyes and glanced at her watch. Still another forty minutes until she'd be free to initiate the survival plan, she'd conceived at Quiet Pines: finding a writing coach, seeking out publishing advice, anything to help her save herself.

"We've discussed before how violence is never the answer," Dr. Leighmann droned on. "Here, in a neutral setting, far from your triggers, let's review some techniques to store in your tool chest for situations like these."

Grace threw her head back in frustration. "Yes, I'm aware of all of them. Count to ten. Remove yourself from the scene. Force yourself to smile and concentrate on something else, anything else. It all sounds so good in theory. But when I get angry, it's like this giant wall slams down, separating the commonsense part of my brain from the part that demands respect, expects to be treated like an adult."

"Which is difficult for us to do, when you still act like a child."

Grace blinked. Something had hit home.

"Don't worry, Grace. I'm sure your recent behavior must concern you. But you're not some lost cause. We can fix this. Some people develop a tolerance for certain medications. That might explain these recent outbursts, your agitation today. Over the next few months, we'll ramp up your dosages and monitor your progress. Along with adding some new coping strategies, like role-play."

"That could work. But how about we fly my father up, involve *him* in some of that role-play. Give him a taste of what a jerk he can be toward his own daughter."

Dr. Leighmann scrawled something down on her pad. "Barrington's almost ninety. He's not about to change, and excuse my bluntness, he doesn't appear to value your relationship as one worth improving. In any case, he's not my patient; you are. If you follow my suggestions, he'll have less to rail against next time you visit. It may not equate to respect, but things might end more peacefully."

The rifts in her family dynamic were old news, but having the doctor reiterate her father's indifference brought tears to Grace's eyes. She grabbed a tissue and dabbed them away. "I have no plans to go back."

"You say that now but you're all he's got. You'll regret it if you're not there for him when he needs you most."

"He's got his billions to keep him company."

Dr. Leighmann's expression turned somber. "Indignance can be costly. Would you rather those billions go to you when he passes, or to the local animal shelter?"

If Eliot has his way, that money will bypass both me and the ASPCA and go right into his pocket. Unless I do something quickly. Unless I act now.

Chapter Seven

Grace feared she might not survive Thanksgiving without imploding. Still unnerved by her recent hospital stay, the last thing she needed was Barrington's traditional holiday greeting. When his call interrupted her turkey basting, she seethed with resentment.

"Happy Crappy," he chuckled from across the miles, amused by his own cynicism. "Got the antacid ready for the troops?"

Since her doctor's warning, she'd redoubled her resolve to maintain her cool around her father, no matter how acerbic his comments. But without her meds, she was less numb to verbal assault than in the past, and less willing to swallow whatever vitriol he threw her way.

"Dad, can you point to one time I cooked for you and you became ill? In fact, considering your team of chefs, I don't remember ever having cooked for you at all."

"I have an active imagination, Spot. Why should you be better at cooking than anything else you do?"

Grace started silently counting to ten, but Barrington interrupted her at four.

"Spot, put on my grandsons. I want to talk to them before the clock hits 'Ptomaine Time.'"

He seemed intent on goading her into an argument. Had boredom launched him into this sadistic holiday diversion? Or did he want to provoke a new excuse for Eliot to stick her back at Grasmere? Whatever her father's motivation, she only had one option if she didn't want to detonate. "Dad? Dad? Are you there?"

"Yes, you idiot, of course I'm here. What's wrong with you? You deaf?"

"Dad, there seems to be something wrong with the line. If you're still there, we all wish you a happy Thanksgiving. Bye!" And with that, she slammed down the phone, proud to have ended the encounter with a modicum of dignity.

Eliot and the boys had planted themselves in front of the television, as they did every year, cheering for the Lions and yelling insults at the opposing team. So, when the doorbell chimed right after she'd hung up on her father, it was clear they considered it her duty to answer, no matter how full her hands might be.

Grace slogged from the kitchen, through the living room and foyer, and flung open the door. She was stunned to find a weary-looking laborer on the other side, his unzipped jacket covering stained overalls and his face darkened by an afternoon shadow a few hours premature. A toolbox lay by his feet. "Can I help you?" she asked.

"I dunno, you tell me. You're the one who called, hysterical about a broken pipe flooding your bathroom."

"I'm so sorry to tell you this, considering it's Thanksgiving, but you've got the wrong house. We have no broken pipes here."

The man frowned and reached a grubby hand inside his coat pocket, pulling out a pink sheet of paper. "Work order," he explained as he unfolded and reread its contents. "You Grace Rendell?"

"Um, yes. That's me."

"Your address 626 Kalb Avenue, Glen Valley?"

She swallowed hard. "Yes, that's right.

"Your phone number 201-555-3373?"

"Right again. But I didn't call a plumber."

He let out a huff and shook his head. "I don't know what to tell you, lady. This work order says a woman by your name called thirty minutes ago, begging us to come over and help. We're not in the habit of popping in for the hell of it, especially on a holiday."

Grace was in no mood to be told she was wrong so soon after dealing with her father's holiday venom. She was about to tell the plumber where to stick his plunger when Eliot intervened.

"Good afternoon. Is there a problem here?"

"Yeah, you could say that. I'm here to fix the broken pipe that Mrs. Rendell now claims never existed." The plumber did not even attempt to mask his contempt.

"What is the charge for a service call, sir?"

"It's normally $125, but seeing as today is Thanksgiving…"

To Grace's horror, Eliot reached into his wallet and pulled out two one-hundred-dollar bills. "Will this cover your trouble?"

"Eliot, do NOT pay this man. We're either victims of some practical joke, or this is some new scam fake plumbers are using to bilk people out of their mon—"

Eliot ignored Grace and handed the money to the plumber. "Again, our apologies. Enjoy the holiday."

The man jammed the bills in his pocket. "With this, I just might. Thanks."

Eliot closed the door and without saying a word, returned to the living room couch. Grace, however, had no interest in remaining silent, and positioned herself in front of the television to block his view. "What the hell, Eliot? I told you not to pay him." She quaked with outrage. "Don't I have any say around here?" Damian and Xander both looked up in surprise.

"Grace, honey, why don't you finish making dinner? This is not the time or place to have this discussion, especially in front of the boys."

"Dinner can wait; you owe me an explanation." Grace increased her volume, unwilling to be muzzled into compliance. "Why is it when I mention something I am absolutely certain about, you consider it less credible than the allegations of a stranger?"

"Drop this, Gracie. Please. I beg you."

"No, I will not drop it. I'll show you my call log. That will prove I'm telling the truth."

Grace sprinted back into the kitchen and scanned the counters. *WTF?* A quick search of the den, dining room, bedrooms, and car yielded the same result: no phone. Where the hell did she leave it? She picked up the home phone and dialed her mobile number and then repeated the search, frantically listening for the ring. Nothing.

She marched back into the living room. "Well, I can't find my phone, but I am positive I never called."

"Grace, for the last time, drop it."

"Why can't you side with me for once? Admit I could be right? That I know what I'm doing?" She stamped her foot for emphasis.

Eliot rose, fists clenched, his pitch raised higher than she'd ever heard before. "Because. This. Is. Not. The. First. Time. This. Has. Happened. Okay? Let it go. I've already forgotten about it." The boys stared at the television screen, intent on avoiding eye contact.

Grace blinked, at a total loss for words. Humiliated, she returned to the kitchen, waited for the tremors to subside, and forced herself to concentrate on something positive. *I won't permit anything to ruin our wonderful family Thanksgiving. Even if it kills me.*

Mind-numbing busywork to the rescue. She basted the turkey, prepared the corn souffle and green bean casserole, and synched both ovens' temperatures so everything would finish cooking in tandem. Once she'd loaded the dishwasher and set the table, a half-hour remained until serving time. She told her family she was heading up to take a quick shower and change.

"Sounds good." Elliot's eyes remained on the game. "Call if you need anything. We'll be here, excited about diving into that turkey. Right, boys?"

She heard their grunts of agreement as she climbed the stairs.

The hot spray pelted over her, each massaging drop erasing the memory of Barrington's maliciousness and Eliot's betrayal, but not her own recriminations over the plumber's visit. "It's so ridiculous. We've never had a broken pipe. It wasn't even our usual guy. How would I have found this joker's number, anyway? And now, on top of everything, I have to waste time and money buying a new cell phone."

Locked in the bathroom, she willed the cascading flow and wafts of steam to calm her nerves. Only when she turned off the faucet and heard the shrill of the alarm and the frantic calls of "Mom!" did she realize that something had gone terribly wrong.

Grace grabbed her robe and dashed barefoot into the hall, thick with billowing smoke. No sign of flames. She loped down the stairs and into the kitchen, where it became impossible to breathe without coughing. The oven door was open, allowing the heaviest plumes to escape. The boys were busy unbolting doors and raising windows throughout the main level to clear the stench; Eliot was on the phone in the living room, assuring the alarm company he had the situation under control. A fire extinguisher lay discarded by his feet.

Grace observed the scene in disbelief, waving her hand to ward off the fumes, torn between rage and consternation. "Everything was right on schedule. What did you do?"

Eliot put his hand over the receiver. "What did *I* do? Are you kidding me? I'm sitting with the boys, minding my business, watching the game, when a wall of smoke floods into the living room and the alarm drowns out the announcer. What *I* did was run in, shut everything off and extinguish the flames."

"You set the temperature to 500 degrees on everything, Mom," said Xander. "I saw it myself as Dad twisted the knobs. Every cooking show on Food Network says you're not supposed to leave the kitchen with something in the oven."

"But I wasn't—"

"The grease caught fire, Grace," said Eliot. "How many sticks of butter did you use, anyway?"

"It's like the slippers," Damian told his brother. "It's not Mom's fault she can't remember things anymore." Then he turned to her, his eyes filled with pity. "Don't feel bad. It's not you, it's your disease. I wasn't hungry anyway."

"I did check everything," Grace spluttered, running back into the kitchen, only to find her prized bird now a charred disaster. The side dishes were also burnt beyond edible.

"It's a fifteen-pound turkey roasting at 325 degrees since noon," she explained, returning to the living room. "It had about forty minutes to go. I coordinated the temperature for the side dishes nowhere near 500 degrees. I am sure of that."

Eliot gave her a sad, patronizing smile that screamed, "You're wrong but you can't help it." Maybe when medicated she could tolerate looks like that; now it stung like antiseptic on a fresh cut. It took every ounce of restraint not to slap it off his face.

Eliot patted the boys on the back. "Let's go out to eat. It'll be a new tradition. I'm sure the Vietnamese place downtown won't be too crowded, and by the time we get back, all the smoke should be gone."

Throughout dinner, Grace kept quiet, unwilling to make matters worse. But Eliot's recent allegation—how she couldn't survive without him—kept pounding in her brain. He'd cited her misplaced slippers. And tonight, Damian echoed the same concern. She doubted that level of forgetfulness, plumber visit and burnt turkey to the contrary. Over her Chè Chuối dessert, she decided it was time to put those slipper allegations to the test.

After returning home, disposing of the ruined food, and closing the windows, Grace waited until Eliot made his usual "business call" to Sheryl before climbing up to their bedroom. She followed her nightly routine, but instead of placing her slippers in her usual spot under the bed, she hid them in the nearby blanket chest.

Footsteps sounded in the hall. She ran to the dresser and pretended to be searching for something when Eliot walked in, pills and water in hand. "You've been so agitated today, Dr. Leighmann said it would be best if you took these." He set the medicine on the bedside table and waited.

"I'm fine, Eliot. The last thing I want today are more drugs."

"Non-negotiable, Grace." His resolve made the hairs at the back of her neck stiffen. "Things are getting out of hand. If you don't want me to call Grasmere, I need you to take these tonight."

He'd played the asylum card. She knocked back the pills, loath as she was to introduce medication back into her system. He made her open her mouth to prove she hadn't stowed them in her cheek.

Overcome by a level of animus she usually reserved for her father, she willed sleep to quell her racing thoughts and bring this awful day to a close. Eliot nestled down beside her, watching the sports recap on his cell. After a half hour, she became woozy, disoriented. Almost in a dream she heard the low ring of a cell phone, followed by a muddle of words too muffled to understand.

"Hey, how you doing? Sounds better than what I've been through...Yeah, I can talk, she's asleep at last but God, what a day. She's fucking driving me nuts...Yes, I took your suggestion, full court press, but I'm not sure how much longer I can tolerate this...I wish I'd been there too...Uh huh, it'll be great...I'd better head downstairs, lock up. You going to be around tomorrow? Great, talk then. Love you too. Night."

■　　■　　■

The next morning, Grace woke up muzzy, eager to shake off the lingering fear and sorrow triggered by her sedative-induced nightmares. Mercifully, she didn't remember the content; she had no desire to revisit whatever left her so rattled.

While Eliot showered, she reached for her slippers. Then, remembering her experiment, she looked inside her blanket chest. There, in plain view, were the pair that any other morning would have gone missing.

Interesting. It might be because I focused on them, which helped me remember where I'd left them. I'll be fascinated to see what happens tomorrow.

That night, she left the slippers under the bed and the next morning, they were again missing. "I was just as focused," she told herself, rubbing the base of her neck. "Maybe some lingering drug withdrawal symptoms are affecting my memory."

Grace prepared breakfast and once everyone had left the house, she ran back upstairs, determined to discover the depths of her dementia. She ransacked the bedroom, peeking in every nook and cranny, emptying dresser drawers, searching inside bathroom cabinets, anyplace a scatterbrained person might mislay an article of clothing. Nothing.

Grace sat on the bed, hugging her knees to her chest and rocking back and forth, seeking to recapture any level of comfort. She'd been so sure. What if Eliot were right, that she couldn't function on her own? Perhaps it was best he watched over her, made sure she didn't become a danger to herself or others.

Then she remembered Thanksgiving night: how he'd sent her cascading into oblivion by force-feeding her an unwanted dose of depressants; the cruelty in his tone when he threatened to commit her to Grasmere; the ensuing nightmares that left her jangled. Was his presence more of a help or a hinderance?

Her resolve from Quiet Pines resurfaced, the idea to weaponize her writing to fend off potential homicidal attacks. "I wonder if any of my old short stories might be a jumping-off point?" With renewed vigor, she ran downstairs to find the stepladder and lugged it back up to the bedroom closet.

The ladder had only three steps, but it terrified Grace to climb even a foot without having someone nearby to spot her. Perhaps it was residual fear from years of medication-induced unsteadiness. It must have been a decade since she'd touched the top shelf of the closet. Yet she persisted, forcing herself step by shaky step up the ladder. *Amazing what you'll do when you fear for your life.* There, toward the back, she spied the box, sitting where she'd left it years earlier, its red "Off-Season" label beckoning her on. But what lay beside it turned her legs to jelly, forcing her to grab onto the shelf for support.

Not since Charles Trask's treachery against Adam in *East of Eden* had Grace experienced as strong a sense of betrayal as she did when she spotted her pair of slippers, hidden away in a spot she'd never have reached by accident. The discovery pushed her off the cliff of naïveté, her past flashing before her eyes, but now in sharper focus. It had been Eliot hiding her slippers all along. Eliot, who must have nabbed her phone and arranged for some woman to impersonate her and summon the plumber. Eliot, who turned up the oven while she was in the shower, incinerating Thanksgiving dinner and leaving her with the blame.

She reflected on all the times she'd defended actions and decisions she'd known to be correct. The afternoons she'd shown up at soccer practice to pick up the boys, only to find herself at the wrong field. Eliot always had a reason at the ready: either she'd forgotten, or heard him wrong, or confused it with the address he'd given her the week before. She'd accepted his explanations without question. Then, there were the times she'd purchased groceries that her husband later claimed could not be found. And that just scratched the surface.

Every week, hour, minute of their marriage, Eliot had manipulated her into thinking of herself as an inadequate wife and a failure as a mother. Now the truth was inescapable—her life was in jeopardy. Her husband was intent on keeping her unbalanced, so she wouldn't leave him until her father died. Then he planned to murder her and collect the inheritance.

But, who could she tell? Who wouldn't chalk up her claims of hidden slippers to paranoia, and commit her for good?

No one. This was something she had to remedy herself.

After the initial shock subsided, she pulled out the box, removed its contents, and placed it back in its original spot, careful not to reposition the slippers. Then she stored away the ladder, cleaned up the mess she'd made, and called her boss, apologizing that an anxiety attack had left her too unsettled to work. Never was an excuse so true. She scooped up her old stories, and with a determination that bordered on the maniacal, ran to the living room and started to read.

Chapter Eight

These Things Happen
By Grace Pierrepoint

It was 1956. Every girl wanted to be a Mouseketeer, listen to Elvis on the radio, and go parking with a boy who owned a coonskin hat. Every girl, except for Ruth Tappen. All Ruth wanted to do was walk again. But prospects looked slim.

The illness had come on so suddenly. Right after her sixteenth birthday, she'd woken up, wondering who had turned the radiator up to boiling, and why her neck and back felt so stiff. It was hard to breathe, and even harder to swallow. She complained to her mother, who turned white and rushed her to the doctor.

Dr. Goetz examined her, gave her a pitying look, and consulted with her mother in the hall. All Ruth could hear were cries of, "If I had known, I would have gotten her the vaccination. I thought they'd found the cure, that everyone was safe."

Her mother took her home and confined her to bed, feeding her chicken soup and reassuring promises that very few polio cases became serious enough to affect the spinal cord. But a week later, Ruth could no longer walk. Her routine now consisted of being fed by her mother, who cleaned out her bedpan several times a day.

During all this time, Ruth's father had been on a business trip in Europe. He'd left behind a vivacious daughter with a promising future, but returned to find a cripple, being nursed by the woman he expected to be at *his* beck and call. Ruth wondered why he refused to look her in the face, much less visit her sickbed. At night, she'd hear her mother apologizing to her father for her illness, bawling after his vicious rants, moaning after he beat her with his belt.

On top of depression over her paralysis, Ruth suffered tremendous guilt over ruining her mother's life. She begged for forgiveness, blaming herself for catching the disease. Her mother, sporting a black eye and bruised arms, smiled sadly and said, "These things happen."

"It's not fair," said Ruth. "Why is he so mean to you? Why don't you leave him?"

"That's your father you're talking about. Don't be disrespectful. He is the head of the household. Women belong to their husbands. Women have to abide by what their men decide."

Her mother's response left Ruth even more desolate, but she was certain that this problem was not without a solution. After much soul-searching, she realized that helplessness was more of an attitude than a reality, and she came up with a plan to help them both.

The next day, she asked her mother to put a phone in her room, claiming that talking to her friends would cheer her up. Her mother agreed, but explained it was costly and begged Ruth to hide the phone under the covers if her father ever entered the room. It was a visit both women doubted would ever occur.

The next time Ruth heard her father beating her mother, she used her new phone to alert the police. Twenty minutes later, the ruckus was impossible to ignore as the authorities broke down the front door and bounded upstairs toward the sound of her mother's cries. Much to Ruth's dismay, her mother protested their attempts to rescue her, saying she wouldn't press charges, that she'd deserved everything she'd gotten. They offered again and again, but she refused any help. Then they departed.

Ruth tried to fight her spiking terror as her father's approaching footsteps reverberated in the hall and her door creaked open. "Were you the one who made the call?" he asked without emotion. Trembling but defiant, she answered yes. He slammed her door and headed back to his room. She expected the assault against her mother to begin anew but she was wrong. The ensuing silence filled her with hope.

The next morning, as Elvis crooned "Don't Be Cruel" over the airwaves, her mother came in, accompanied by her father. It worked, Ruth thought, overjoyed. The officers' visit was a wake-up call. He realized what he was doing was wrong and their marriage will be better now. Even if I never walk again, at least I'll be part of a happy family where my mother is safe.

One look into her father's unyielding eyes revealed they did not reflect this new, optimistic reality. "Do it. Do it now," he instructed her mother as he maximized the radio's volume.

When her mother walked to the bed and lifted Ruth's head, Ruth assumed it was to plump her pillows. She grew confused when her mother removed the pillow instead and laid her head back down. She held it above her daughter's face, tears brimming in her eyes. Then she spoke and Ruth's confusion cleared.

"I'm sorry, I'm so sorry. You left me no choice. It's you or him. I can't lose him."

That's when Ruth realized there would be no Mouseketeer ears in her future, no necking in the backseat with a Davy Crockett wannabe. She didn't struggle when the pillow smothered her face, so consumed was she with sadness, that her father might beat her mother again tonight if this didn't go as planned. How tragic that in a minute, she would be dead, yet it was her mother who had never lived.

These things happen.

The End

Grace was so convulsed by uncontrollable sobs, she could barely read the final paragraph. While the writing style was juvenile and filled with clichés, it reflected how she had interpreted life in her teens. Passive, a victim, forced to accept whatever life threw at her. A societal expectation to endure whatever cruelty a heartless father or husband deemed acceptable. The idea that a wife shouldn't accuse her husband of wrongdoing, no matter how oppressed or demoralized she might become. Unexplained ailments that developed from nowhere, invoking a parent's ire rather than his compassion. The high cost of rebellion. The final message: die rather than rock the boat.

Ruth Tappen may have given up and allowed herself to be suffocated, but Grace Rendell was not going down without a fight. Nothing in this story might fit into her novel, but it was the greatest incentive she could have found. Motivation to overcome her own paralysis and run toward a bright, new future. One that did not include being murdered for her money. She didn't need Jonas Salk to rescue her. She had her wits and her belief that "these things" needn't happen. Not then. Not now. Not ever.

Part Two

Chapter Nine

On the Tuesday evening following her post-Thanksgiving epiphany, Grace stood outside a small ranch home in Westwood, heart racing, as she drummed up the courage to knock on the door. Inside, the members of the North Jersey Burgeoning Writers Meetup expected her. Well, not her as Grace Rendell, but as her new author persona, Ruth Allen. She'd spent hours concocting what she considered to be a clever yet authentic-sounding pseudonym, a play on her name created by mashing together Gracie Allen and Ruth Rendell. She couldn't risk Eliot discovering her plan and stopping her. That's why she had no intention of letting anyone associate her real name with her novel, at least not until a copy was in the hands of every reviewer, reporter and police precinct in New Jersey. She'd even bought a burner phone so unbeknownst to Eliot, she could communicate with anyone who could help her publish a book and save her life.

Grace had spent days studying the craft of writing from authors like Stephen King and Anne Lamott, the titles hidden from view thanks to the privacy of her Kindle. But theory was one thing, execution was another. So, she'd scoured Google for writing classes—free, so Eliot wouldn't question the expense—and soon learned that any combination of the words "free" and "writing" was a joke. Writer's organizations were champions at dreaming up ways for aspiring authors to spend their money. Workshops on plot, character development, dialogue and more flooded the Internet—hell, promoters charged sixty dollars for a class on how to select a class. How ironic: a former Pierrepoint unable to afford a writing class because her father was punishing her for marrying a "commoner." She remembered Barrington's first words to Eliot after they returned from eloping in Las Vegas: "Good luck, buddy. She's your problem now." Through her research, she'd found this free Yahoo Meetup where members gathered weekly to critique each other's work.

Nervous, intimidated, and desperate, Grace summoned all her courage and knocked.

"C'mon in, it's unlocked."

She pushed open the door. To her left, five women sat laughing and chatting around a dining room table overflowing with Merlot, Chardonnay, and Entenmann's finest.

"You must be Ruth," said a willowy blonde through a mouthful of kettle corn. She waved Grace forward. "Come sit down and join the party."

Grace was torn between relief and upset. They seemed like a friendly group, but she wasn't there to get drunk on wine or high on sugar. She wanted, scratch that, she needed knowledgeable advice on how to start a novel. Writing was the cornerstone of her survival plan, along with calling her father each week to check on his health—her welfare now interwoven with his. She'd also flushed her pills down the toilet and replaced them with candy capsules. As long as her prescription bottles were full and Eliot didn't examine them too closely, he'd never notice the difference. Now more than ever, she needed her mind to be at its sharpest, not dulled by antidepressants and antipsychotics.

"Hi, I'm Vera. We spoke on the phone. Did you bring anything to read?" asked a heavyset woman in her fifties, her long, silver hair streaked with lavender.

"Ugh, no. I'm sorry. I had no idea I was supposed to—"

"No problem," interrupted a giggling redhead. "You'll bring it next time. Today, just listen and give us your comments on our work. That's what we're all here for anyway. Well, that and the Merlot."

Everyone around the table broke into laughter. Grace, cheeks burning, found the only empty chair. "I didn't think to bring snacks either."

"There will be plenty of time to correct that. Most of us have been meeting for years. Hence the extra poundage. Help yourself to whatever," said a younger, African-American woman. "By the way, I'm Ava. I write multi-cultural romance. What's your genre?"

"I...I'm writing a mystery. My first." Grace strained to hear her voice over the beating of her heart. "What about you all?"

The women around the table introduced themselves.

"Pixie Pendleton," said the willowy blonde with a warm smile. "Yes, it's my real name. I write Christian westerns and Ultra-Cozies."

"Ultra-Cozies?" asked Grace.

"Yeah, most people aren't familiar with the category. They're short mysteries with only two or three characters, take place in one location, and have very little action. Maybe a theft of something inconsequential, like a trash can. They're for readers so traumatized by the current political climate, they can't tolerate too much drama."

Vera rolled her eyes. "Paranormal erotic comedies. I won the Bergen County, New Jersey division of the Reader's Preferred, Universal, E-Book Summer Award two years ago. But I still apply my blush one cheek at a time, just like the rest of you."

The redheaded, Merlot drinker shook her head. "Ignore her, she's kidding. I'm Jaye. I write YR."

"What's that?" Grace was dizzied by the variety of genres.

"Oh, I'm sorry. It's Yoga romance. My latest, *Chakra Full of Nuts,* hit number one in the category last week. It's about two Yogis who fall in love at a cashew farm."

The last person to introduce herself was an Asian woman in a red pantsuit, seated to Grace's left. She had black hair with dark eyes that, in contrast to the other writers, studied the newcomer with a less-than-friendly expression. "I'm Lynn Andrews and I also write mysteries. Have you heard of the Clara Cardone series?"

Up shot the hair on the back of Grace's neck. This woman didn't want any competition, and the last thing Grace needed was trouble. But she remembered what her mother used to say about keeping friends close and enemies closer…and about catching more flies with honey than vinegar.

"Lynn, oh my God, *you* wrote that series?"

Lynn's visage softened.

"Yes, that is one of several series I've written over the past twenty years." Still a haughty tone, but perhaps a little less so than before.

"Wow. I can't believe someone as accomplished as you would still be in a writing group."

Grace's stomach jumped as Lynn's smile overtook her scowl, and the author put a hand over hers.

"No matter how much success any of us have enjoyed in the past, with every book, we feel as vulnerable as you must feel right now. None of us are one hundred percent certain we can do it again. So, follow our rules, help us with your honest commentary, and we'll do the same. I promise."

Vera waved Lynn off. "Don't mind her. She's more rigid and hardcore than the rest of us. Plus, she's dealing with some unpleasantness at home. Any updates on your brother, hon?"

Lynn sighed and shook her head. "Things have settled down over the last few months, but Joe Hackford is the last thing I want to talk about right now. Can we please get on with it?"

"Sure, no problem. Sorry to rub salt in the wound."

Vera proceeded to read six pages that held Grace in awe—primarily because they were barely coherent. She might be new at writing but not at reading; this was schlock. The paranormal erotic humorist finished her final paragraph and looked around the table with a satisfied smile. "It's rough, I realize that," she said, but Grace sensed it was with misguided false modesty.

The critique started at Vera's left, with Ava straining for something positive to say.

"Well, it's terrific, of course, but Vera...you may have some point of view issues going on. First, you're in the vampire's POV and then you're talking as the hooker..."

"That was the next paragraph."

"Still, it's inconsistent."

"Got it. Next?"

"It's wonderful," Pixie cooed. "And you know I'm your biggest fan, but the tone...it's off. First, it's snarky, next it's full of innuendo and then it's flowery and romantic. And that's only the first page. But I'm sure you'll catch that in the revision."

Jaye's turn was next. "You had three "fangs" too close together. Other than that, I've got nothing. How about you, Ruth? Ruth?"

Grace realized they were speaking to her and she jumped to attention. "Oh, sorry. I...I'm new at this. Let me keep listening and learning. I'm sure I'll have more relevant comments next week."

Vera twisted her lips and turned her gaze to her final critique partner, Lynn.

"I gotta give it to you straight, Vera. It sucked. You're so much better than this. I can't fathom what you were thinking, bringing that dreck in here. Flush it down the toilet, where it belongs."

The room grew as silent as the second "n" in "condemn." Then two beats later, Vera burst into hysterical laughter and the others around the table joined in.

"You're absolutely right. It does suck. I'll revise it and bring it back next week."

It was at that moment Grace realized she could write and publish a novel, but only if she had someone as brutally honest as Lynn Andrews in her corner.

Chapter Ten

Joe couldn't believe his bad luck. What should have been another quick in and out— grab a few valuables pictured in the background of social media posts and then vamoose—had gone south in a hurry. And it wasn't as if the last three successful "outings" had lured him into a false sense of bravado. He was a Robin Hood for the Internet age, careful to digitally track his targets before making a move, taking from the rich to help the needy—in this case, himself. And these folks had posted from Cancun as recently as this morning. Pictures of the beach at sunrise, shot between mimosa flutes lifted in a romantic toast. He should have suspected something was wrong when he found the door unbolted.

Now they were calling him a thief. But that's not how he saw himself. Nope, Joseph Montgomery Hackford—or Hack to the friends who admired his shortcuts and fast talk —was just someone who was a little down on his luck. Someone trying to extricate himself from a tiny misunderstanding he'd had with some vindictive individuals. Lesson learned, never borrow money from shady people to repay gambling debts, and then try to double it at the track. When longshot "Jeddy's Folly" came in last, he'd lost every penny, leaving him unable to repay his initial debts, much less what he now owed to loan sharks. The money was due last week and when he came up empty, said lenders casually mentioned something about leg breaking. Hack liked his legs and planned to do whatever was necessary to maintain them in their original condition.

But Hack could tell the importance of intact limbs held little interest to Mr. and Mrs. Houlahan, who'd caught him red-handed in their living room, stuffing some jewelry and a Ming vase into his duffel bag. They appeared more intent on blocking his exit than listening to excuses, with expressions that read, "Repent now, clarify later."

"What's your name, kid? How old are you? Mr. Houlahan's face was right out of the American Gothic painting they'd recently studied in Art History. But without the pitchfork.

Hack resented the guy talking to him like he was an errant adolescent. Then it occurred to him that his youthful appearance might be his way out of this mess. "I'm Joe Hackford. And I'm sixteen...sir," he lied, slicing two years off his actual age. To further the illusion, he opened his eyes wide and jutted out his lower lip like the pathetic waifs in his late mother's ancient jigsaw puzzles. These two looked like they were in their seventies. Grandparental. How could they resist such a respectful, remorseful young man?

"Well, Joe, have you done anything like this before?" His faint brogue coated the question in an almost cinematic patina, like something from an old cops and robbers movie.

"No, sir, never. I don't know what came over me."

Houlahan glanced at his wife, wavering. Hack's tale of woe had plucked a heartstring or two. "Mo, if we call the police, we could screw up his entire future. That's a heavy price for a kid who made one damn mistake."

Hack turned his quivering pout toward Mrs. Houlahan, trying to project a vibe that combined fright with contrite. Which wasn't too far off the mark.

"Liam, we caught him with my mother's pearls in his hand. My sainted mother's pearls. Irreplaceable. If we let him walk, what's to stop him from pulling this stunt again sometime down the road? You want to tell the Moldows they were robbed because we went soft?" She sniffed with indignation.

Hack winced, his smidgen of hope disintegrating like Alka Seltzer in water, but without the relief.

"Mo, what if we call his parents? Have them come here, pick him up. That way, we can make sure they hear the entire story. Leave it to them to discipline their own kid. Which, if they'd done from the start, would have prevented this whole mess, I'm sure."

"You can't call my parents."

"Would you prefer we call the Bergen County police, and have you hauled down to the precinct?"

Hack estimated his distance from the door. What were his odds of outrunning this guy? He looked in good shape, for a geezer. But Hack was fit, wiry and had youth on his side. Still, if he didn't make it, he'd have bought himself a ton more trouble. Not to mention, he was a good ten miles from his house. The plan had been to run twenty blocks and then pick up the Uber where it had dropped him off thirty minutes before. He decided to bet on the Houlahans' compassion instead.

"You can't call my parents because they're dead. Plane crash about nine months ago." He wondered if he'd ever be able to say those words without stinging from the loss.

Houlahan's face fell. "That's tough, kid. My condolences. But if you're sixteen, who's your guardian?"

"I suppose you could call my sister but...she's a very busy author. I'm sure you've heard of her. Lynn Andrews?"

No recognition registered on either of the Houlahans' faces. *Illiterates.* Time to change course.

"Look, why don't we do this...I'll shovel your driveway and the pathway up to your front door all winter if you let me go. You've got my word on it. And if I renege, well, you'll have my sister's phone number. The almanac is predicting a terrible winter."

It was a stretch, even for Hack, considering the unseasonably warm mid-November afternoon. Immune to the teen's powers of persuasion, Houlahan insisted on the number and then let out a snort of incredulity as he punched it into his cell.

"Good evening, Ma'am. We haven't met, but my wife and I live over at 39 Mulberry in Hackensack. We have a situation with your brother, Joe...no, he isn't injured, but he broke in and has been trespassing and...well, no, we were going to, but we decided against it. My wife and I wondered if you could swing by for a talk...um, sure. One second." Houlahan held out the cell phone to Hack.

"Joe, I'm in the middle of my critique group. What the hell is this all about?" Andrea screamed so loudly, it hurt Hack's ear.

"It's one big misunderstanding...I'm sure if we sit down and discuss this rationally, we can work everything out."

"Cut the BS, Joe. At least they're not calling the police. I expected better of you than this. Stay put. I'll be right over and see about getting you out of this mess." *Click*.

"Yeah Sis, they *are* blocking the door." Hack pretended to listen for a few more beats. "I agree. I'll tell them. Thanks."

He handed the phone back to Houlahan, trying to quell the slight tremor in his hand. "My sister is convinced you're overreacting, sir. Let's hope she doesn't sue for false imprisonment, you keeping me here against my will and all. She sounded annoyed. But, there's still time to do the right thing and let me go..."

Houlahan's harrumph quashed Hack's attempted con. "We'll take our chances on that one, son. Why don't you sit down and make yourself comfortable while you still can. If you were my kid, you wouldn't be able to sit down again for a week after the whooping I'd give you."

Hack shrugged his shoulders as if to say, "It's your funeral. I warned you," and plopped down onto their oversized leather recliner, unsure of his next move. None of his go-to strategies were working today. The Houlahans sat opposite, also at a loss for words. Mrs. Houlahan ducked out to finish clearing the dinner table. Her husband scrolled through emails. The grandfather clock marked the seconds as they ticked by, exacerbating the teen's unease.

Hack cursed his fake ID for causing this whole mess. Without it, he wouldn't have gotten into the Jersey casinos or the track and lost his shirt. Or the bars, where he'd met bad men with money to lend. He made a mental note to get rid of his as soon as he turned twenty-one.

After fifteen minutes, his sister arrived and shot him a look the Defense Department could register as a lethal weapon. She spent the next quarter-hour apologizing so profusely, the Houlahans agreed to forget the whole incident, as long as she sent them a free book or two. Hack figured that was the end of it, but once in the car, Andrea proved him wrong.

"Honestly Joe, what the hell is wrong with you? It's probably our fault. We should have never agreed to let you stay in the house unsupervised after Mom and Dad passed. The shock of losing them has obviously affected you worse than we gathered."

"You all live outside my school district, busy with your own lives. Did you expect me to finish my senior year as the new kid in class, surrounded by strangers? Anyway, I was eighteen when they died. Legally an adult."

"Barely eighteen. A typical, irresponsible male adolescent. And not much has changed. Drag races this past summer. Peddling stolen cell phones on the black market a few months before that. What were you thinking, breaking in? I got you off the hook with the police the last few times, but something like this? No way."

"Sis, don't you remember what life was like when you were my age?" Hack brandished his most ingratiating smile.

It was her soft spot, and he massaged it as often as possible. Guilt over neglecting him during his youth. His siblings were all adopted and at least twenty years his senior, with Hack the surprise menopausal baby his parents had been told they'd never conceive. John and Elaine Hackford had spent his adolescence slaving away to afford the retirement they'd never lived to enjoy, and most of his siblings hadn't pitched in to help, leaving him to his own devices. Andrea had been the exception, mothering him as often as her schedule would allow, though between her meeting planning and writing careers, it wasn't as often as he needed.

"I remember it well. I went to school and wrote stories and saved my money. What's your excuse?"

"I guess things are more expensive now than they were in the Dark Ages."

Hack couldn't come clean about his gambling issues, or his tailspin existence since the day a malfunctioning jet engine turned his parents' one-week vacation into forever. That was the moment he realized that no matter how good the person, or how pure their lifestyle, it could be over in one, inexplicable instant. And if nothing anyone did during their short stay on Earth mattered, why not try everything while you were still around to enjoy it? His "everything" had been an unfortunate and expensive exercise in self-indulgence that had done little to fill the void left by his parents' death or imbue his existence with any real meaning.

He'd talked his siblings into letting him stay alone in their family home and cover the property taxes until high school wrapped up. With house values down and the mortgage already paid off, it hadn't been that hard a sell. But when his excesses depleted most of his inheritance, he'd converted the six-bedroom colonial into a SleepStay—an Airbnb wannabe but with less vetting—to make the extra cash he'd need until graduation when his siblings sold the place. Between food and utilities, even that wasn't pulling in enough. If Andrea and the others found out about his real estate venture, they'd pull the house right from under him—or worse, want their share of the profits—which was financially unfeasible right now. He forced himself to sound more repentant.

"The last two times, I agree. I was bored and it was stupid. This robbery was to win an argument. I told a friend that thanks to everyone announcing their whereabouts and displaying their belongings on social media, burglary was now as simple as taking candy from a baby."

"Looks like you proved yourself wrong."

"Come on, sis. Who knew they were after-posters? God, I hate when people pull that. Either post your photos in the moment or skip it. Don't fricking make everyone believe you're away when you're not."

Andrea pulled up in front of the house, shaking her head. "You're blaming them? Please. Just promise me you won't do anything like this again."

Hack looked down at his lap. "I promise." Even if she doubted him, he knew that as her favorite sibling, she'd always give him a pass.

"Are you going to invite me inside?"

No way, not with his tenants milling about. "I'd love to, but the place is a wreck, and this whole mess has left me exhausted. Raincheck?"

"I suppose it will have to be. See you soon. How about dinner Sunday?"

Hack couldn't escape the car fast enough. "You got it. Thanks for everything, Andrea. I promise, I'll do better."

"I certainly hope so."

He ran up the front walk, keys in hand, and unlocked the door. Mackenzie O'Malley waited in the foyer, clad in skinny black jeans and a black button-down blouse—the height of militant chic—which complimented her buzz cut and facial hardware. Kenzie had been his tenant and confidant for the past two months, the only one he didn't hit up for rent because she helped with the other guests while he was at school.

"What the hell took you so long?" Her greeting matched her looks, blunt and no-nonsense.

"I got caught." He longed to crawl under the carpet.

Her face grew solemn. "Oh my God. Did they...?"

"Call the police? Press charges? Almost. Andrea got me out of it."

"Thank God for that. Did you manage to get anything?"

Hack shrugged. "I almost got a Ming vase."

"I'm worried about you, Hack. You're involved with some bad people and you can't pay off your debts with almost."

"Truth. They even kept my duffle bag."

She gave him a hug. "This can't be easy for you, with your parents gone and all. I'll try to drum up more cash. I appreciate you not charging me to stay here."

"And I never will." When not cleaning up after his guests, Kenzie split her time between waiting tables at the local diner and volunteering at Matthew's Retreat, a shelter named for Matthew Shepherd that provided refuge to marginalized teens escaping bullying and other forms of persecution. Vulnerable himself since his parents' death, he wasn't about to take a penny from someone dedicated to such a worthwhile cause. In fact, when things turned around, he planned to make a big donation.

She walked into the living room and plopped onto the couch. "So, what's the plan going forward?"

I'll have to figure a way out of this. I always do. It's just going to take a little ingenuity. That's all."

And time. And money. Two items that were currently in short supply. For the first time in his life, Hack may have dug himself a hole so deep, it could easily become a grave if he didn't act soon.

Chapter Eleven

For the first time in her CPA career, Grace appreciated her firm's sizeable number of self-employed clients. Their need to file quarterly returns made it easier to justify ten to twenty hours of overtime each week and hiring Keira to chauffeur the boys around. If Eliot questioned the missing imaginary pay, she'd tell him she'd been compensated off the books and then used the cash to cover some equally imaginary house repairs. If he ever caught on, it would likely happen after she'd published her book and no longer needed to sneak in extra hours to add a few hundred words each day to her growing manuscript.

Her boss sympathized with her faked panic attacks and didn't protest when she asked for a lighter workload. She'd always been a consistent producer, so he had no reason to doubt her. The challenge of carving out some dedicated writing time was far less daunting than conjuring up the actual prose. She hunkered down in the back of the Westwood Public Library where no one would recognize her save for the authors from the critique group. When the narrative eluded her and writer's block set in, she'd zip over to Conrad's Confectionary for some chocolate or a quick afternoon coconut ice cream.

A second visit convinced Grace to bag the writer's meetup. When her turn came around, she'd read her first chapter and endured their criticisms—too many repeated words, some point of view issues, too many passive verbs. Only Lynn cheered her on, reminding the others that Grace was a newbie, and this was a first draft. But it wasn't the comments that upset her; it was exposing her plot to a group of near-strangers and potential rivals. What if someone suspected it was autobiographical? Or figured out who she was, and word got back to Eliot? What if one of them stole her idea and published it under their own name? Who would distribute her "plagiarized" version then? Her efforts would have all been for naught, and her days numbered once her dad passed.

Grace's fears fueled a newfound boldness. After her final critique meeting, she walked Lynn Andrews back to her car, an evening flurry dotting their hats and coats in white. Lynn had been dead-on with her criticism that night, offering nurturing and complimentary comments when appropriate, but unafraid to shred her fellow authors' less-talented work with her acerbic wit. The meeting convinced Grace that as a mentor, Lynn wouldn't allow her to publish anything that wasn't bulletproof. She had to tread cautiously, though. Aspiring authors must inundate someone so skilled and famous with requests for help. She needed to offer Lynn something of equal value. Adoration seemed like a good place to start.

"Lynn, I was shopping online yesterday and noticed that *Clara Knows Honor's Face* was out of stock."

"I'm sure that's true. As the contracts expire, I've been grabbing back the rights so I can self-publish. I'll have it out with a new cover next month." She pulled her coat tight to deflect the snow, which had intensified from flurry to squall.

"When? It's one of the only Cardone books I haven't read."

"Tell you what. Email me all the titles you're missing, and I'll see if I have any extra copies lying around at home."

"That would be wonderful, thanks." Grace waited a beat, unperturbed by the freezing wind. She was, after all, a woman on a mission. "Look it's cold, and I don't want to keep you out in this weather. But there is so much about writing I don't understand yet and Lynn, you're such a font of knowledge. I need some tutoring and some objective help with my manuscript."

"What you read today was promising, Ruth. Your talent may be raw, but it impressed me."

Grace's heart fluttered. If someone like Lynn Andrews had faith in her prospects, anything was possible. "That's wonderful to hear, but I'm having real trouble getting past these first few chapters. Do you ever consult with authors? Help them edit and publish their books? I'm not rich, but I've scraped together a few hundred dollars as a deposit, and then later, I'd be willing to share any of the profits I make." She'd promised money she couldn't really afford to spend. But if she laid off the cleaning lady for a few months and vacuumed and dusted while Eliot was at work…

"A royalty share? Hmm. That might be interesting. I'm leaving town tomorrow for my other job, but I'll be back on Monday. Can we meet then and discuss this, before I make any rash decisions?"

Grace grew optimistic. Splitting her income—or royalties as Lynn put it—was the perfect way to remove any incentive for Lynn to plagiarize her plot. One less thing to worry about. "Yes. Let's exchange cell numbers so we can touch base when you get back." She pulled out her burner.

"If it works out, we can meet over at my house in Ridgewood." Lynn climbed into her black BMW. "Two rules though: if you work with me, you must accept my manuscript revisions without debate. I don't have patience for ego."

"Got it. What's the second thing?" Grace asked through rattling teeth.

"I hope you like cats. Denver, Aspen and Vail have the run of the house."

"I love cats. I'm sure it won't be a problem," Grace lied. She wasn't about to skewer her chances of working with a famous mystery author by admitting to an allergy. A few sniffles and hives in exchange for a publishable manuscript and a reprieve from her death sentence? It was a no-brainer.

"Get out of the cold, drive safe. We'll talk soon." Lynn shut the door against the flakes invading her leather interior.

A growing excitement warmed Grace as she watched the author pull away onto the snow-blanketed street. She looked down at her Movado. Time to hurry home before Eliot noted the lateness of the hour. She couldn't jeopardize her alibi now that all the pieces were falling into place.

Chapter Twelve

Two weeks to go before Christmas and Grace had a lot on her mind: presents to buy, a tree to decorate, a life to save.

Lynn was back in town and had scheduled their first meeting for three o'clock that afternoon. But what might have seemed overwhelming a few weeks ago was much easier to handle now, thanks to a clear head unhampered by psychotropics.

Grace hoped to get a little more writing done beforehand, proud of having eked out two more chapters of *Salvaging Hope*, the title she'd chosen for her *chef-d'oeuvre*. The story of Hope, an heiress with a history of paranoia, certain her husband planned to murder her once she inherited her father's fortune. A target, frantic for a guardian angel, yet ignored due to her mental fragility. Forced to adopt extraordinary measures to save her own skin.

She imagined it wasn't that different from what many older, neurotypical women experience. How many wives over forty were trapped inside loveless marriages, ignored by their husbands, invisible to employers, disrespected by society at large? Wasn't that like death in a way, the slow suffocation of a soul? How many lingered, yearning to escape but unwilling to decimate their finances and the lives of their children in the process? Maybe her book would find an audience as a feminist allegorical manifesto.

Grace had changed a few autobiographical details to pass the book off as fiction. For example, rather than two boys Hope had three girls, and lived across the bridge in Westchester County. But Eliot would know. He'd read the plot and realize she'd exposed him and foiled his plans. That if he proceeded, everyone would view his wife's opus as a warning to the world, her "accidental" death inspired by his insatiable greed and lifted from her own manuscript.

Everything that Tuesday seemed pitted against her. The boys insisted on omelets for breakfast, and the extra preparation time caused them to miss their bus. As she bundled up to drive them to school, Eliot dropped the bombshell he planned to work from home and suggested escorting her to Dr. Leighmann's for her weekly appointment.

"Why not grab lunch at Pastitsio's first, get some decent spanakopita? You've been working so many late nights, I never see you anymore, darling. I miss you."

She'd planned to skip both work and her therapy session and instead, grab her favorite desk at the library to edit what she'd already written. Now that was off the table.

After chauffeuring the boys, she headed over to Davidoff, Weiss & Greenburg, her CPA firm. For once she was thankful her husband always steered clear of the place. There'd be no "Hey Eliot, long time no see" comments from her co-workers, no damning remarks like, "We've missed Grace the last few weeks, where have you been keeping her?" Still, she'd asked him to call a few minutes before he arrived. That way, she'd wait for him by the front door, never give him a chance to step inside.

To her dismay, her boss Seth ambushed her by the coat closet as soon as she arrived that morning. "Thank the lord you're here, Grace. Mounica and Francine are home with the flu, and we're *snowed* under, so to speak. I have a few pressing files for you to *plow* through." She forced an obligatory smile, acknowledging his wintery *puns du jour*, and reacquainted herself with the workstation she hadn't visited in the past week. True to his word, Seth dumped several folders onto her desk with a grunt, then retreated to his office, shutting the door behind him.

The first return was so complex, it crushed any hope to split her attention between 1040s and her manuscript. She plodded along, scanning the W-2s and 1099s, but her mind kept wandering back to her novel, wondering how to describe the epiphanic moment when Hope conceived the perfect solution to save herself. A bolt of inspiration hit. She grabbed her notepad and scribbled: "Hope couldn't write to save her life, but now it was the only way she could." Satisfied, Grace returned her focus to accounting, and hummed with pride as she completed Mr. Haber's return.

She started to work on Ms. Helprin's when her cell buzzed, and she realized lunchtime approached.

Eliot jabbered throughout their meal. His bosses had completed his annual review earlier than expected and offered him a $20,000 raise. "We should stick it right into the boys' college fund, Grace. It's only two years away and with Damian's grades picking up, Trinity would be a slam dunk. Why shouldn't we cash in on that legacy advantage?"

His enthusiasm was so contagious that for a moment, Grace let down her guard and got caught up in the possibility of her son heading off to Eliot's alma mater. It would have been her alma mater too, if things had gone differently twenty-five years earlier...

After Grace slogged through her first two years of college via video classes and distance learning—all thanks to Barrington's unwillingness to expose her paranoia to an ever-prying paparazzi—she parlayed her 4.0 average into an escape route. Without his knowledge, she applied to a slew of top colleges, the so-called Little Ivies, sight unseen, with Trinity in Connecticut at the top of her list. The brochure, highlighting the school's Long Walk and gothic-style chapel, enchanted her. She dreamed of spending her junior and senior years meeting people her own age, unmonitored and unencumbered by her father's rules and snide criticism.

Her grades and high-profile name garnered her acceptances wherever she applied. Some even offered scholarships. More shocking still, after hours of heated discussion and reminders of her tenuous mental state, her father and therapist relented and permitted her to attend. She'd been ecstatic, barely able to sleep. Freedom was a mere few months away, a chance to make her own decisions and live an independent existence. Heaven.

That illusion lasted about one week. A few days after orientation, Grace had been in the school's bookstore, crouching to pull a novel off the bottom shelf. When she stood back up, she bumped into a freshman passing behind her, knocking a mug from his hands onto the floor, where it cracked into dozens of ceramic shards. She spluttered an apology, insisting on paying for the damage, but the student refused. His hair was black as Poe's raven, his eyes as green as Anne's gables, and his Bantam-adorned Trinity tee-shirt did little to conceal the sculpted muscles underneath. "You can't pacify a Rendell with mere words," he said with mock affront. "Only a beer or two at College View can appease our ire."

Thanks to romance novelists like Jude Deveraux and Julie Garwood, Grace recognized a good line when she heard one. She flirted right back, donning a British accent and matching his archaic vernacular.

"Ah, good squire, pray forgive that my clumsiness may have offended ye. Let us sally forth that together we might partake in a pint of conciliatory ale."

"Who is this Sally and why is she horning in on our date?"

Grace found it hard to resist the twinkle in his eye. He introduced himself as Eliot, hailing from the exotic climes of the Bronx. And from that moment on, they were inseparable.

Collegiate infatuation turned out to be even more exhilarating than freedom from her father. They married soon afterwards, and she dropped out of college to keep house and support his studies, finishing her own degree by mail.

"Earth to Grace." Eliot yanked her attention back to the present. "Are you on board with sticking that extra money right into the college fund?"

"Sure, sure...sounds like a plan."

"Grace, what's going on? You don't seem like yourself today. Is it work, or do you have a lot on your mind to discuss with Dr. Leighmann?"

She appreciated the question; excuses were more believable when served up by the accuser. "Both. I have a pile of files on my desk that Seth predicts will soon double. It looks like more overtime...I hope you don't mind." A little contrition never hurt when trying to make a lie sound authentic.

"Not a problem. I can pick up the slack. Since my company's so happy with me, they might consider letting me telecommute a few days a week until tax season ends. I'll ask when I get back to the office."

So sweet. To the unsuspecting eye, anyway. But she knew the truth that lurked beneath that solicitous exterior.

"Eliot, I can grab a cab from here if you don't want to waste time schlepping me around." It was worth a shot. If he agreed, she'd cancel with Leighmann, blaming a work emergency, and recoup a few writing hours.

"I would never consider time spent with you a waste."

Hopes squashed, she chomped on the rest of her salad in silence.

Her resentment grew deeper over the following hour of therapy. Eliot waited in the car while she stared up at the ceiling and endured her weekly grilling. She loved Dr. Leighmann and appreciated her help, but right now, she had a plot twist to flesh out.

Leighmann focused on the looming holidays, and the memories they dredged up. Her visions started around Christmas. It had been a difficult time of year ever since, and the therapist wanted to head off any angst.

"So, Grace, how are you making out?"

"What can I say? I'm coping." It was an understatement; she was thriving. All this intrigue—sneaking around, claiming time for herself—invigorated her. It was almost as if she were as normal as any other suburban New Jersey housewife.

"So, no recurrences? No bad dreams or night tremors?"

Grace shook her head.

"Eliot called and reminded me how distraught he still was about Thanksgiving dinner and the plumber incident. You sure you're being diligent about your medication? You're aware how essential it is for your stability."

She nodded, but Leighmann's words struck a nerve. Now that the doctor had increased her dosage, Grace had a mandate to tone down her emotion and verve. She blurred her focus and slackened her jaw.

"I haven't missed a pill. Guess they're working. Worried about losing your star patient?" She sat up, unwrapped a hard candy from the bowl on the coffee table, and popped it into her mouth.

"Nothing would make me happier than if you lived a normal, unmedicated life, where you never again worried the world was out to get you."

Grace studied Leighmann's face. Her smile seemed sincere. She questioned if this might be a signal to come clean, tell her therapist everything.

"How are things with Eliot?"

Funny you should ask, Dr. Leighmann. He's planning to kill me. She visualized the aftermath of that little admission and stared back off into space, eager to maintain the illusion of overmedication.

"Grace?"

"Huh? What?"

"I asked how things were going with Eliot."

"Oh, sorry. Same old, same old. And the boys are as disrespectful as ever."

"That is your interpretation. All teenagers consider their parents idiots and treat them accordingly. You shouldn't take it personally. And while we're on the topic of parents, have you spoken to your father recently?"

"I call Caprice on her cell. It's less upsetting that way. She says his memory loss and disorientation haven't worsened since my last visit. I suppose that's the best we can hope for at this point."

Dr. Leighmann scrunched her brow. "Is he seeing any doctors down in Florida who deal with dementia?"

Grace noticed how her therapist's concern amplified when the conversation turned to Barrington. *He's the one paying the bills, after all. No one wants to see their meal ticket marked void.*

"No idea. I guess he's Caprice's problem now. I mean, she's enjoying the fruits of his wealth, she might as well fertilize the soil it grows in." Grace laughed. "Gotta sift through a lot of manure to tolerate Barrington." Writing daily had upped the quality of her metaphors.

Leighmann frowned. "Do you know anything about Caprice? Her past?"

"Are you worried she's a gold digger?"

"I wouldn't know, I haven't met her. You have. What's your opinion?"

"She appears genuinely concerned about his health and safety. More so than the other moppets he's talked into his bed. Currency can be a powerful aphrodisiac."

"Grace, you still seem on edge." Leighmann pulled out her prescription pad. "Hostile at the mere mention of your father's name. I'll add some Dilantin to your cocktail but let me know if you experience any twitching or nausea."

Great, another drug I won't be taking.

"In the meantime, have you considered flying down there to make amends? Not only are the holidays a great excuse to get together, but they can be nostalgic, bring out everyone's softer side."

Ah yes, the magic of holiday reunions. Combine several different personalities, add the stress of forced gaiety, a pinch of anxiety over money spent, and you had all the makings of a mental breakdown. Literally, a serving of fruitcake.

"I'll consider it. Eliot's attending an advertising convention in Dallas the week before the holidays. The boys will be out of school too. If the three of us fly down, who knows? Maybe Barrington's grandsons can coax out his softer side."

She had no intention of flying south again and congratulated herself for delivering such a convincing lie. Better to appease her therapist now and come up with a last-minute excuse later.

"That's an excellent idea, Grace. Notify me when you've booked the flights so I can cancel that week's appointment. I don't want you charged for a no-show."

Grace wondered if anyone still sold refundable airline tickets. It was essential that she continue to appear cooperative.

Eliot was deep in conversation when she returned to the car. He disconnected mid-sentence as she slipped into the passenger seat and shot him a knowing glance.

"You didn't have to stop talking on my account." *I'm sure a prepubescent paramour like Sheryl can dish up a complex conversation. Why is the sky blue? Why is the grass green?*

"I didn't. We were wrapping up when you came out."

"Just how expensive *are* Justin Bieber tickets this year, anyway?"

He threw her a curious look. "Got me. This client is in engineering, not entertainment, and can't distinguish his advertising ass from his elbow. Back to your office, madam?"

"Please." She didn't want to go back— hell, she hadn't intended on going to work that day at all. To her relief, Eliot turned on ESPN, eliminating the need for further chatter. He dropped her outside her office at 2:45 p.m., leaving her just enough time to run to her Volvo and floor it down the Garden State. Barring any speeding tickets, she was only fifteen minutes away from receiving the writing advice she craved.

Chapter Thirteen

Dozens of multicolored porcelain cats crowded the living room of Lynn Andrews's Tudor home, their ceramic stares making a nerve-wracked Grace fidget more than usual. "You're not fooling anyone," their expressions chided. "You're not Ruth Allen. And you're no author." Lynn's live felines, equally unimpressed by the budding novelist, scrutinized her from their various perches before meandering back to the kitchen, where their owner reviewed her initial chapters.

For Grace, waiting for Lynn to finish was like a winter spent walking barefoot on carpet and then touching metal doorknobs. Born was a newfound respect for every author who'd overcome this initial hump and made it onto the shelves.

Her gaze wandered past the cats to study the rest of the home's flea market decor. Antique typewriters, clocks, teapots, and chess sets, all covered by a thin coating of dust, lined the tops of coffee tables, bureaus and the shelves of a cherry curio cabinet. Multi-hued scarves adorned the backs of mismatched recliners and rocking chairs. The resulting vibe was both disheveled and welcoming. *Haimish*, as the owners of her CPA firm would say.

"You can come back in now, Ruth," Lynn called from the other room.

Grace poked her head into the kitchen, her heart jumping like a Riverdance audition. "You ever read *Tea and Sympathy*?"

Lynn broke into a smile. "Yeah, yeah, don't worry. I'll be kind. Come and sit down."

Grace pulled out a chair, winced, and prepared for the worst.

Lynn reviewed the screen of her turquoise MacBook, covered in stickers from exotic climes. "Okay, Ruthie, you have some solid prose here.

It's clear you can write. We need to work on the pacing and some of the dialogue. It's got to sound natural, not so stilted...Hey, don't get upset. If you take my advice, I can help you fix this."

Grace's eyes *were* tearing, but not because of her cat allergy or any hurt feelings. Criticism didn't faze her; she'd spent a lifetime buried under a pile of her father's "well-intentioned" critique. No, these were droplets of joy—Lynn Andrews believed she had talent!

"I'm so glad you think it has potential." Grace pulled a tissue from the box on the table and dabbed her cheeks. Then she opened the note section of her phone. "I'm listening. Shoot."

"If I help you write this thing, I'll need a synopsis and an outline. Have you figured out the entire plot and how it ends?" Lynn pointed to a plate of toll house cookies to Grace's left. "Take a few. Old Chinese recipe for stress relief."

Grace stopped typing, opening her eyes wide. "You serious?"

"About the Chinese part? No, that was a joke. Though most authors agree that sugar has great reparative qualities. Which is why we cram our critique table with junk food."

"And wine."

"Alcohol doesn't heal the sting of the criticism, but it sure helps you stop giving a damn."

Grace relaxed, elated that she'd cracked Lynn Andrews' intractable exterior. In fact, despite her initial sidestepping of eggshells, she couldn't remember ever having this level of comfort with another woman. It was almost like she was a normal person, not a psychiatric case study. One of the perks of being Ruth Allen instead of Grace Rendell.

"So, have you? Worked out the ending?"

If only. "I figured it would come to me as I wrote. Doesn't that happen with some writers? They plot as they go?"

"Pantsers, yes. They're called that because they write by the seat of their pants. Don't sweat it; we can sort it out together. Tell me, where did you get the idea for the story?"

This was the question Grace had been hoping to avoid. "Err...it's something I've been mulling over for a while."

Lynn nibbled on a cookie, oblivious to Grace's unease. "It's an unusual concept. I like the heroine writing herself out of danger. Publishing rather than perishing. But we'll need some side plots, a few secondary characters. She should have a sidekick, maybe an enemy-turned-friend who can help her carry out her plan, escape her fate. And perhaps her mother or a maternal-like character should appear in a chapter or two. Someone trustworthy, a go-to person in moments of anguish. What's your take?"

Grace had never considered side plots or secondary characters and gave silent thanks she'd chosen to align with someone who'd been through this before. "Great idea. It makes sense to balance such a desperate character with someone she can rely on for support." Grace wondered if Lynn would evolve into that character in *her* life.

"Everyone needs someone to turn to. And if that character cares about your heroine, then the readers will take that as a cue to care about her too."

"Point taken. I'll work on it. If we meet a few times a week, how soon until *Salvaging Hope* hits the bookstores?" She reached down to pet the Scottish Fold rubbing its torso against her calf.

Lynn held up a finger while she swallowed the last of her snack. "Oh, wow, we're a few years away from that. Between revision, editing, querying agents and advance marketing, publishing is a glacially slow process."

Grace's chest tightened. She didn't have a few years to wait. Her father's eighty-eighth birthday was only weeks away, and dementia multiplied his risk of mortality. She remembered the conversation they'd shared after the critique meeting. "What about self-publishing? How long would that take?"

Lynn considered the question as she filled a kettle with water and set the flame on high. "Once we edit the book? If we order the cover art ahead of time and work with a fast formatter, it might be ready for release as soon as a week after final revisions. You want some tea?"

"That would be great, thanks."

Lynn busied herself with the kettle, giving Grace a few moments to consider her timeline. "Self-publishing sounds like the way to go. I want *Salvaging Hope* to be in readers' hands by early summer."

"That's highly optimistic." Lynn handed her a steaming mug.

"I have faith. And I'm willing to work as hard as necessary to see things through. Are you available to meet more often than we originally discussed?"

"As long as my brother Joe doesn't do anything stupid and nothing crazy happens at work, I'm sure I can free up some extra hours here and there. You'll have to be flexible about the hour, though,"

"I can always fabricate a credible-sounding story for my boss. You tell me what to do and I'll find a way."

Grace prayed everything in Lynn's life remained stable, and that her mentor was as committed to their joint project as she was. Her life depended on it.

Chapter Fourteen

Bleary-eyed, Hack tried to make it through sixth period history without dozing off. The after-school jobs he'd taken to repay his gambling debts were taking their toll. The last thing he needed were texts like the one he'd just received from his realtor sister-in-law. He raised his hand, excused himself, and called her from the bathroom.

"What's going on, Joe?" Sammie's voice was a few octaves higher than usual. "I was at a listing presentation for the Kaplans. They mentioned seeing two young girls leaving your house this morning and asked if you were running your own personal harem. What gives?"

Damn. The nosy neighbors had noticed a few of his tenants. Hack grappled for a plausible response. "Yes, two girls slept over, it's true. We studied for midterms until midnight, and they were too exhausted to drive home. I put them in Gwennie's room. Do I have to send out a newsletter to the entire block whenever anything happens out of the ordinary?" He hoped that sounding offended would add some believability.

"No, but you have to be conscious of appearances. We want to sell as soon as you graduate. We can't have anything stigmatize the house. Let's talk about it over dinner next Sunday."

Hack rolled his eyes. Between classes, dog-walking, and his evening ride-share gig, he didn't need to see his family; what he needed was a week of uninterrupted sleep. "You got it. I'm looking forward to hanging with you and Chuck."

The call brought attention to an issue he hadn't contemplated—no secret on Wolver Hollow Road stayed secret for long. The last thing he needed were gossips like the Kaplans ratting him out and exposing his real estate venture. This was a tricky one. He couldn't expect boarders to confine themselves to the house. Kenzie was shrewd. She might offer a suggestion or two.

One thing Sammie said struck him as odd, though. Kenzie was the only female currently staying at the house, and they didn't expect any new guests for a few days. After eighth period, he squeezed in a trip home to find out what was what.

Kenz set down her coffee cup as he entered the dining room, a slew of official-looking papers spread across the table. "Hey Hack. You're back early. No work tonight?"

"Not for a bit. I need to ask you something. A neighbor told my sister she saw two girls leaving this morning. We have someone new check in?"

"No, I'm sorry, that was my fault. We're so crowded at the shelter that we turned our office into an auxiliary bedroom. I had to meet with someone from the Gay Grid about a grant, so I asked her to meet me here instead. I hope that's okay."

Hack shrugged and walked toward the kitchen. "Screw the neighbors. I'll drop by later and feed them some excuse. You want a soda?"

"Nah, I'm good."

"What's the Gay Grid?" he called out as he opened the fridge.

"The umbrella organization that oversees and funds the various shelters and transports that belong to the Rainbow Railroad. They receive tons of money from donors sympathetic to the cause. I'd like to get a slice of that for Matthew's Retreat."

Hack returned to the table and sat beside her, still confused. "That would be great, but what's the Rainbow Railroad?"

"You remember the Underground Railroad? From history class?"

"Like Harriet Tubman?" He downed a gulp of soda.

"In Toronto, they've formed something similar. It helps LGBTQI and other at-risk individuals escape persecution, violence and death by transporting them to more accepting environments."

"Canada is dangerous for gay people?"

"It's a worldwide effort that's headquartered in Canada, dumbass." Kenzie's snicker suggested he was a lost cause. "And it's not just for gays. They rescue transgender and bisexual people too."

Hack still missed the connection. "We're in the United States, Kenz. What does all this have to do with us?"

"Some secret groups on social media have adopted the Rainbow Railroad model here. They've organized a network of emergency shelters across the country and linked them to drivers willing to rescue at-risk teens from less-accepting towns, bring them to safe houses like ours. The Gay Grid helps support that effort. I'm applying for the grant so we can expand, take in more refugees."

"You're amazing. I admire your passion." A wave of embarrassment washed over him. Kenzie was doing so much good, while he spent days at the track racking up debt. If his parents were looking down from heaven, how disappointed they must be. He envied Kenzie and her dedication. At least one of them had found a mission in life.

Her expression grew sober. "The world can be a dangerous place. I won't rest until society stops trying to quash those of us who are different, and silence us whenever we say something they don't agree with. Everyone deserves respect and acceptance, to live comfortably in their own skin. Sermon over."

"I agree with every word...yet I feel so powerless. I wish there was some way I could help."

The bell chimed. "If you're serious about that, the answer to your prayers is on the other side of that door. Like I said, we're out of room at the shelter. There was a new guy who showed up today and instead of turning him away, I hoped he might spend a few days here until some space opened up."

"Um...sure, Kenz—whatever you need." Hack walked to the foyer with feigned enthusiasm, unsure if this was the help he had in mind. Giving up a bedroom would siphon off potential income that he needed now, more than ever. If Kenzie sensed his trepidation though, it would make him look like a hypocrite.

He opened the door, uncertain of what to expect. On the other side stood a lanky, olive-skinned, bearded man around Hack's age, wearing a yarmulke. He pointed to a rip in his shirt. "You're in luck. I'm the holy man you've been hoping would show."

Hack stifled a laugh. "Holy man, huh? Are you sure you're at the right house, Rabbi? The nearest synagogue is several towns away."

"You are the shelter, no?" Hack detected the hint of a Yiddish accent.

"Not exactly. More like the shelter's waiting room."

"Sarcasm! I like it. My name is Zev Einhorn. Kenzie gave me this address. Okay if I come in and sit down?"

Hack looked down and noticed with surprise that Zev was empty-handed. "No suitcase?"

"No, everything I own I'm wearing. Oh wait..." He reached into his back pocket and pulled out a toothbrush. "There's this. But if you're waiting for a secret handshake or something—"

"No, no—I'm sure you're legit. Come on in, make yourself comfortable. Kenzie's in the other room." It was hard not to like Zev, even if the guy might cost him a few nights' profit. Would asking the shelter for reimbursement be out of line?

Kenzie headed them off in the living room, holding a clipboard and a bottle of water. "Hey Zev. How's it going?"

"Better, since the landlord doesn't appear pogrom-happy." He winked at Hack. "It'll be nice to have a place to stay tonight."

Kenzie sat on the couch and gestured for Zev to join her. "I'm sorry it was so crazy at the shelter earlier, but before we can move you in, I have to complete your intake forms. Are you up to doing that now?"

Zev sat and broke into a cockeyed grin. "You want my story? I'm honored. Are you sure you can handle all the drama?"

Hack joined them. "I'm sure we've heard worse."

"Okay, you asked for it." He cleared his throat for maximum theatrical effect while uncapping his bottle of water. "My father is a well-respected man in the Satmar community in Boro Park. Strict but fair. Meanwhile, my mother Malka grew up in a more liberal Hasidic community in Milwaukee. I guess whoever arranged the marriage didn't realize there might be slight cultural differences.

"My mother is a believer but," he held out his hand and tilted it from side to side, "not so much as others in the area. From the day I started yeshiva, she told me life was too short to accept only the word of one man, the Rebbe. She had no intention of raising a son who couldn't think for himself."

"Smart lady." Kenzie scribbled so quickly, Hack worried her fingers might cramp.

"She bought me a notebook computer, installed a hidden Wi-Fi router in the basement, and gave me a debit card with a $100 monthly limit.

'Subscribe to whatever interests you,' she said, 'Don't tell me the details. Read the Torah, but also read and listen to everything else you can find. The word of God alone won't pay the bills.'"

"That's unusual for your community?" asked Hack.

"Unheard of. She couldn't have other children, so I was her one and only. She wanted me to have the best chance at life. I devoured books and magazines almost as fast as the publishers printed them. Binged the popular shows on Netflix, educational videos on YouTube, conflicting opinions on Twitter. I discovered there are many different ways to live life—loving women, loving men—everything was on the table and I wanted to try it all."

Hack leaned in. "And no one ever caught on?"

"Nope. I was very careful. Everything was going okay until last year, when my father arranged a *shidduch* for me with a girl from London. An arranged marriage with someone from thousands of miles away who'd been ripped from her family and friends. Someone who expected a *frum* husband to study in *shul* all day and then help raise their twelve children at night. It wouldn't have been fair to either of us. So, I did the one thing that would let me escape my social responsibilities while still protecting my mother's secret; I came out, told my father I was gay."

"Well," said Kenzie, dryly, "that's partially true, no?"

"Partially." Zev winked again. "He told me to forget all that nonsense and lead the life *Hashem* had provided for me or leave. So, I cut off my *payot*—my side locks—abandoned my *shtreimel*, along with my prayer shawl and *tzitzit*, kissed my mother and friends goodbye and left. Well, kind of left. I got some handyman jobs around town—the non-religious areas, anyway—made some friends at local clubs, spent a year couch-surfing. Even took some acting classes. Occasionally snuck home to see my mother, eat some decent, homemade food."

"Stripped of options—having nowhere to go, no one to take you in—I know a little something about that." Kenzie stared down at her clipboard. "I'm glad you had the guts to find a better life for yourself."

"Well, for the short term, anyway. When my friends' hospitality dried up, along with my savings, I slept in a public homeless shelter for a few nights. The anti-Semitism was off the charts. They stole my suitcase, left me with nothing. I took refuge in the library during the days, researching the Internet until I found out about Matthew's Retreat. But like Joseph and Mary in that *other* book of the Bible, they turned me away, no room at the inn. So, here I am. How do you like my story? Oscar-worthy? Suppose Spielberg will direct?"

Hack recognized an opportunity when he saw one. "I'm not sure about an award, but I might have a job for you. You said you did some handyman work. So, you're good with hammers, nails, power tools?"

"I don't host a show on HGTV, but I can get by."

Hack grinned. "Kenzie does a great job around here, checking in the guests, making beds, cleaning up the bathrooms. But I need someone for general maintenance. I'd trade free rent for that kind of help. What do you th—?"

An object shattered the window on the other side of the room, interrupting Hack's question. It sent slivers of glass scattering in all directions and rolled across the carpet before coming to a stop by Zev's foot. Kenzie shrieked in surprise, but Zev seemed impervious to the intrusion. He reached down and picked up what looked like a note held to a rock with a rubber band.

"Someone's an iPhone short. Doesn't communication like this only happen in cartoons?" He reached across the coffee table and handed the object to Hack. "Here, I believe this is for you."

Hack held the rock in his trembling hand, already suspecting who had delivered the missive in such a histrionic fashion. When his nerves calmed, he pulled off the rubber band and unfolded the note, which read, "Thursday. 4:00 p.m. Jerry's Diner."

Zev smiled, taking the ultimatum in stride. "In case you were wondering, I can replace windows. I hope the job offer is still available."

Kenzie was far less cavalier. She grabbed the note from Hack's hand and looked it over, her expression a study in terror. "If they can do this, it's proof they're capable of real violence. Hack, what are you going to do?"

Zev cocked his head. "Who is doing what to whom?"

"I'll fill you in later," said Kenzie.

Hack shook his head with resignation. "What can I do? I'll see what they want...and then I'll find some way to give it to them."

Chapter Fifteen

It was six o'clock and Grace was busy revising her manuscript to include Lynn's suggested supporting characters when she had an unfortunate encounter with an antagonist of her own. Sheryl, her husband's secretary and supposed mistress, popped by to see Eliot, who had taken off early from work to escort the boys to basketball practice. She claimed they needed to discuss a blistering client email she'd intercepted right before it reached senior management. It was the first time the two women had spoken since the holiday gala, where Grace had first overheard the widespread rumors concerning their dalliance.

"Aren't you the diligent one, reviewing emails during your off-hours." Grace practically choked on her own sarcasm. "He's out right now, but why don't you join me in the living room? We can get better acquainted over a cup of coffee while you wait." She pointed to the couch as she headed into the kitchen.

"That sounds…nice." Sheryl's pause reflected a smidgen of unease. She staked out a spot on the far end of the sofa, guarding the folder on her lap as if it contained the nuclear codes.

Grace peeked out from the kitchen and watched with satisfaction as her guest fidgeted. She prolonged the awkward moment, grinding the Arabica beans instead of tossing some pods into the Keurig. Meanwhile, the wait afforded her the opportunity to size up her competition. No Miss America, but attractive. Yet, so boyish—slim-hipped, an A-cup. She wondered if she were jealous or merely catty.

"It looks like it might snow again," Sheryl called out, unnerved by the extended silence. "They're predicting a polar vortex later in the week."

A secretary and *a meteorologist. And here I thought Eliot only liked you for your "data entry" skills.*

"Things certainly are frigid around here." Grace returned with two mugs of coffee on a silver tray, along with a china creamer and matching sugar bowl. Only the finest for such an important guest.

"I wouldn't have interrupted your evening if I hadn't deemed it vital. Peterson Industries is our largest account right now." Her words smacked just shy of sincere.

"Were you so dedicated with all your bosses?" Grace enjoyed navigating the tightrope between feigning interest and downright accusing the woman of adultery. She was on home turf. Why not hang this little interloper out to dry?

Sheryl lifted the mug to her lips and blew the steam in Grace's direction. She too appeared adept at barbed repartee, letting Grace's comment dangle in the air for a minute before responding.

"Mrs. Rendell...Grace. To be honest, when I work for someone, I belong to them. Totally and completely." Her stare was a guided missile, her tone serious as a heart attack. "I would do anything to protect them from competition, angry clients, or anyone else that threatened their position with the firm."

Grace glared back with equal intensity. "I've heard you're very ambitious, Sheryl."

"I get what I want."

Grace visualized herself slapping the smug expression off the secretary's face. She leaned forward, dropping the pretense of friendly chat. "And what *do* you want?"

Sheryl set down her mug and opened her mouth to respond when the sound of bootsteps and chatter erupted in the foyer. "Where's the cocoa, Mom?" Damian and Xander ran past them into the kitchen. "It's freezing outside."

The front door slammed shut, signaling Eliot's return. Sheryl grabbed her folder and sauntered out to greet him as if she owned the place.

"Sheryl, this is an unexpected pleasure. What brings you out to the suburbs on such a cold afternoon?"

He sounds surprised. What a great actor I married.

"Eliot, we need to talk. As I explained to your wife, I came across this email from James Peterson—"

"Let's go into the study Sheryl, where we can discuss this without disturbing the others."

"Mom, the cocoa? Did you forget?"

Grace trudged into the kitchen, picturing her husband and his secretary groping each other a few doors down. "He's all yours, Sheryl," she said under her breath. "Enjoy it while you can. He won't look half as attractive when my book comes out, and you discover what kind of monster has been sharing your bed."

Chapter Sixteen

Jerry's Diner was more deserted than Hack would have expected for a weekday afternoon. It was still an hour shy of the early-bird special, with only a few high-schoolers scarfing down grilled cheese and sipping egg creams. Absent, to his dismay, were a league of credible witnesses to forestall whatever heinous punishments his "bankers" might have planned.

Boris and Ving were waiting for him in a corner booth. Hack had met the weaselly-looking Boris a few months back at his favorite bar when he'd gotten drunk and mentioned his gambling losses. The stranger commiserated and then introduced Ving, his bald, muscle-bound companion. "The guy has lots of discretionary income," he'd said, without mentioning the source of his assets. Based on their subsequent discussions, and both men's eternally bloodshot eyes, Hack surmised they dabbled in the local drug trade when they weren't shaking down delinquent borrowers.

"Good afternoon, gentlemen." Hack turned on his usual charm as he slipped into the booth opposite the two thugs.

"Where's our money, pal?" Boris sounded unamused. Where was all that compassion now?

"As you know, I've made partial repayments and I'm working on the rest as we speak."

Ving cracked his knuckles. "How reassuring. Interest has a nasty way of skyrocketing when you miss payment deadlines."

"You're into us for $2,500," Boris added.

"How is that possible? I only borrowed $1,000. And I've paid off $250."

"Like I said, skyrocketing like the national debt. Too bad I don't see any Chinese businessmen around to bail you out." Both men cracked up at Ving's reference to international investment patterns. "Next week, it becomes $3,000. And so on. In a month, you'll owe so much, we'll need to go after your big celebrity sister for the money. You don't want that, do you?"

Hank's stomach plummeted at the mention of family members. "How the hell do you know about her?"

"It's a small world, Hack. People like us make it our business to stay informed about our clients. And their loved ones. It's like taking out an insurance policy. So why don't you do what's best for them and clean out that savings account of yours? Like, today."

The moisture forming on Hack's forehead dripped into his eyes, and he rubbed them dry, lest the two geniuses opposite him mistook the droplets for tears. When he opened his eyes again, he took a double take. Three rotund, bearded, Hasidic men in full religious garb—black hats, white shirts and long coats—were approaching their table. Odd, since this wasn't a kosher restaurant and the closest orthodox community was in Teaneck. Were they lost and looking for directions?

"*Antschuldigs mir*. I'm afraid you are sitting in our seats," said the largest of the three in a heavy Yiddish accent, though "largest" was an arbitrary distinction. Each must have weighed at least three hundred pounds. The trio glared down, causing Boris to squirm.

Ving was less intimidated than his partner. "You've eaten a few matzo balls too many and they've gone to your brain, buddies. This is our hangout and we sit where we like. Isn't your diner a few thousand miles west, over in Jerusalem?"

The Hasids raised their eyebrows. "*Er hot azoy fil seykhl vi in kloyster mezuzes*," the second of the three whispered to the third, and the two chuckled.

"Please excuse my associates, Pinchus and Mordechai, for their rudeness," said the man who had initially addressed them. "Since you are so familiar with Jerusalem, I probably don't need to translate for you, but will do so for the others at the table. What Mordechai said was that you had as much sense as a church has mezuzahs."

"What the hell is a mezuwhatever?" asked Ving, unimpressed with the proverb.

Pinchus spoke up for the first time. "Do you have any idea who we are? Ever heard of the Jewish mafia?"

"No such thing. Mafia is Italian, through and through." Ving beamed with pride; Boris remained silent but grew paler by the minute.

Mordechai laughed. "Ya? You ever hear of Mayer Lansky? Lepkele Buchalter? Bugsy Siegel? They sound like nice Italian boys to you?"

Now Ving grew angry. "Yeah, I heard of 'em. What of it? They're long gone. You'll be following soon if you don't get out of our grills and let us finish conversing with our friend here." He gestured toward Hack.

"Well, let me introduce myself," said the first man. "The name's Shulem Siegel. Bugsy was my great grandfather. This is Mordechai Lansky and Pinchus Buchalter. Like the Kavod Brothers, we are delighted to have followed in our family's footsteps. You've heard of the Kavods, no?"

Ving gulped and shook his head.

"They make coffins," said Pinchus.

Boris stood then, uninterested in becoming a future Kavod patron. "Man, let's get out and let them have the booth. We got our message across." Then he shot Hack a threatening glance. "I'd take care of what we discussed, kid, if you want your whole family alive at the annual Easter egg hunt." They edged out of the booth, pushed past the Hasids, and hightailed it out of the diner.

Hack stood too, but Mordechai waved him back down. "No hurry. Eat. Enjoy." His accent had switched from Yiddish to British. The three of them burst into laughter as they peeled off their sidelocks and beards.

Hack's chin dropped. "Who *are* you guys?"

"Actors from the Jewish Repertory in the city," said Shulem. "We understand you are doing a favor for a friend of ours. We don't forget favors and we repay in kind. Call us if you need anything else." He handed Hack a card that read, *"Schmuel Lavendar, Character Actor."* They each shook the teen's hand and departed.

Now that the danger had passed, Hack became more aware of the racing pulse pounding in his ears. Hasidim notwithstanding, this had been his Come to Jesus moment. Zev's friends, God bless them, couldn't protect him forever. His bank account was on life support. The rent income barely covered the costs of food, heat, and water. His part-time jobs weren't repaying his debts fast enough. And these two bozos were more dangerous than he'd assumed.

The situation was turning Code Red. He'd stretch it out as long as possible, but unless he brainstormed a better solution or won the lottery, he'd run out of options. Soon, he'd have to set his ego aside and call in the only person who would love him no matter what he did, Namely, his sister Andrea.

Chapter Seventeen

Other than the run-in with Eliot's paramour, and her obligatory weekly calls to Barrington, Grace was enjoying some of the happiest days of her life. She did spend some time at Davidoff, Weiss & Greenburg, but during every spare second, she was hard at work, bringing Hope's story to life. How cathartic, airing grievances accumulated over four decades. The arguments, accusations, hospitalizations—she flung them all onto Hope. But much of her joy also sprang from the creative process itself. Every hour she spent with Lynn, editing her manuscript, brought her one step closer to joining the esteemed ranks of the authors she'd idolized for so long, those who slaved over blank pages or computer screens to provide readers with a few hours of escape. Before embarking on this project, she'd never considered that by saving herself, in some small way she might save others.

Another unforeseen benefit: her nightmares had disappeared. No visions for a few months now, not since she'd gone off her medication. No constant self-doubt, just laser-beam focus, pulverizing negative comments from Eliot as the mutterings of a man with an agenda. A man killing time until circumstances changed, and he'd kill her instead.

During their weekly sessions, Dr. Leighmann hammered away at the source of her good mood. Grace cited the miraculous effects of exercise— something she'd invented to justify her lack of lethargy—and flashed a health club membership card to emphasize her newfound dedication. She'd anticipated such an inquisition, investing $10 in a one-week gym trial. Money well-spent.

Leighmann pursed her lips. "Don't get lulled into false optimism again, and do something unwise, like going off your meds. With psychoses like yours, cycles of depression often alternate with mania and periods of delusion. You've experienced it yourself. Remember that time you insisted on going to Trinity for your junior year, how giddy you were? Or after you got married and decided you had to get a job instead of staying safe at home? You were so excited; you couldn't think straight. Consider the aftermath when those short-term fixes fell apart."

Grace scraped her fingernails against the insides of her palms, refraining from the urge to rip the pages from her therapist's notebook. "Well, in case number one, I met Eliot and put a hold on my studies. In case number two, I got pregnant. I wouldn't label those events as "aftermath" or even relapses, I'd call them life. A little bit of normalcy. Do you begrudge me that?"

Even though Dr. Leighmann had her best interests at heart, she left the appointment with a mouth sore from jaw clenching and tongue biting. Would it be so difficult for her trusted confidante to step aside for once, and let her luxuriate in her newfound bliss?

Mid-February brought another pleasant surprise: freedom. Eliot had to attend another week-long advertising convention, this time in Atlanta, and his parents volunteered to host the boys in Tucson over winter break. Even Dr. Leighmann was going away on vacation. Grace would have an entire week to herself. Time to let the muse roam free.

Eliot hovered over her at the dinner table like a mother leaving her baby with a sitter for the first time. "Will you be okay in the empty house? Why not fly down and visit your dad? Finally broach the subject you keep avoiding."

"Mom, I agree with Dad. What if you have an attack and there's no one around to help?" Xander's eyes reflected his concern.

"I doubt it will be an issue. Between working my way through tax returns and spending hours at the gym, I won't have time for a nervous breakdown. But if it makes everyone happier, I promise to check in with Dr. Leighmann's service every morning. Would that help?"

Eliot reached across the table and rested his hand on hers. "That, and a promise to call me every day. I'll only be two hours away by plane if anything goes wrong. Nothing at that conference is as important as your well-being."

Oh brother, laying it on thick today, aren't you? "I appreciate your concern. If I sense an attack coming on, I'll call Keira to stay with me until

I can get professional help." She had no intention of disturbing their sitter, but her lie put an end to the discussion.

No husband and no kids. She hoped it would mean having more time to spend with Lynn. Grace hadn't had a lot of friends in her life. The hours she'd spent with her mentor—someone smart and funny to confide in, ask for help, share a few laughs—had been a bittersweet reminder of all the years gone by without social connection.

What she hadn't counted on was Lynn's travel schedule, which had her Europe-bound that week. She suggested Grace housesit instead. "All you'll need to do is feed Denver, Aspen and Vail every day, make sure their water dish is full, and clean their litter box. Consider it your own little writing retreat." Grace picked up a set of keys the next afternoon.

The prospect of a mini holiday at a "secret hideaway" was exhilarating; she'd never stayed anywhere on her own unless you called a week at a mental hospital a vacation. She kept the keys hidden at the bottom of her handbag, far from Eliot's inquisitive eyes, but occasionally, she'd reach down and roll them between her fingers, causing her stomach to flutter with excitement.

Lynn left a second parting gift before taking off for Europe: the name of one of her sources. Grace needed expert advice on which poisons Hope's husband, Elias, might use to murder her. She'd searched the Internet but wanted a more intricate understanding than a generic Wikipedia article could provide. Lynn set up a lunch meeting for her with Tom Druthers, a forensic toxicologist whom she'd consulted for the Clara Cardone mysteries. Grace was a little wary of being seen dining with a man who wasn't her husband. If anyone asked, she figured she'd explain Tom away as a tax client with a complex return.

The morning of her family's departure, Grace quivered as she slipped Lynn's key into the lock and turned the knob. It was like starting Trinity all over again. The living room, with its hodgepodge of souvenirs and memorabilia, greeted her like a long-lost cousin and in response, she pirouetted with delight.

By Wednesday, aided by antihistamines to ward off her cat allergies, she'd added over 5,000 words to her manuscript. As she ironed the hem of her favorite blue dress in advance of her lunch with Druthers, her hand froze: what if he found her questions stupid? What if he wasn't as knowledgeable as he claimed, or Lynn had instructed him to feed her false information, so she'd have less competition from another mystery author? Grace would be a literary laughingstock, the gravity of her message diminished. She unplugged the iron and considered canceling the lunch date.

After some deep breathing, one of Dr. Leighmann's centering techniques, Grace reviewed her qualms in a more rational light. Readers held Lynn's books in high regard. Would that be true if she used sources who weren't credible? And why would Lynn sabotage her work when she'd be sharing fifty percent of the profits? As for stupid questions, he expected her to be lacking in knowledge. That was the whole point of consulting an expert. Thrilled she'd talked herself out of an anxiety attack sans therapist, Grace applied her lipstick, braced herself for the February chill, and drove off to meet Mr. Druthers.

She arrived at Julianne's Café at one o'clock, shivering more from nerves than the artic frost. As the hostess led her to Druthers' table, she tried to pick out the well-groomed, professorial type she had imagined. The disheveled person who greeted her was the opposite: bald, about fifty pounds overweight, sporting a chin of grizzled stubble. His button-down shirt looked like the host hotel for a wrinkle convention. But his kind eyes and warm smile reminded her of a neglected, middle-aged teddy bear. Neither hand bore a wedding ring. It made sense—no self-respecting wife would let her husband leave the house in such a state.

"Ms. Allen? I'm Tom Druthers. Lynn has told me great things about you."

His firm handshake immediately impressed her, and his earnest expression eased her apprehensions. "And you as well. Thanks for interrupting your day to meet with me." The waiter filled their water glasses, then hurried off.

Her plan was to start slow, get acquainted before bombarding him with sensitive questions. "So how long have you known Lynn?"

"Wow. It's been what, ten years, now? She got my name out of some scientific journal. Plied me with questions about toxic gases right around the time she was divorcing her husband. I wondered if she were writing a mystery or a how-to manual. Since then, whenever she enquires about some variety of poison, I ask which boyfriend she's killing off this time."

They shared a laugh.

"Do you consult with a lot of authors?"

"A few. You writers amaze me, creating something out of nothing like you do. In toxicology, there isn't a lot of room for imagination. It must be very freeing."

Grace's skin tingled. It was the first time anyone had labeled her a writer.

"My real job is straightforward, like yours. CPA. Cold, concrete figures that always add up. Unless something is very wrong."

"So, your books are your escape?"

"In a way, yes." Never was a statement more accurate. *Salvaging Hope* was her flight from a doomed future.

They continued to chat for another ten minutes. What Grace most appreciated was how Druthers never patronized her or scrutinized her insights for signs of psychosis. It was liberating to converse with a man without being studied like a specimen under an ever-present microscope.

The maître d' finally strolled by and asked if they'd seen a menu.

"Yes," answered Druthers. "But not from this particular restaurant."

The well-earned sarcasm delighted Grace, especially when not directed at her like some underhanded jab. Eliot was not a man who quipped. He was a sour drop compared to Druthers' chocolate kiss. She wished lunch could go on forever.

After the waiter finally served their meals, a cheeseburger platter for him, a Cobb salad for her, Druthers got down to business.

"What is your interest in poisons, Grace? Who's kicking the proverbial bucket?"

"I need the name of a substance one person might slip a spouse over time that would eventually lead to death. Something undetectable or could be considered accidental."

The waiter shot Grace an alarmed look and moved on to the next table. She stifled a chuckle at the notion of her homicidal inquiry being taken seriously.

Druthers munched on his burger and considered the question before responding. "There's cyanide in bitter almonds, eating as few as twelve might prove fatal, but they're scarce in the U.S., so it would be difficult to claim serving them as inadvertent. And no one's grabbing a handful of apple or cherry pits or rhubarb leaves as an afternoon snack. Some folks mistake daffodil bulbs for onions, but rarely eat enough of those to keel over."

Grace looked past the dribble of ketchup dotting Druthers' chin and listened with great interest.

"If the character owned a portable air-conditioning unit, and someone punctured a hole in its coil, the victim might die of asphyxiation from a Freon leak. But the room would have to be a small, confined space, and the death would be quick."

"Unfortunately, that won't work." Grace dipped a piece of lettuce into the dressing she'd ordered on the side. "Most modern houses have central air. I really need something administered over a period of months."

Druthers remained quiet for a time, chomping on his liberally salted French fries. She wondered why someone so knowledgeable about poison would permit an avalanche of sodium, carbs and fat into his diet. But that would have to remain a discussion for another day.

"Does your doomed character have a weak heart?"

Grace pierced a piece of blue cheese. "I hadn't considered it. Why?"

"An NSAID, like ibuprofen, causes a person to retain water and salt. It impedes blood flow and can therefore boost heart failure if the patient also uses diuretic drugs to treat high blood pressure. Cancer meds, stimulants, and antidepressants can also be hard on the heart."

"If she isn't suffering from a weak heart, what else ya got?" Grace signaled for the waiter to refill their water glasses.

"This is fun," he said with a grin. "Does the victim-to-be take any medications?"

"Possibly." Grace was unwilling to let too much of her plot become public knowledge, at least not until the book launched.

"And might one of those drugs be, say, Klonopin?"

A shiver went up Grace's spine. Was she that transparent? Klonopin had been one of her regular drugs until she'd swapped them out for sugary placebos. But with so much at stake, she had no hesitation about playing dumb.

"I haven't heard of that one. What does it treat?"

"It's a Schedule IV controlled substance, which means it requires a physician's prescription. Doctors use it to treat epileptic seizures, sleep issues, and panic disorders, which would give you more of a general umbrella of ailments. Because it's addictive and has side effects like lots of these other benzodiazepines, it might beef up the drama in your story. I mention it because medical journals have reported some recent cases of Klonopin toxicity."

How interesting. She'd have to read up on Klonopin. Grace had never taken the time to research anything Dr. Leighmann had prescribed; instead she had downed the pills like an autotron.

"What caused the toxicity, Mr. Druthers?"

"Call me Tom, please."

Grace sensed he might be flirting. The prospect of being considered attractive at forty-five brought heat to her cheeks.

"Caffeine can create problems if it's administered in a pain medication that also contains aspirin and propoxyphene. And alcohol can be deadly. So, if someone 'accidently' served a character on Klonopin or Darvon a drink where grapefruit juice, for example, masked the taste of the alcohol, it could be lethal and still look unpremeditated. If you can get around the slow-acting aspect of the plot, it might work for you."

It was a lot to take in. Not only had Druthers given Elias the means to murder Hope, his suggestions were excellent tip-offs for any of Eliot's future homicidal attacks. Overall, a productive conversation. Plus, she might have made her first male friend.

The waiter removed their plates and offered them dessert menus. Grace heard the phone buzzing in her handbag. She ignored it, considering it gauche to answer a call while dining. When the buzzing continued through three ten-ring cycles, it was obvious someone wanted to reach her, and badly. Were the boys hurt? She apologized and fished through her purse for the cell.

The Caller ID read "Caprice." She gulped, forcing back her mounting panic, and clicked the answer icon. Her father's girlfriend started blubbering before she could even say hello. Through sobs, Grace made out the gist of the message. Stroke. Unresponsive. Ambulance. She asked for the name of the hospital and told Caprice she'd be on the next flight.

"Sounded important." Druthers puckered his brow.

"That's the understatement of the century." The walls were closing in and she squinted to navigate the din. The bill. She had to pay the bill. She rooted through her bag and threw fifty dollars on the table. "That should cover the lunch and tip."

"What's wrong? Is there any place I can drive you? Anything I can do to help?"

"I appreciate the offer but my car's right outside. I...I have to get out of here. You've been a lifesaver. I can't thank you enough, but I've got to go."

He stood up as she pushed back from the table. "Please call, let me know how things are going. I'm here if you need a sympathetic ear." He pressed his business card into her palm.

She stuffed the card into her coat pocket and forced what she predicted would be her last smile for some time. If her dad died, she would have to check over her shoulder every moment until her book hit the shelves. The time for pleasantries was over. The clock was ticking.

Chapter Eighteen

Javier greeted Grace as she entered the baggage claim area, bearing a sign that read the pre-agreed upon, "Mrs. Jones." Head swathed in a nondescript scarf, eyes hidden behind cheap sunglasses, only her polyester pants distinguished her from the other women heading toward awaiting chauffeurs.

It was anonymity by design. The last thing she wanted was attention drawn to her arrival. If she'd had any doubts, they vanished when she passed a newsstand near the arrival gate, the headlines screaming, "Stroke of Financial Genius" and "Barrington's Brain on the Blink." The tabloids were starving for any hint of drama, and she imagined that soon, they'd dredge up all the details of the scandals that had driven him out of New Jersey. In the meantime, she didn't plan to throw the media vultures any raw meat by announcing her presence.

Once she and Javier ensconced themselves in the limo, a black Rolls this time, Grace unleashed the torrent of questions that had plagued her since Caprice's call. "How did this happen? Was he alone? Is he awake, alert, talking? What do the doctors say, what's the prognosis?"

"Ah, Ms. Gracie, I am sorry, I do not have these answers. I take you back to the house to pick up Ms. Caprice and she can tell you everything she knows. Is good?"

"Then you're taking us both to the hospital?"

"Yes, Ms. Gracie. It's an hour south. Ms. Caprice, she guessed you'd want to freshen up, eat dinner before the long drive."

Grace prickled at the mention of her father's chippie calling the shots, but then remembered she was the outsider here. Caprice had helped her keep tabs on Barrington's dementia over the past few months and had been on her side during the arguments that devastated her last visit. An unlikely ally, but one she still needed.

Caprice, clad in a black blouse and pencil skirt, waited outside the courtyard to greet them. Dewey and Dutchess, tails whipping up a breeze, clamored for attention as Grace emerged from the car. If only Barrington had fed off his dogs' enthusiasm, learned about unconditional love from their example, their relationship could have been so different. She knelt to stroke them and endured their Springer slobber while listening to Caprice alternate between gushing appreciation and a more somber appraisal of her father's condition.

"Thank you so much for coming, Grace. I've been carrying on here alone and I'm at loose ends. It's important to have a blood relative weigh in on medical decisions, don't you agree?"

Grace stared at Caprice's mourning apparel. "The black...it's a little premature, no? He's not dead yet, is he?"

Caprice misinterpreted Grace's sarcasm for concern. "Oh, no. A hospital is a serious place. It wouldn't be appropriate to wear bright colors and shorts. Does that make sense?"

"You're the color consultant." Grace swallowed her snark, recognizing it for what it was—a distraction from her anxiety over her father's condition. She stood up, much to the spaniels' dismay when Silverio, the butler, called the two women into the house for a late dinner.

Caprice led the way, the white courtyard stones crunching under her pumps. "I had Marquesa make you something special as a light welcome *cena.* That's dinner in Spanish."

Grace hesitated. "I'm not sure we'll have time to eat. I want to get to the hospital before they close. How late do visiting hours go?"

"Quiet time starts at nine, but St. Laziosi's is a private facility. For a patient who's been as generous a donor as Barrington, they told me to visit any time that was convenient."

"Ah, the benefits of wealth." Grace followed Caprice into the dining room.

"Yes, we're all very lucky." Oblivious to the dig, Caprice gestured for Marquesa to serve the meal. "Not that he'll notice us there, being in a coma and all. Though I've heard that deep down, they can sense when a loved one is near. Do you suppose that's true, that he'll feel our presence and take some comfort from it?"

Grace went on high alert at the mention of a coma. "He's still unconscious? Why didn't anyone tell me that?"

"I'm sorry. I was so crazed when I came home yesterday and found him, I guess I wasn't thinking." They took their seats at a table large enough to host dinner for a small country. "Everything happened at once. I had to call 911, arrange for the best doctors, dodge the press, it was all very overwhelming. I didn't even remember to call you until today, when things stabilized a little."

"Came home? You mean you weren't here?"

Before Caprice could respond, Marquesa entered, carrying two plates of *ropa vieja* and rice. The women discontinued what had escalated into a heated discussion until the servant returned to the kitchen.

Once they were alone again, Caprice sunk her fork into her flank steak. "I could kick myself for not being here when it happened. Do something, catch it early enough to limit the damage."

"What was so important that you had to leave?" Grace regretted sounding unsympathetic, but this bimbo knew her father suffered from the beginnings of dementia. Watching over him was her one job, and she'd failed at it. Miserably.

"Nothing, actually. It was the oddest thing. Barrington insisted I go, claimed he owed me an early anniversary gift. Paid for a full day at the Breakers spa. Facial, massage, mani-pedi, lunch, the works. Hired a private limo to drive me there early in the morning and not bring me back until late afternoon. It was glorious while it lasted. Who'd have guessed I'd come back all relaxed, only to find him splayed out on the living room floor?"

Grace pushed her plate away after only one bite. This discussion had massacred any chance of her digesting the meal. "Weren't any of the staff here to help?"

"It was their day off." Tears brimmed in Caprice's eyes. "That's what was so strange about the timing. I always stay home on Tuesdays when they're gone. But he was so insistent. What choice did I have?" She erupted into sobs and ran off to the bathroom.

Grace had to admit, Caprice came across too genuine to trade in crocodile tears. Perhaps she was a better person than Barrington deserved. But what had he been up to, clearing out the house on a Tuesday? A meeting of Fathers-Burdened-with-Paranoid-Daughters Anonymous?

The speculation would have to wait. Javier poked his head in and asked if they were ready to leave. He'd chosen the extended limo for the trip, giving both women more than enough space to stretch out. They sat perpendicular to each other, the minibar in front of Caprice, who promptly poured herself two fingers of Glenlivet and offered Grace a soda. "Because of the meds," she explained. Caprice polished off her first drink and poured herself a second. Barrington's consort did not appear to be taking his condition in stride. Grace, eager for inside knowledge, decided to exploit her budding inebriation.

"Has he been eating the right foods? Under any unusual stress?"

"You sound like the doctors." Caprice slurred the final "s." "He's remained steady. Forgetful but coherent. Just his usual nasty self. But that's nothing you haven't seen firsthand." Caprice leaned forward and poured herself a third drink. It was as if the very prospect of seeing Barrington was something she wanted to obliterate from her consciousness. "Can I confide in you?"

Grace activated the soundproof glass partition between themselves and Javier. Then she moved to Caprice's left and placed an arm around the woman's trembling shoulders. "You can tell me anything. Consider this your safe place."

Caprice's eyes opened wide. "Honestly?"

"Of course."

The truth came pouring out. "It's gotten so bad the past few weeks. We had an epic argument at the end of January. It was about the dogs. He said he'd grown tired of them constantly expecting to be pet and played with. That they distracted me from paying attention to my primary responsibility—him. He ordered me to take them to the vet and have them put down."

Grace's jaw dropped. What kind of monster euthanizes dogs for expressing affection? Then she recalled her own sorrowful childhood and a knot formed in her throat. She grabbed some tissues from her purse, handed a few to Caprice, and kept the rest for herself.

"Naturally, I refused. I threatened to move out, take them with me, so none of us would bother him any longer. And he...he..." Caprice's sobs broke free and it was several minutes before she continued. "He threatened to shoot all three of us while we slept and...and...bury us in the backyard. Reminded me I had no family, no one to notice if I went missing...I looked into his eyes...they were so cold...it was clear he meant what he said."

Caprice's confession left Grace speechless, her bare arms covered in goosebumps. How could she play the dutiful daughter when she suspected Barrington was capable of such a statement?

She recalled the research she'd done after her last Florida encounter. "He's an old man fighting dementia. When they become angry, they yell, throw things, display combative behavior. I doubt my dad would resort to hitting, kicking or pushing, much less murder. His sadism has always been more verbal than physical."

"You think that was it? Because his words were so hateful. I've done nothing to deserve that, nothing at all. Except to push back when he threatened the dogs."

Grace squeezed Caprice's shoulders a second time. "You're not dealing with a coherent mind. But consider yourself lucky. At least when *you* disagreed with him, he didn't commit you to a mental hospital."

Caprice shook her head and finished off her scotch.

"Alone in the house with all his demons, the upset might have spiked his blood pressure and brought on the stroke." Grace wondered which of them she was trying harder to convince. "That's on him, not you. One thing's for certain. He's no longer in any condition to hurt either one of us for a while."

It was after ten-thirty when Javier pulled up to the palm-fringed entrance to St. Laziosi's, its complex of yellow and blue buildings jutting out in all directions. They ventured up to the fifth floor, where private suites lined the perimeter of the Intensive Care ward, occupied by the more elite critical care patients. Caprice led Grace to Room 562, where she spotted Barrington through a battery of blinking and bleeping machines, some connected via tubes to her father's mouth, arms and stomach. "One's for oxygen, one's an IV and the third is a feeding tube," the night nurse explained after Grace introduced herself. "There's also a catheter which leads to a container we keep hidden from view. I'll go find a doctor who can update you on his condition."

Grace had never seen Barrington look so weak and vulnerable. All her life, he had towered above her, barking out his callous criticisms while she turned herself inside out to satisfy him and earn his respect. He hadn't deigned to concede it then, and by the look of his current condition, he'd go to his grave without granting her even a nod of approval. She struggled between empathy for his condition, anger over decades of unrequited attempts at reconciliation, fear over what Eliot might do if her father died, and an unexpected sense of empowerment. Here she stood, for once the stronger and more capable of the two, far beyond the reach of his disdain.

Standing by his bedside, watching the red line dance across the face of the heart monitor, she remembered the preparations for her mother's funeral. He'd forbidden her to invite anyone who might provide her with an ounce of comfort, even Dr. Leighmann. "We don't need their phony sympathy. They weren't your mother's friends. They'd only show up looking for a handout or to network with the more influential of our mourners." When she'd cried, aghast at his insensitivity, he added: "Buckle up, Spot. You're a Pierrepoint. We don't turn to others for help, especially those so far beneath us."

It's your turn to buckle up, Barrington. Though I hope you never experience the loneliness that I did back then.

The nurse returned with a young, bespectacled resident, covered in khaki-colored scrubs. "This is Doctor Amari. He's one of the team who's monitoring your father's condition."

"Any idea of what caused this?" Grace asked, bypassing any introductory pleasantries.

"Ms. Pierrepoint, it's a delight to make your acquaintance. Your father has been a great friend to our facility, a very generous contributor."

Grace grew impatient with the resident's prattling. "Again, any idea of a cause?"

Dr. Amari's expression morphed from congenial to solemn. "Your father suffered what we call an acute ischemic stroke. That means a clogged or burst artery compromised the supply of blood to his brain. He's lucky to be alive. Patients with dementia run twice the risk of dying from a stroke as those without."

"And how long will he remain like this?" She gestured toward Barrington's limp, motionless body.

"It's impossible to be certain. The event increased his intracranial pressure, causing a loss of oxygen and a buildup of toxins, all of which can lead to a coma. How long that coma lasts depends on the size and location of the stroke, and the general health of the patient. We're running tests to determine all of that."

"But he's stable for the time being?" Grace grasped for any crumb of reassurance.

"We've seen no downturn. If nothing else goes wrong, I'm confident he'll soon be on the road to recovery. Though that may require weeks or perhaps months of round-the-clock monitoring, rehab, the works. I hope you intend to leave him in our capable care, Ms. Pierrepoint."

"It's Rendell and yes, we can leave him here for now. I'm sure whoever's got the checkbook..." She looked over at Caprice, who was busy rearranging the flowers on Barrington's nightstand. "Caprice, who handles the books?"

"Uh, uh, one of his attorneys, I guess. I've been living on pocket change the last few days. His name is...Castle something...Raymond. Raymond Castleberry. That's it. I met him once when he came to the house. His office is in....uh... Cityplace Tower."

"You can advise the business office that I will speak to Mr. Castleberry and make the necessary arrangements." Grace glanced again at Caprice, who was now straightening Barrington's blanket—a bundle of nerves compared to her own level of lucidity and calm. No hysterics, no second-guessing herself. The picture of competence. *Take that, Dr. Leighmann.*

Now that she'd seen her father and spoken to someone in charge, she'd rest a little easier. He was stable and hopefully, would remain so for the near future. She'd have to step up her writing schedule, just to be safe.

"Caprice, are you done with your visit? I'd like to drive home, get some sleep and grab the first flight back to Newark in the morning."

"Give me another minute or two." She fussed over Barrington, running her hand across his forehead and pushing back a few unruly strands of hair that had fallen over his closed eyes. Her earlier crisis of faith a distant memory, Caprice's blind devotion had returned, transforming her back into the role of doting trophy girlfriend.

"Take as long as you need." Grace headed into the hall to check her email. She shot Tom Druthers a quick note, apologizing for her abrupt departure and thanking him again for his help. It would be nice to see him again, get a few more questions answered, like what poison might cause a stroke in an elderly man suffering from dementia. One that conveniently occurred when help was nowhere nearby. Could something other than old age have caused her father's infirmity—perhaps a threatened girlfriend who feared for her life? Things weren't adding up, and being a diligent CPA, Grace was determined to keep examining all avenues until she found the right solution.

Chapter Nineteen

After a turbulent flight, Grace drove back to Lynn's house. It was only Thursday which meant she had three full days left to concentrate on her writing before Eliot returned from Atlanta and the boys from Tucson. Three more days of freedom from obligation and sneaking around. She intended to enjoy every minute.

She made her perfunctory daily call to Dr. Leighmann's service, prepared to explain why she'd missed her Wednesday check-in. To her surprise, her therapist answered. "I heard about your dad. How awful. Thought you might need me, so I grabbed the first flight back. No reason for you to worry, though. Barrington made provisions for this. He prepaid your sessions a few years in advance, so there's no need to stop treatment."

Therapy continuity hadn't been foremost on Grace's mind, and Dr. Leighmann's mercenary comments left her stunned. She decided against briefing Eliot and the boys since Barrington's condition was stable. She didn't need her husband hounding her over the contents of her father's will. He'd have to wait a little longer to discover the amount of his prospective windfall.

Grace threw herself back into her writing, only to be interrupted by the ring of Lynn's house phone. She let the machine answer, but when the caller announced his name as "Tom Druthers," she seized upon the opportunity to chat with him again.

"Lynn isn't here. I wanted to apologize again for my rudeness yesterday, running out on lunch like that. I assure you, I'm not that kind of person."

"Hello to you too. I was actually calling to speak to you, not Lynn. Thank you for your email. I never for a second considered you rude, I promise.

How did things turn out? Is everything okay?" The pleasant timbre of his voice and his caring message put Grace at ease.

"It may take some time to sort out, but everything should be fine." Then, like an adolescent schoolgirl, she fumbled for anything to keep the conversation going. "And again, thank you for all the information you shared over lunch. It was all very helpful."

"I'm so glad to hear that. Did you get enough? Is there anything more I can do?"

Was he angling for another meeting? And would that be so awful?

"You gave me a lot. But if I find I'm missing anything, would it be okay to call?" That worked—appreciative and yet open to more.

"Day or night. I enjoyed our time together. I'll look forward to hearing from you. Good luck with the book."

"Thanks so much. Have a great day."

She smiled as she hung up the receiver. Day or night. A nice invitation. If only her circumstances were different...

She pushed romantic speculation aside and got back to work. She was deep into Chapter 20, where Hope's father suffers a stroke—*thanks for the plotting help, Dad*—when the doorbell rang. Wow, first the phone and now this. Lynn had left no instructions about visitors, nor had she mentioned any expected deliveries. Grace debated answering, but after another four chimes, it was obvious she needed to deal with this intrusion if she were to get any more work done.

She glimpsed through the peephole and saw a tall, good-looking kid decked out in a faded green parka, shifting his weight from foot to foot as if eager to relieve himself. Thieves and murderers rarely ring the bell, she reasoned. Maybe he's been in an accident and needs to use the phone. Or a bathroom.

She pulled the door open a crack. "Can I help you?"

"Who the hell are you? Where's Andrea?"

Flustered by his brash response, she tried to shove the door closed but he slammed his hand against it.

"You m-m-must have the wrong house. There's n-n-no Andrea here," she stammered, but being the stronger of the two, he pushed past, barging inside.

"I think I know where my sister lives. Andrea Hackford Lin?" The boy scanned the room as if on a hunting expedition. "The question remains, who are you? And what are those?" He pointed to Grace's luggage, still in the hall. "You planning to clean her out?"

"I could ask you the same thing," Grace shouted, now panicked. "My friend—Lynn Andrews, the author—invited me to stay here and housesit her cats while she's out of town. I'm sure she'd verify that by phone. And that's my suitcase and toiletry bag you're asking about. The woman you're claiming is your sister didn't have anywhere for me to unpack my clothes."

The boy rolled his eyes back, adopting a less aggressive stance. "I get it. Andrea Lin. Lynn Andrews. She gave you her sue...sue—"

"Pseudonym?"

"Yeah, her writer's name. To keep her lunatic fans from tracking her down. Now you probably assume *I'm* the lunatic." He held out his hand. "I'm sorry for yelling. My name is Joe, but everyone calls me Hack. And you are...?"

"Apprehensive." Grace kept her hand by her side. "She's mentioned a brother, but you look nothing like her."

"I get that a lot." Hack reached into his coat pocket. "My parents adopted my brothers and sisters. Andrea was one of the first babies brought over from China in the early '90s. Did she tell you that?"

Still flustered, Grace stared at his jacket, praying he wouldn't draw out a knife or a pistol. "No, we're working on a book together. We've never discussed our pasts. Which I guess is obvious, since I wasn't even aware of her real name."

To her relief, he pulled out his phone and swiped a few times. "This was us two Christmases ago. The whole multicolored crew."

Grace studied the picture displaying an older man and woman, surrounded by six adult children of various ages and races. Hack was standing in the middle, his arm around Lynn's shoulders. She exhaled, satisfied that his story was on the level. "You look like one happy family. Your parents must be wonderful people."

Hack's face grew glum as he slipped the phone back into his jacket. "I guess Andrea didn't tell you that either. They died last February. Plane crash."

Blood raced to Grace's cheeks. *What a stupid faux pas!* "Oh, how awful. I'm so sorry. Would you like to sit down? I can get you something to drink." She walked to the fridge, eager to change the subject. "Think I could help with whatever you needed from Ly...Andrea?"

"Thanks, but no. And I don't have a lot of time. Do you have any idea where she is?"

"Madeira, on business. She seems to travel a lot."

"That's my sister, the meeting planner, gallivanting around the world. After the divorce, she claimed she felt claustrophobic. Never wanted to stay in one place for too long. Nice life, eh?"

"Without a doubt. Look, if it's important, I can try to get her on the phone. Otherwise, she's due home Sunday afternoon."

"I need to speak to her face to face. Listen...wow, I never even got your name..."

"It's...Ruth, Ruth Allen."

"Listen Ruth, if she calls, can you pass along a message? I need to meet with her as soon as she comes home. It's important. Critical even. Can I count on you?"

"I'll be leaving before she gets back, but I promise I'll scatter a few notes around the house so she can't miss them. You should call her though, just to be sure."

"If she's away and working, I don't want to disturb her. There's nothing we can do about the situation until she gets back. I appreciate the help." He extended his arm. "Nice to meet you, Ruth. Again, sorry about before. I wish you lots of luck with your book."

This time, she shook his hand. "Likewise. I hope you can sort out whatever the problem is."

Hack chuckled as he turned to leave. "I hope so too. Otherwise, I might end up as part of the plot in one of her novels."

■　　　■　　　■

Sunday came far too soon. Grace spent the morning doing what she'd done every morning since leaving her father's bedside: feeding the cats, sneezing from their dander, and devoting every second to increasing her novel's word count. She'd made some amazing progress and to reward herself, she treated herself to some of Lynn's...or was it Andrea's...exotic varieties of tea, along with some croissants she'd found at a nearby bakery. She sipped her oolong, reflecting on how much had changed since the fateful night of her husband's office party, how even treachery can leave something positive in its wake. She bid the cats a wistful adieu, threw her bags in the car and headed back to Glen Valley.

When Eliot and the boys walked through the door that afternoon, she gave her husband's cheek a perfunctory kiss and signaled for him to join her in the study, out of hearing range of the kids.

"I waited until now to tell you because I didn't want to disrupt your trip, but while you were away, my father had an event. He's in the hospital."

"What kind of 'event'?" His calm response surprised her; she'd expected reprimands for not alerting him immediately.

"He had a stroke. He's in a coma. I flew down and spoke to the doctors. They said he was stable, at least for now."

Only then did his tone reflect concern. "You went down there? Alone? Did you check with Dr. Leighmann first?"

"That's what you're worried about? Not my father's health, but the fact I flew alone? You had no issue with me getting on an airplane right before Thanksgiving."

"Back in November, we had your itinerary. We were prepared if anything went wrong."

"So, you're suggesting I'm incapable of traveling to Florida without having a nervous breakdown?" She realized she was instigating a fight, not the most sensible course of action, but the last few months had left Grace too confident and sentient to accept being micromanaged and second-guessed.

Eliot raised an eyebrow. "All this yelling, all this rage...you sound crazed. We should schedule therapy for first thing tomorrow."

"You and my dad. You both want to anesthetize me the second I express one iota of emotion. I do not need a doctor's appointment. What I need is for you to treat me like an adult." Grace's face flushed hot, but she had no intention of stepping off her high horse or capitulating to his veiled threats and ultimatums. It was invigorating to speak her mind.

"Where did you...never mind. It's been a long day and I'm tired. Just tell me one thing. Do the doctors have any idea what caused this?"

Torn between frustration over his patronizing tone and relief he was changing the subject, Grace debated sharing her suspicions about Caprice. But no, rather than adding insight, he'd insist she was being paranoid, that there was nothing unusual about an aging man in failing health wanting a few hours of privacy. Best to keep it to herself.

"Caprice found him on the floor and called the ambulance. Everything I've read says that Alzheimer's patients have an increased risk of stroke. I'm figuring that was the cause." Without waiting for a response, she left to tell the boys to empty their suitcases in the laundry room.

She'd tossed a detergent pod into the washer when Eliot reemerged, rattling her nerves once again. After a week spent on her own, now the very sight of him was like a mouthful of unsweetened cocoa.

"Tomorrow, Dr. Leighmann. 9:00 am. She'll be waiting."

"Maybe for you. Not for me. I've got work in the morning." She dialed the machine to permanent press without giving him a second glance, guessing Eliot would find her composed yet flippant response far more exasperating than an argument. He couldn't exactly call the men in the white coats, demanding, "Come quick! My wife is too calm! Throw her in the loony bin!" A defiant strategy so brilliant, it made her want to tap-dance with glee.

"I'm not having this argument tonight. If you truly imagine the shock of seeing your only living parent comatose isn't stress-inducing and won't affect your care of me and the kids, then skip your appointment and go straight to work. You say you want the world to treat you like an adult? Here's your chance. Show everyone the choice a coherent adult would make."

Grace saw Eliot's passive-aggressive ploy for what it was, an exasperated, last-ditch attempt at control. She wasn't falling for it anymore. And while he delivered it in a cool tone that matched hers, she noted with satisfaction how the throbbing vein in his neck belied his attempt to mask his fluster.

"Thank you for your vote of support. I *am* a coherent adult. One who, thanks to four decades of psychoanalysis, can now cope with stress and still look after my family. Right now, for example, I've got laundry to do, and then I need to get back to work and meet a client. Everyone and his brother wants to file early this year and I've been up to my ears in difficult returns."

Let him argue that almost forty years of therapy had been ineffective, because if he did, she'd have an excuse to quit seeing Dr. Leighmann altogether. She had him by the short hairs and they both knew it.

Eliot may have been exasperated by her unapologetic response, but rather than take the bait, he sighed and left the room. Grace pressed the start button, told the boys to order a pizza, and with her laptop under her arm, left before her husband fabricated a reason to stop her. She was dying to ask "Andrea" about her trip and discuss her new manuscript pages. Grace was halfway through the third act. One or two more chapters and the three-month project would be ready for her co-writer to edit and help bring to market. And not a minute too soon, considering her father's medical condition.

■   ■   ■

Andrea answered the door only seconds after Grace rang the bell. "Come on in, stranger. Join me in the kitchen. I'm preparing an early dinner for the gang."

Andrea ripped open three packets of gourmet nuggets and poured the contents into each kitty's personalized china bowl. "Madeira was scenic, but I swear, these travelers leave their brains behind when they step onto an airplane. Calls at 2:00 a.m. because someone misplaced their gloves on a tour bus. Not that they needed gloves in Madeira, even in February. But do they think I'm cabbing it halfway across Funchal to a deserted parking lot to search the seatback pockets for a pair of frigging gloves?"

Grace didn't want to undercut her friend's complaints with stories of her own trials over the past week. "Can't be easy."

"Hang out, be right back." Andrea's exit to the foyer was followed by some *oomphs* and clatter. "Where did I pack this damned thing...ah yes." She returned and presented Grace with a box of cookies labeled "Broas de

Mel." "Enough of my complaining. Try these, they're Madeira's most beloved honey cookies. Everyone on the trip was raving about them so I picked some up before heading to the airport. So, tell me about you. How's the book coming along?"

"It's about three-quarters done." Grace pulled a cookie from the box. "I've emailed you what I've finished up through this morning, so you can start your edits. To be candid, I'm not sure how much more I'll be able to write the next few weeks. My dad suffered a stroke. I may have to fly down south if his condition worsens."

"What a shame." Andrea set the bowls on the floor, spurring a feline stampede. "What's the prognosis?"

"He's stable. With any luck, he'll be fine."

"Thank God for that. I didn't realize your father was still alive. Kind of like Hope, huh? Is he a billionaire, with your husband counting down the minutes until he kicks?" She laughed.

Grace managed a weak smile, not wanting to let on how close Andrea had come to hitting the mark. "I wish. But if I were the daughter of a billionaire, would I be wearing these *schmatas* and slaving over a manuscript, or would I be off in the South Pacific, wearing a designer swimsuit and sipping champagne? Oh my God, this cookie is delicious."

"Told you so. And good point about your imaginary riches. Was Tom Druthers any help to you?"

The mention of Tom made Grace's face grow hot and she wondered how Andrea would interpret her blushing. "He was great. Gave me some creative methods for Elias to bump off Hope. I incorporated them into the story."

"Well, I can't wait to read it." She collected the cats' empty bowls and set them down in the sink.

"Assuming my father's condition doesn't deteriorate, I'm aiming to get more done by Thursday. Do me a favor and hold me to that, okay?"

"Accountability all the way. I got your back, sister." She held up her hand and they high-fived.

"Oh, speaking of siblings, your brother stopped by Thursday. I meant to leave you a note, but it slipped my mind."

"Brother? Which one? Was he white and young, white and bald, or Hispanic?'

"I saw a photo of your family. Quite a mix."

"It was like Heinz 57 at our house. All we needed was a little person and a paraplegic and we would have cornered the market on diversity."

They burst out laughing.

"He was white and young. And he told me your real name is Andrea."

"Lynn, Andrea, call me whatever. That visitor was my fast-talking, hustler brother, Joe. I may have mentioned him once or twice. Don't worry about not relaying the message. I already know what he wants."

"You do?"

"A friend of his showed up earlier today as I was getting off the airport shuttle. Said she needed to talk to me." Andrea shook her head and rolled her eyes. "Called it a matter of life and death."

"You sound skeptical, but he seemed pretty serious when he stopped by."

"He always acts serious when he needs a handout. This friend, her name was Kenzie, told me that my brother racked up a bunch of gambling debts and turned our family home into some kind of Airbnb to help pay them off. But the rentals aren't generating enough income, so she asked if I would consider lending him some money."

"How can you be so calm? I'd be out of my mind with worry." Grace reached for a second cookie.

"Well, I would be if I weren't so pissed that he's renting out our family's biggest asset without mentioning it to anyone. He's singlehandedly put our joint inheritance at risk. I have to discuss this with the rest of the family and decide what to do. My guess is we'll shutter the "Hotel Hackford" and then sell it, let him pay off his debts with his share of the proceeds. If those debts even exist. Knowing Joe, he sent his friend over with some cockamamie story, so I'd be faster to cough up the money when he stops by."

"Is he capable of something that deceitful?" Grace tried to ignore Vail, purring and rubbing against her calves. Her constricting throat made her wish she hadn't left her antihistamines at home.

"Joe? He's capable of just about anything."

"Well, then I'm not as sorry about forgetting to tell you. My condolences on the loss of your parents."

"Thanks. It's been almost a year now." Andrea pulled a cookie from the box for herself. "Kenzie had a lot to say about *her* parents when she was here. We chatted for around an hour. She came out when she was fifteen, and the stories of the bullying she endured, and her parents' total rejection of her lifestyle, would curl your toes."

"Sounds like one courageous lady. I'd like to meet her sometime." Grace could commiserate with any oppressed, marginalized child, discarded by her elders.

"Kenzie might have given me the makings for my next novel, though in my story, somebody's got to die."

Grace laughed, but it soon evolved into a wheeze. Without Zyrtec, her bronchial tubes were no match for three shedding cats. "I'd better get going, let you have some downtime. Thank you again for letting me stay here. It meant more than you can imagine."

"My pleasure. Consider yourself welcome to move in anytime I'm away. Do you mind letting yourself out? I want to grab a shower. Don't forget. Finished manuscript by Thursday. *Comprendes*?"

Grace slipped on her coat. "*Absolutamente.* I can't wait to wrap up this project." Never was there a truer statement. She couldn't wait. Her own denouement was fast approaching.

Chapter Twenty

After leaving Andrea's, Grace stopped by a café to get a little more writing in before packing up her laptop and heading home. It was around nine o'clock when she turned the corner onto Kalb Avenue. The first thing that struck her as odd, even from several houses away, was that light shone from every window. That only happened when her sons' friends stopped by, except for that one time when...Grace recalled a harrowing night from a few years back. The memory bathed her in a cold sweat, leaving her gasping for breath. Calm down, she told herself. *The "new you" can handle anything, remember?*

She clutched the wheel and inched down the street, bracing herself as she studied the vehicles parked along the curb. Sure enough, there it was, two doors away from her house so as not to attract her immediate notice. The blue Audi A6. Miles from its usual parking spot outside Dr. Leighmann's office. She drove to the end of the block where, as she'd feared, she found a parked ambulance bearing the name Grasmere in small print on its side. Just like last time, when she'd questioned Eliot about a few hundred dollars missing from their bank account, and spent a week doped up and "nursed back to mental health" for her curiosity.

Grace sped away, heart racing as fast as her engine, stopping only after she'd put a good ten miles between herself and Eliot's attempt to catch-and-commit. She pulled into a deserted office parking lot and idled behind one of the larger buildings, her Volvo hidden from view. She needed time to process.

Eliot must have called the office looking for her. Whoever worked late shift would have told him they hadn't seen her for months. Thirty seconds later, an emergency call to her therapist. Grace unmonitored! She wondered if anyone had checked her pill containers and noticed the switch to sugar tablets. That would have upped the ante. Grace loose and unmedicated! Hide the children, bury the silverware! One thing was for sure. Home was off-limits for now and the foreseeable future.

Her hands still trembling, she turned on the overhead light, looked around the car, and rifled through her purse. All she had on her was $137 and her laptop. If she used her credit cards or phone, they'd be able to track her movements, pinpoint her location. At least she'd always used the burner to call Andrea. The burner…oh, God. Where was it? She rummaged through her handbag a second time and then slammed it down on the passenger seat, spilling its contents in all directions. *Damn it, Grace, what a stupid, careless mistake.* She prayed she'd hidden it in her night table where Eliot might not ordinarily look.

She closed her eyes and centered herself. What to do? Or better still, what would her favorite literary detectives do? Strong, gutsy women like V.I. Warshawski, Kinsey Millhone, even Lynn Andrews' character, Clara Cardone. A germ of an idea propelled her into action.

Grace drove toward Valley General and its covered lot, where she parked in the spot farthest from the hospital's entrance. She crammed all the displaced items back into her oversized bag, shoved in her laptop, and then strode as confidently as any fictional sleuth into the emergency room entrance.

Patients crowded the waiting room, even at this late hour, which was perfect for her plan. "Excuse me, Miss," she addressed the harried receptionist, "I'm here to see Cornelius Phipps, which room is his?"

The receptionist looked up from her intake forms with an expression so sour, it was as if Grace had ordered her to perform a one-armed tracheotomy. She scanned her patient list. "There's no one by that name here," she said with unmitigated contempt.

"Damn, I was positive she said they brought him to Valley. Before I play hospital hide-and-seek, would you mind if I borrowed your phone? Mine's dead and I have to call my brother and double-check."

The receptionist harrumphed and pointed to a house phone against the far wall. "Dial nine and then one, followed by the area code and number. Just don't be too long. Those phones are reserved for doctors' use only." She turned back to her paperwork.

That was easier than I imagined. Grace reached into her coat pocket and studied the number she'd received a few days prior. Then she picked up the receiver and called the only person whose number wouldn't show up in her burner because she'd never dialed it before. "Hi, it's Gr...Ruth Allen. You *did* invite me to call day or night. This may sound crazy, but I'm in kind of an odd situation. Could you pick me up in front of the emergency room at Valley General? No, I'm not injured. But I am in danger and you may be the only one who can help me...yes, twenty minutes is fine. I'll wait by the entrance and explain everything once you get here. And thanks. I appreciate it. You're a godsend."

.   ∎   ∎

Tom Druthers pulled up to the hospital curb. "There was an accident on the Garden State, but I got here as fast as I could. You said you were in danger. How can I help?"

Grace jumped into the passenger seat and scrunched down so passersby wouldn't notice her. Then she looked up, saw the concerned expression on Druthers' face, and forced a smile to set him at ease. "I must look like the ultimate drama queen, but it's not like that. I can explain."

"When you're ready. In the meantime, relax. You're safe with me."

Gone was his flirtatiousness, assuming it had existed outside of her imagination, replaced by an aura of protectiveness. She straightened up after he pulled out of the parking lot and onto the street, less concerned that anyone they passed at fifty-five miles an hour might recognize her.

"I hope my call didn't disturb anything."

"Nope, just me and the crew watching a video. Nothing we can't go back and catch later."

She wondered if the "crew" included a special someone, and if that someone had freaked out when a stranger summoned Tom to meet her after dark.

They parked in Maywood outside a small Cape Cod and he escorted her to his front door. As he pressed his key into the lock, an intimidating chorus of barking from the other side added to Grace's anxiety.

"Are they friendly?"

"That's my crew. All bark, no bite. Two of the sweetest guard dogs you'll ever meet." He turned the knob and cracked open the door, pushing back one black and one red Doberman Pincher, both wagging their stumpy tails and longing for attention.

"That one's Thunder." He pointed to the black one as she pulled off her coat. "The red one is Rain."

Memories of Barrington's Springers, Dewey and Dutchess, tugged at her conscience. She'd have to figure out a way to check on her father's condition without being traced.

He extended his arm and she handed him her coat, leaving her free to crouch down and pet the appreciative duo. "Tom, if I give you some money, would you pick up a burner phone for me tomorrow?"

"I'm sure it won't be a problem. Make a list of whatever you need. And don't worry about the cost."

A sense of relief flooded over her as she watched him hang her coat in the closet. It was the first time she'd let down her guard since she'd seen hints of the "surprise party" her husband and doctor had planned.

Grace scanned her surroundings. More modern than many Capes she'd seen, this one had an open, airy floor plan. Myriad ferns and lush fiddle leaf figs lined the window ledges in green, with bromeliads adding occasional touches of yellow, orange and pink. Like Druthers, the décor was ragtag, yet warm and welcoming. He gave her a quick tour, their four-legged bodyguards following close behind.

"I sleep upstairs but there are two bedrooms on this floor. Take your pick. They're both a little cramped, but the mattresses are comfortable. You're welcome to stay as long as you like."

She peeked into the first; it was crowded with boxes piled to the ceiling. If each hadn't been so neatly stacked, with a list of contents marked on the side, she might have labeled him a hoarder. Still, if a dog were to bump into them...

"Those aren't likely to topple over, are they?"

He brushed past her and pulled the first carton from the top of the pile. "I doubt it, but why don't I move them to the other room anyway? Sorry for the mess, but I never found the time nor the inspiration to unpack after the divorce."

Grace wanted to apologize for being a bother, but it seemed a little late for that. She'd asked a relative stranger to drive twenty-five miles on a freezing night to rescue her. Rearranging a few boxes seemed trivial in comparison. She grabbed the carton now topping the pile and maneuvered between Thunder and Rain to transport it next door.

"You've got a lot of things you're not using."

"I used to collect stuff at flea markets and yard sales to resell on eBay. Anything my ex and I didn't need anymore, I added to the inventory." He lifted a third carton. "Even some of the clothes she left behind after taking off...then I got busy and...well, long story short, I suppose I'll get around to listing them one day."

She sensed his former marriage was an off-limits discussion and that was okay. Her life already teemed with drama; she didn't need to top it off with anyone else's. After five minutes, her bedroom was clear, the other one impenetrable. They retired to the kitchen table and the dogs lay down nearby. He asked if she'd like a hot drink.

"Tea, please, decaffeinated if you have it. But you've been so nice, I don't want to put you to any more trouble. Let me make it."

"It's no trouble, Ruth." He reached into the cupboard and pulled out two mugs. "I'm afraid I don't have any biscuits, but I'll go shopping tomorrow. Please write down any snacks you like, and I'll add them to the list."

She heard him call her Ruth and realized there was something she needed to get straightened out right away. It was only fair. "My real name is Grace. Grace Rendell. And I'll pay you back, I promise."

He gave her a surprised look as he set down a carton of milk. "Please don't worry about the money, Grace. it may not sound all that prestigious, but some of us toxicologists make a decent salary, and it's not like I've had anyone to share it with. Not for a while, anyway. The dogs are great, but it's nice to have some human companionship for a change." He placed a handful of sugar packets alongside the milk. It wasn't fine dining, but she was grateful for the effort.

"Now that you've got my real name, I guess I owe you the rest of the story." As he set their drinks on the table, she realized if there was ever a good time to trust anyone, this was it. Were anything to happen to her, at least someone else could bring Eliot to justice. Over the next hour, Grace sketched out a mini biography, describing her tyrannical father, her hospitalizations, her suspicions about her husband, and the book she and Andrea were writing. With every sentence, the enormous weight on her shoulders shrank by a few ounces until it disappeared.

"For what it's worth, you don't seem paranoid to me." He reached out and put his hand on hers. "If you were, would you call someone you barely knew to help you out?"

She hung her head. "After a lifetime of being told something, it becomes your reality. But since I stopped taking the meds, things look different. It's like a haze has lifted."

"Grace Rendell, at lunch the other day, you seemed as normal as a robin in springtime, and you've done nothing since to dissuade me." He pulled his hand back and they drank the rest of their tea. "Don't worry about anything. I'll get you the burner and whatever else you need. The dogs will keep you safe while I'm at work."

"I'll only need a nightgown and a change of clothes, something cheap. I can always order them on Amazon, if you have an account. And I'll make dinner every night, anything to earn my keep. What dishes are your favorites?"

"I'll eat anything you set in front of me. I'm not picky. But there is one thing...if you'd let the dogs out into the yard a few times each day while I'm away, it would make a nice change for them. It's fenced, so you don't have to worry about walking outside and being noticed."

"It would be my pleasure." She glanced over at the two sleeping Dobermans. "We've already become friends."

"I wish my ex had felt that way." His words were spiked with sadness.

She sensed a minefield and sidestepped with a yawn. "Thank you for the tea. Today has taken a lot out of me. I'm going to turn in."

"Before you do, I have something for you." Tom ran up the stairs and returned a few minutes later, holding a scrunched up, blue flannel shirt. "I'm sure it's ten sizes too big, but maybe it can double as a nightshirt until you pick out something else online. I washed it yesterday. It may be rumpled, but it's clean."

Grace accepted the shirt and gave Tom a kiss on the cheek. "You've made me more comfortable here than I feel at my own house. Whoever said chivalry was dead never came to Maywood."

"Whatever it takes to get that book written, Grace. You'll be the brains, but I'll provide the muscle. Don't worry. Together, we'll get it done."

Chapter Twenty-One

Hack left school early and stopped off at the coffee house before heading over to his sister's house in Ridgewood. It didn't seem right discussing his issues over the phone, not when a calculated pout might garner him the extra sympathy this confession warranted. And while he had given her a few days to recover from jet lag, he had no more time to waste; Boris and Ving had made that patently clear. He cased the venue from the window before he entered and checked over his shoulder every few minutes. Complacency was not an option when you owed dangerous people money.

While waiting to pay for a double expresso, he noticed a pile of tabloids by the register. The oversized headline and lead photo aroused his curiosity: "Paranoid Schizoid Heiress Missing." She looked familiar. Hack picked up a copy and staked out a corner table.

A closer look at the photo revealed a mother coddling two toddlers, her eyes clouded over by melancholy. He shuddered with recognition. A few years had passed, but it was her, the woman he'd met at Andrea's house, though the article named her as Grace Pierrepoint Rendell, not Ruth Allen. He scanned the article, noting it was "unclear if she'd been kidnapped, lost, or in hiding from some imaginary adversary" and how she might be "a danger to herself or others. Approach with caution and please call the police with any information." The last line of the article piqued his interest most: "$5,000 reward for any tips leading to her whereabouts."

That sum of money would come in handy right about now. Then again, it had been a few days since their encounter. His information might be irrelevant by now. And she'd seemed stone-cold sane when they met. A little tense, but no psycho. Not pure of deed himself, if she were on the run—for whatever reason—he didn't want to be the hypocrite who turned her in.

And the biggest reason Hack was reluctant to come forward: he needed to avoid any interaction with the law. If anyone saw him going into a police station—say, someone pressuring him to repay an illegal loan—he'd be labeled a snitch and dealt with accordingly. Nope, as tempting as that reward money sounded, he needed to give the authorities a wide berth.

.   ■   ■

Andrea answered the door in mismatched clothes, her hair tousled and uncombed. Hack had rarely seen her so out of sorts. "I hope you're not bringing me any new predicaments, Joe. I've got my own crisis of faith to deal with."

Hack glanced at the newspaper spread out on the counter. "You saw, then? Your ex-house sitter, missing in action?"

Andrea threw up her hands, as if she'd abandoned all trust in the world. "I've worked with that woman for months now. There was something so authentic about her, so vulnerable. It wasn't even about the money as much as the joy of cultivating raw talent. I was determined to help her make it. I liked and trusted her; we'd become friends."

She plopped down at the kitchen table and grabbed a sorrow-dousing chunk of banana bread. Hack joined her, listening and biding his time until the right moment arose to segue into his request for a loan.

"Now it turns out I didn't even know her real name. Or that she comes from money. Hell, she could have hired a thousand editors. I even entrusted my house to her. My babies..." Andrea reached down and lifted Denver onto her lap. The exotic cat studied his "uncle" with suspicion. Once satisfied Hack was harmless, he returned his attention to his owner, purring and rubbing his shimmering fur against her. "Do you have any idea how rare Denver is? Or how much I adore him? If anything had happened to this little guy..."

Hack snorted as he grabbed part of his sister's snack. "Pot, meet Kettle. I hate to break it to you, but she didn't know your real name either, *Lynn*. And for what it's worth, when I spoke to her, she didn't strike me as anyone who would hurt an animal. I saw what you saw. Someone trying to make it, grateful for your help. Pierrepoint money and all, maybe someone abducted her."

"Pretty inept kidnappers, then. The papers say her dad's in a coma. Not like he'd be running to the bank to cut a check. And anyway, I'm sure no one kidnapped her. She called me this morning. To make sure I wouldn't worry."

Hack gave his sixth sense an invisible thumbs up. His intuition was seldom off the mark. "What did she say? Did you tell the police?"

Andrea slumped back in her chair. "No way. I might be disillusioned and utterly gobsmacked but I'm no rat. I'd never turn her in. She's my friend. Or rather, *was* my friend. Regardless, I don't want to deal with the police more than necessary. God knows, they already hate me for the way I portray them in my books."

Hack snickered. "If they were competent, then Clara Cardone would be out of a job."

"Isn't that the truth. All Grace said was that she'd cloistered herself away to devote every spare second to finishing the novel. She was on the phone for less than a minute." Andrea got up and poured them each a glass of milk.

"With your temper, I bet you told her to take her book and shove it."

"Nope, just listened. I've invested months on this project. Time I borrowed from writing my own book. It would be nice to see it come to fruition. Even if I didn't do it primarily for the royalty split, that money would buy a lot of catnip. But if she's this goddamned flighty, what assurance do I have she won't publish it without me? I never insisted on a written agreement. What a fool I've been."

Andrea shooed Vail from her last bite of banana bread when they heard banging at the front door.

Hack looked up. "Think that's her?"

"Doubt it." Andrea lifted Denver from her lap and placed him on the floor. "More likely, the police found out about our connection and decided to question me. I don't want you involved in all this. Why don't you slip out the back door?"

"Sure thing, sis."

Hack was a desperate man. He had no intention of leaving without a promise of the money he needed. He waited until Andrea left the kitchen and then snuck into the dining room, where louvered doors afforded him a perfect vantage point without the risk of being noticed.

He watched Andrea peer through the peephole and then crack the door open. "Can I help you?"

"I'm Eliot Rendell. Grace's husband. May I come in? We need to talk."

Andrea opened the door to a slender, dark-haired man with bedraggled clothes and green eyes that even from a distance looked like he hadn't slept in days.

"Please, make yourself comfortable." She gestured toward the sofa. "What makes you believe I might be of any help?"

Eliot ignored her invitation and instead paced the room, wild-eyed, taking inventory. "Let's not waste time, okay? I found her phone; went through all the numbers she's called. Yours came up repeatedly. I ran a reverse search online and found this address. Are you claiming you two never met?"

Eliot's aggressive stance and controlled hysteria made the hairs on Hack's arms stand at attention.

"I'm not "claiming" anything. I've spoken with her a few times." It was clear from her tone that Andrea shared Hack's dislike and distrust of this nasty intruder.

Eliot rambled on as if he hadn't heard a word Andrea said. "She left a message on our machine, claiming she was taking some 'me time' to clear her head and didn't want anyone to worry. But that's not like Grace at all, running out on me and the boys. Someone could have abducted her and forced her at gunpoint to make that call. If you've been spending time with her, can you please tell me where she might have gone or whom she might be with?"

"No idea. Sorry I can't be of more help." Andrea walked toward the door, but Eliot didn't take the hint.

"After months chatting, you have no concept of where she might be? Do you expect me to buy that?"

To her credit and Hack's surprise, Andrea suppressed her notorious, hair-trigger temper. "I don't care what you 'buy,' Mr. Rendell. I'm telling you I don't have a clue as to your wife's whereabouts. But if she took time to contact you with a reasonable explanation, why isn't that good enough for you? Why not accept she needed to reflect and find herself, instead of riling up the police and newspapers with this convoluted suggestion of kidnapping?"

Eliot rubbed his hand against his greasy scalp. "You live too far to be part of our school district. So, what business did she have with you, anyway? What's more important than going to work and taking care of the kids?"

Andrea's nostrils flared. "If you must know, she wanted my help writing a novel. And last week, she pet-sat for me while I was out of town. There. That's the whole story. I think it's time you left."

"A novel?" Eliot erupted, his yell loud enough for the entire neighborhood to hear. Alarmed, Hack grabbed a broom and readied himself to protect his sister.

"Are you aware of how screwed up my wife is? She can't see anything clearly. When she's unmedicated, her reality becomes distorted. She's got a long history of delusions, nightmares, mental hospitalizations. She may appear sane for long stretches of time, but you must tread gently because if she senses betrayal or frustration, she becomes violent. Give me a pad and I'll list a dozen doctors and asylums who can confirm that. You trusted her to pet-sit? I hope your pets can feed themselves, lady, because last week, she flew down to Florida."

Andrea's face blanched at the mention of her neglected felines. "I wasn't aware—"

"Not only that. Any negative things her addled mind might concoct about her father—published in a novel or anywhere else—could sink the stock at Pierrepoint Industries and hurt thousands of employees and investors. The last thing they need right now is a ton of bad publicity that he can't refute while he's in a coma. So, I'll ask you one last time, where is she?"

Andrea remained close-lipped, but her balled-up fists convinced Hack that inside, she was seething. Eliot was apparently not a fan of the silent treatment and Andrea's lack of response prompted one last-ditch effort.

"Give me something. Anything. I'll double the reward money. Ten thousand dollars, for any clue to her whereabouts."

"Would you prefer I lie and rattle off some imaginary location? Fine, she's hiding out at the library." Andrea's patience had dwindled to zero, and her indifference pushed Rendell to raise his fist. Hack flew into action, charging through the louvered door, broom in hand, stunning both his sister and her unwelcome visitor.

"Look buddy, she said she doesn't know. I'm sorry about your missing wife, but you've overstayed your welcome."

Eliot glared at Hack, who was two inches taller and at least twenty years his junior. "So sorry I disturbed you," he grumbled as he stomped out of the house.

Andrea locked the door after him and then threw Hack an angry stare. "I distinctly remember telling you to leave." Her voice wavered, a clue he'd disrupted the interchange at exactly the right moment. She might act fearless, but his sister was not superhuman.

They wandered back into the kitchen, where Andrea replenished their supply of banana bread. Both munched away, purposely avoiding the topic of Grace and her overwrought husband. Still, Hack couldn't oust the memory of Eliot's generous reward.

"Andrea, you realize that ten thousand dollars is a lot of money."

"Indeed, I do. But having spent as much time as I have with Grace, I don't trust a word he said about her mental condition. And I don't want a penny of his blood money. He's too much like the jerk of a husband in Grace's novel..." Andrea's eyes grew wide and she fell silent as if she'd experienced an epiphany.

"But you expect some compensation, right? Only minutes ago, you regretted never drawing up a contract and were afraid you might not get paid for all your hard work."

"Joe, that's true but no matter what Grace has done, she's been a friend. A friend I now realize may be in real danger. Even if I discover where she's hiding, I'd never share the location with that lunatic."

"And still, she's the heiress to billions, but offered you how much to help her write her book?"

Andrea pursed her lips. "Two hundred dollars plus a promise of half the royalties."

Hack watched his sister's limbs stiffen. One or two more gentle pushes would incite her legendary wrath and make her more amenable to what he had in mind.

"Only two hundred, huh? And how far back did you push the release of *your* next book?"

"A month, maybe more."

"And how much does that translate into, monetarily?"

Andrea looked down at the floor. She was in author purgatory, torn between expressing altruism toward a fellow writer, and punishing herself for wasting time she'd never recoup.

"It's not like I need the money, Joe. It's the principle of the thing."

"Consider this. What if both were possible—keeping her safe and still ensuring you got paid?"

She looked at him askance. "How would I do that, pray tell?"

"You ever hear of ransomware?"

"Vaguely. Only in ads I've seen online for software that protects your computer against it."

"You've got Grace's email address, right?"

"That's how she sends me her pages to edit."

"Does her computer have virus protection?"

"No idea. Doubt it though. She doesn't seem to be all that tech-savvy." Andrea's eyes narrowed. "What's that to you?"

Hack's body vibrated with excitement. "What if we hack into Grace's computer and install some ransomware? She won't be able to access her manuscript until she meets our demands. Let's ask for five thousand, the same amount her husband's offering as a reward, and tell her to pay us in Bitcoin so it's untraceable. Send it to some anonymous email address we create. If she's as rich as the papers say, and so desperate to release this book, she'll hand over anything we ask. That way, you get paid in advance for your help without lowering yourself to tip off the authorities. A little insurance policy. If she ends up cutting you in later, you can always hand back your half of the money."

Andrea lifted an eyebrow. "My half? Where's the other half going?"

Hack had gotten away without revealing his hand this far. A tiny lie now wouldn't hurt. "A friend of mine runs a shelter for marginalized teens. I want to make a donation. Deal?"

Andrea shot him a glance that reeked of skepticism. "A donation, huh? You and I are going to have a heart-to-heart discussion about your finances and the disposition of the house when all this is behind us."

Hack's stomach fell. His secret was out. But how? Maybe it didn't matter. Once he paid off his debts, he might not need the SleepStay income any longer. And he was so close; she was wavering on the precipice of capitulation.

"Whatever you want, sis. But will you do this one thing for me? And for you, of course. For both of us. But mostly because your time and your work deserve proper respect and compensation."

Heart racing, Hack watched Andrea consider his proposal, her eyes darting from side to side. She had to agree, she just had to.

"You're such a BS artist, Joe. But it *is* an interesting proposition. Grace is a billionaire's daughter, looking for cheap editorial handouts. I won't betray her confidence, but if this is all a game to her, why should she have all the fun? Question is, who will help us? I doubt installing ransomware is something they teach you at the Genius Bar."

Hack cracked a smile. "It's all in the family, sis. We'll get Gwennie to help."

"Joe, she's an Ethical Certified Hacker. Emphasis on the word 'ethical.'"

"We'll tell her it's to lure Grace out into the open. For her own good. Grace will have to route the cryptocurrency through a BTM, that's like an ATM for Bitcoin. We'll tell her which one and when. As far as Gwen's concerned, when Grace gets there, we'll arrange for the medics to grab her. There's no way our moralistic sister will pass up an opportunity to use her skills for good. It's not our fault if the medics get 'confused,' go to the wrong BTM, and Grace gets away."

"And goes back into hiding, unharmed. A little poorer until she cuts me in for my half of the royalties and I refuse. Under those conditions, I'm in. And now it's all so clear."

He cocked his head. "What's clear?"

"Why everybody calls you Hack."

Chapter Twenty-Two

Grace hummed as she loaded the dishwasher after yet another wonderful breakfast with Druthers. A few weeks off the grid, without once being second-guessed, criticized, contradicted or patronized. Tom was respectful, valued her opinions, laughed at her jokes. Unlike Eliot, he never treated her like some Stepford wife, sounding the medication alarm if her demeanor strayed from flat, submissive, and robotic. Who would have guessed that being "on the lam" could be so relaxing and enjoyable?

Another bonus—her possessions stopped disappearing. In the morning, her slippers were right where she'd left them the night before, without having to hide them where Eliot wouldn't look. She remembered with a pang of regret how she'd accused the boys of playing tricks on her. The boys...

Sure, Grace missed her sons, but she no longer felt compelled to hover over them every minute. They were teenagers now. Eliot could handle whatever came up, with Keira nearby to pick up the slack. If her absence forced Damian and Xander to become more self-sufficient, even better. Anyway, it's temporary, she reminded herself as she set the dishwasher on its rinse cycle and let Thunder and Rain out for their morning romp. She'd return to them as soon as her mentor edited her manuscript and released it for the world to read.

Andrea had been her anchor and sole support system these last few months. A pang of guilt over deceiving her friend fizzled Grace's good mood like a fire extinguished by a heavy downpour. She bristled, remembering their conversation a few days after she'd sequestered herself at Tom's house. She'd taken the trouble to call Andrea and assure her she hadn't fallen off the map, and to renew her commitment to completing the book. In response, Andrea had uttered a frosty "uh huh" and an "okay" or two. Her indifference wounded Grace, but didn't Andrea have every right to sound shell-shocked after the newspapers unmasked her untruths?

If Andrea was that upset, could Grace still count on her collaboration? She didn't seem like the vindictive sort. They'd forged a friendship based on more than edits-for-royalties. Or had they? All questions worth considering—later. The threat of discovery still loomed, and apart from cooking and cleaning to repay Druthers' hospitality, she refused to deviate her focus until her manuscript was complete.

She called the dogs back in, gave them each a biscuit, and retired to her makeshift office, a card table that Druthers had set up in a corner of the living room. With Thunder and Rain nestled at her feet, she booted up her laptop, ready to unleash her creative juices.

"What the f...?" She gasped as a yellow skull and crossbones graphic filled the screen. Its caption read: *We've blocked your computer. If you ever want to access your files again, bring $5,000 to the Bitcoin machine at 312 Dwight Street in Englewood on Mar 29th at 3:00 p.m. and send it to wallet code 1dawSLRHtKNngkdXEzXbR76k53LETtpyT.*

The note torpedoed Grace's earlier cheerfulness, scattering remnants of lost optimism across the room. The dogs jumped up and started pacing, sensing her agitation. How many times had she ignored Norton's constant solicitations for anti-malware software? Or put off subscribing to services that auto-backed up files and stored them in the Cloud?

Now what? It was the first time since arriving at the Maywood house that she'd panicked. That laptop was her life preserver. Who knew what this hacker had done to her manuscript? Shared it? Altered her words? Deleted it from her hard drive? She didn't have access to ransom money, nor any idea of how to save her files without paying off the extortionists. There was only one option. She phoned Druthers and begged him to rush home.

Together they used his desktop to comb the Internet for instructions on how to remove ransomware. Druthers even called in a programming expert. Grace hid in her bedroom while he checked out her machine and reported the hacker had encrypted the files, and that installing any anti-virus software would only protect her work moving forward. "Don't pay the ransom," he warned Druthers. "There's no guarantee you'll get your files back and it only encourages more attacks."

Once he left, Grace slid to the floor and curled into a sitting fetal position. All those weeks of dedication, 60,000 hard-fought words, all for nothing. Her literary insurance policy, so close to completion, confiscated. Out of reach, perhaps forever.

Druthers dropped to the floor beside her. She buried her head against his flannel-covered shoulder. "What do I do now? I can't hide from Eliot forever. Why not swallow a handful of peanuts? I'm as good as dead right now."

"Guess the only answer is to pay the ransom and get you back your story."

"That's not an option," she murmured into his shirt. "How can I get at that money without alerting everyone who's looking for me? I'm sure Eliot's put a tracker on our bank account."

"I have money."

Grace looked up at him, astonished. "You'd loan me five thousand dollars? We only met a few weeks ago."

Druthers gave her a squeeze. "I figure you're good for it. You're friends with Andrea. That's reference enough for me. I'll even go to the Bitcoin machine myself, so no bounty hunters or reporters will spot you."

Propelled by a wave of gratitude, she threw her arms around him and gave him a big, spontaneous hug. Then, without thinking, she pressed her lips to his. It must have caught him unawares, but after a few seconds of non-response, he joined her in a long, luxurious, open-mouthed kiss that allowed their tongues to mingle and explore. Unwilling to be left out, Thunder and Rain wormed their way into the embrace, forcing the couple to separate and share their attention.

Grace suddenly became self-conscious. "I'm...sorry. That was out of line. You've done so much for me already, and I'm not used to anyone treating me—"

Druthers was having none of it, He pushed Thunder aside and pulled her back into a second, albeit shorter embrace. "Don't apologize. It's the nicest thing that's happened to me in a long time. If it doesn't happen again, I'll understand. But don't blame me if I'm delighted it did."

"I appreciate that. I'm just not the type of woman...I would never...I'm married. Not happily but the vow still applies. At least for the time being. But if I were free—"

"Grace, not an issue. I'm a very patient man. If things progress, great. If not, we're friends, right?"

"And associates. Don't forget that, Tom. Your name is in my book under Acknowledgements."

"Hey, that's almost as good." They laughed, breaking the awkward tension. "I've got to get back to work. Remind me Grace, when is the money due?"

"March twenty-ninth. 3:00 p.m. Do you want me to text you the address?"

Druthers rose, prompting a disappointed Rain to paw his thigh. He pacified her with one last scratch under her ear. "That would be great. I can pick up the cash on my way home, before the bank closes. Are you sure you'll be okay here on your own?"

"Positive. I'll use the break to get this place vacuumed, dusted and neat. If that's okay with you."

"I'd be an idiot to turn down an offer like that." He gestured toward the dogs as he headed to the door. "But you'd better check with the bosses first. They get the final say around here."

Chapter Twenty-Three

March twenty-ninth. Payday. An opportunity to get out of debt and reimburse Andrea for the effort she'd invested in Grace's book. For the first time in months, Hack would be free from obligation, other than to study and graduate high school—as long as he convinced his siblings to allow him to remain in the house that long. Maybe if he fessed up about his SleepStay side hustle, cut them in for a share...

Along for the ride was recent handyman hire, Zev, who'd proven his resourcefulness the afternoon he'd dispatched his protective trio of "Hasidic fixers" to Jerry's Diner. It took most people forever to earn Hack's trust; his new friend had done it in record time.

Hack's plan was well underway by 2:45 p.m. when Zev texted him from the designated Bitcoin machine, where he was posing as a random customer. Zev's job was to play Good Samaritan and assist Grace if she encountered any problems converting funds or transferring them to the designated wallet. "Jay-Z blows compared to Drake," read the note, their code for "I am onsite. So far, so good." That was a relief. He drove over to Andrea's to wait for the money to hit.

At three o'clock, his eyes were glued to the Bitcoin wallet when his phone buzzed again. "I heard Travis Scott's new single might not drop on schedule." Hack balled up his fists, a reaction to their code for "She's a no-show. Should I hang out?"

"What's wrong?" Immersed in the intrigue, Andrea had plans to include a similar plotline in a future Clara Cardone mystery.

Then another buzz. "But Kanye's better than them all," which translated to, "Everything's good." *Thank God.* That meant Zev was now following Grace back to her hideout. Knowing that address would give them another shot to collect the reward money if their original scheme fell through.

Hack walked over to the bookcase and pulled out the Scrabble board. "We've got an hour to kill before we can make sure the money's in. Loser pays winner one dollar per point."

"Don't you ever learn your lesson? Go on, set it up."

At four, they left their tiles on the board and returned to the computer screen. After a few tense minutes, the confirmation appeared. $5,000!

One hug and fist bump later, Andrea wrote her brother a check for $2,500, made out to cash, while Hack tried to reach Gwennie by phone to advise her to unblock Grace's computer and decrypt her data.

Ten rings, then to voicemail. No way was he leaving any evidence on a recording. He punched in the number a second time, the perspiration on his palms making it difficult to hold onto the cell. Same result. He'd gone over the plan a hundred times, but a team member going AWOL was one hitch he hadn't foreseen.

"She's not picking up. What should we do?"

It shocked Hack that his normally stoic sister's hands trembled as she turned over the check. "Not a problem. Go to the bank, take care of whatever you need. I'll sit here and keep dialing Gwennie. I bet she's on a coffee break. Anyway, I doubt Ruth, slash, Grace is counting the seconds until her screen becomes unblocked. It'll all be fine. Meet you back here later, and we'll celebrate over spaghetti and cake."

.   .   .

Butterflies swirling in her stomach, Grace sat by her laptop and counted the seconds until her computer became unblocked. By 4:15 p.m., when Druthers reappeared, she'd wasted over ninety minutes holding her proverbial breath. She bombarded him with questions at the door: "What went wrong? Didn't the machine work? Did you miss the deadline?"

Druthers gave her a reassuring hug. "Everything went as planned. My boss called me back into work, which is why I didn't come home right away. I guess I should have phoned, but I figured you'd be busy composing your next chapter."

"It's still blocked." She moaned into his shoulder. "It's like your friend said: these crooks get one payment, see you're an easy mark, and hold you up for more."

He patted her back. "I can imagine how frustrating this must be for you. It might take longer than we figured for the money to get posted to an account. Or the hacker isn't waiting by the computer the way you are. He may be off at his second job—beating up old ladies or taking children's candy—and will release your laptop from captivity as soon as he gets home. You have to be patient."

Druthers played with the dogs while Grace paced the living room floor, rechecking her laptop every few minutes, only to see the familiar skull and crossbones staring back. By four-thirty, she'd had enough. "This isn't working. I'm going to stuff my hair under a cap, take an Uber to Andrea's, and beg her to put her copy of my manuscript onto one of the dozens of flash drives she keeps lying around. It won't have everything I've added since I've been here, but I'm sure I can recreate most of that. Would you mind if I use your computer to edit, once I have my book back?"

Druthers threw a tennis ball across the room, and Rain raced over to retrieve it. "Everything I own is at your disposal. But Grace…let's talk this through; it seems a little impulsive. If you're going to risk being seen, why not at least call Andrea first? Make sure she's there and has everything ready for you."

"I don't want to do that. She acted so offhand the last time I called. If she's mad at me, I don't want to give her a chance to say no. If I just show up, she can't very well turn me away. And anyway, I have her spare key in my bag. If she's out, I'll find the manuscript on her computer and download it onto a flash drive myself. She'll never notice the difference."

He cleared his throat. "That's one way to handle it, I suppose. But at least let me drive you."

"Thanks, but that's unwise. If Andrea sees you, she'll guess where I'm staying." Grace realized she sounded bullheaded, but she had total faith in her plan and had no intention of getting Druthers involved any deeper than he already was.

Rain dropped the tennis ball and started whining. She let both dogs out into the yard to do their business. "Can I borrow one of your shirts? It'll be too big on me, but I'll tuck it in. I might be less recognizable if I'm wearing something out of character."

"I may have a better idea. Give me five." Druthers hurried out of the room.

She called the dogs back in, listening with half an ear to the commotion emanating from the spare bedroom. He returned with two stacked boxes and used a steak knife to slit open the top one, revealing a mannequin head wearing a red curly wig. "Knew I still had this somewhere. Guess it pays to procrastinate, huh?"

Grace snatched the hairpiece and tried it on in front of the bathroom mirror. The color suited her. Best of all, she barely recognized herself.

She walked back in, eager to model the look for Druthers. He was busy unpacking the second box, laying out various articles of women's clothing. Admiration for his resourcefulness and gratitude for yard sales momentarily replaced her alarm over the missing ransom money. "What size are they?"

"Most are twelves. You look about the same size as my ex-wife." He handed her a pair of jeans and a white, button-down silk shirt. "Here, Red, try these on."

"It would be perfect if they fit. I don't own any pants like these, so wearing them would fool everyone."

Grace donned the new outfit and applied heavier makeup than usual, blinking twice as she checked herself out in the bedroom's full-length mirror. Between the wig, the weight she'd lost since quitting her meds, and the compressing magic of denim, she looked about ten years younger and sexy as hell. She studied herself at different angles, pleased at the unexpected transformation. Then she remembered everything at stake and her elation plummeted. *This is no time for a fashion show. This is about saving my butt...which I must admit, looks hot for the first time in ages.*

Druthers' mouth gaped, and even the dogs growled as she reemerged, sensing a stranger in their midst. She held out the back of her palm, praying her personal scent would triumph over the clothes' pervasive mothball odor. After a few sniffs, their stumpy tails started wagging again.

"Tom, this is perfect. I hate to ask for anything else, but would you be a doll and let me borrow your credit card, so I can call a car service? I'm keeping track, I swear."

He walked over and gave her a kiss on the cheek. "I told you once before, your money's no good here. All I've ever wanted was to feel needed, something my dogs understood better than my ex-wife. I'm having a blast knowing that in some small way, I'm helping a damsel in distress. Let me have my shining armor moment, okay?"

"My apologies, Good Sir Druthers." Grace walked to her makeshift desk and scribbled something down on a sheet of paper. "This is how I plan to get there and back." She handed him the note. "Kindly summon the carriage, so I may be off."

He placed his arm across his chest and bowed. "My pleasure, sweet Lady Grace. Your wish is my command. I shall also prepare the computer for your use while you are off on your crusade. Just promise me you'll take caution on your travels, Milady. I would hate to lose thee to the whims of fate."

Grace donned her hooded coat, fighting the twinge of hesitation creeping down her spine. It was the first time she'd left the safety of his fortress since stories of her disappearance hit the media. A five-thousand-dollar bounty might be mere pocket change to someone like Andrea but if she were spiteful, the reward might symbolize something more. Like compensation for Grace hoodwinking her with a pack of lies. Could their budding friendship withstand the temptation?

Chapter Twenty-Four

Cloaked in borrowed hair and garb, Grace's confidence in her camouflage was stronger than the faith she had in her collaborator. Andrea had been so reticent during their last phone call, it renewed Grace's determination to repair any damage she'd caused. Explain how the tabloids had exaggerated the severity of her medical disorders. And why an heiress, whose father was worth billions, had negotiated for edits at bargain basement rates. Even why she'd used the Ruth Allen pseudonym from day one. If Andrea recognized "Ruth's" story as autobiographical, as an escape route, compassion might temper her upset. It all depended on whether she'd trust someone labeled as a paranoid schizophrenic.

Damn Eliot and the media for their persistent and hyperbolic reporting. Every day, a new angle about the missing heiress. Since when did local newspapers publish such brazen headlines? Yes, her husband wanted her back and sure, the papers needed to boost circulation, but at what cost? The relationship with Andrea aside, faced with so much negative press, how could she return home and face her co-workers, her neighbors, her kids? Especially when she no longer bore any resemblance to the addled person the papers described, or the dowdy, overmedicated woman they might remember?

She'd concocted an elaborate scheme to travel the seven-mile route to Andrea's house without detection. A three-block walk over to Benz Court, where she'd asked Druthers to arrange for an Uber to drive her to ShopMart. Then a Lyft from that supermarket to Joshua Drive, four blocks shy of Andrea's. On the return, she'd planned something similar, involving different streets and two taxi services instead of ride shares.

Neither of her initial drivers paid her any mind. Either the wig and makeup were working, or they hadn't read about the reward. By providing this camouflage, Druthers had saved her once again. Too bad she'd left her antihistamines behind. Red eyes would clash with her new hair color.

With most people either still at work, or home cooking dinner, Grace's late afternoon stroll from Joshua Drive was free of strollers, joggers, and dogwalkers. Even if she had been recognizable, there were no bounty hunters around to turn her in. Yet, the sight of Andrea's shadow through the living room's gauzy curtains dredged up memories of her acerbic wit.

Grace hesitated outside the house, her hands thrust deep inside her pockets, her nerve waning. She needed a flash drive, not a sparring session with the queen of candor. What if she begged for forgiveness, only to have Andrea refuse? A desperate person fearing for her life, but denied a simple favor? The thought made her judder with rage. Her pills used to squelch feelings like this, but now she experienced them full force and they scared her. Maybe the safer alternative was to go home, leave things as they were…

.   .   .

Cork & Beans was a hybrid neighborhood hangout, located only a mile from Andrea's house. From sunrise until late afternoon, it served a wide variety of coffees and pastries. At happy hour, it transformed into a wine bar offering both popular and rare vintages until the wee hours. The transition period, between four and five o'clock, was dining limbo. Which is why Hack had selected it for this debriefing, a way to get Grace's whereabouts and compensate Zev for his trouble before meeting Boris and paying off a big chunk of his debt. Once he got that monkey off his back, he planned to return to Andrea's for their celebratory dinner. In the meantime, he ordered a latte and a piece of pound cake and waited. And then waited some more.

At 4:45, his bearded accomplice finally showed, allaying Hack's growing panic. He bypassed the counter and came right to the table. "I'm sorry I'm late. It did not go as planned."

"How so? We got paid. I've got the cash in my wallet."

"First, she never showed. Some bald, *shlumpy* guy came in her place."

A blonde waitress—straight out of collegiate-cheerleaders central casting—interrupted Hack's avalanche of questions. "Can I get either of you gentlemen anything?"

"You paying?" Zev asked Hack.

"Sure, why not."

Zev turned his attention back to the waitress. "Do you have any Kopi Luwak?"

"Um, I'm afraid not. I've never heard of it," the girl giggled.

Zev flashed his most engaging smile. "What a shame. It's made from the feces of the palm civet in Indonesia. It's a little expensive, but delicious and—"

Hack cleared his throat and glowered at Zev, unable to fathom why his friend had chosen that exact moment—in a place he'd selected specifically to escape notice—to discuss something as memorable as cat poop coffee.

"Err, I'll take the house brand, black with sugar."

"You got it." The waitress winked and walked away.

Hack shook his head in disbelief and resumed the conversation. "I suspected our friend might find a substitute. Are you sure he was the one? The money didn't hit for an hour."

"I inched close enough to get a glimpse of his screen. He was transferring $5,000. It would be quite the coincidence if two people transferred that exact amount at the same time."

"Fair enough. But how long did all that take? I figured you'd already be here, waiting for me, not the other way around."

The waitress returned with Zev's order. "I chose a Central American-South American blend. Fairly poop-free, but still pretty good. I hope you like it." She winked a second time and left the teens to their conversation.

"Do you suppose she was flirting?"

Hack sighed. "Is that important right now?"

Zev twisted to take another look. "In my community, boys don't speak much to girls once we reach a certain age. I've got some catching up to do."

"You can chat with her later, Romeoski. Tell me what happened once you left the Bitcoin place."

"I jumped into my car and followed him, just like you asked. And it would have worked if he'd gone straight home. But no, *Shlumpy* drove to some office building and kept me waiting. The longer he stayed inside, the more freaked out I got. After he came back out, I followed him home and then headed over here."

Hack sipped his now-cold latte. "Good. What's the address?"

Zev reached into his pocket and pulled out a crinkled piece of paper. "It's a little place in Maywood. I didn't see any sign of Grace there, so I have no idea if she's staying with him or he's a go-between." He blew on his coffee and took a sip. "Not bad. For the uninitiated."

Hack pulled an envelope out of his jacket pocket and handed it to Zev. "Here's your cut. Try not to spend it all on Blondie there."

"Give me some credit. I'm not the village *schmuck.* I wait until the second date to empty my pockets into their purse."

"Do whatever you want with your pockets. I need to make a call and then meet up with some folks to settle my debt. We'll have plenty of time to chat about your sexual exploits later."

"Prepare for an earful then." Zev finished his coffee and stumbled past his crush before heading out the door.

Gotta teach that kid some moves once this whole mess is over. Hack pulled out his cell to check in with his sister. She picked up after half a ring, as if she'd been waiting by the phone. "I figured you'd have called by now. Everything on track?" he asked.

"Finally. Took forever to get through to our friend, but she said she'd take care of 'our project' as soon as her meetings wrapped up. From here on out though, I'm sticking to fiction. Real-life intrigue is too stressful."

"At least this experience will add some authenticity, right sis? Sis? Andrea, you still there?"

"Joe, hold on a sec. I think someone's in the house. I'll call you back later." *Click.*

Part Three

Chapter Twenty-Five

"Oh my God. Grace. Oh my God. What the hell have you done?"

Stomach clenched tight, Grace stood frozen, trying to comprehend how her mentor could lay inches away, lifeless and awash in red. Only fury over the accusation posed by the man beside her brought her back to her senses. She turned and faced the teen whom she recognized as Andrea's brother.

"Are you crazy? Why would I kill her? She was my friend." The gravity of the situation hit, and she fought back a tsunami of tears.

"You paranoid bitch. Were you afraid she'd double-cross you? Publish the book under her own name and cut you out?" With a trembling hand, he pulled out his cell phone. "I'm calling the police."

"No, don't do that." She yanked the phone from his hand and slipped it into her coat pocket. "I'm only here because I needed something from her computer...she has a copy of my manuscript..." The reasons behind her visit now seemed so far away and unimportant. She tried to focus through the fog of upset at anything but the bloody remains of her collaborator.

"Did you need it badly enough to kill her?"

This second accusation snapped Grace out of her stupor, and what had been bewilderment morphed into anger. "You're quick to accuse, but I could say the same thing about you. I didn't hear any knocking at the door. You may have been here all along. Maybe you two had words when she told you she was kicking you out of that makeshift boarding house of yours, or when she refused to help you pay your gambling debts. You became furious, killed her, then ransacked the place to make it look like a burglary. I should call the police, and have *you* arrested."

Hack's eyes grew wide, and his body stiffened. He opened his mouth to speak, but instead, chose to stand over his sister's body and mourn her loss.

Offense really is the best defense. With Hack preoccupied, Grace grabbed her wig and repositioned it on her head.

"What if the killer is still here?" she whispered, giving him the benefit of the doubt. He did look more crazed than culpable.

"Long gone, I imagine. I noticed the back door open when I ran through the kitchen. That must be how he escaped. You were here first. Did you see anything?"

Grace clutched a chair for support, her forehead damp. The prospect of reliving what she'd observed sucked the last of the oxygen from the room, leaving her lightheaded. But it was the only way to convince Hack of her innocence.

"I was approaching the house when I saw Andrea's shadow in the window, and I lost my nerve. I turned to leave, when out of the corner of my eye, I noticed a second silhouette, someone taller than Andrea, slim like you. Not sure if it was a man or a woman. I stood there, watching like a Peeping Tom. Andrea started flailing her arms and shaking her head—"

"And that didn't alarm you?" The disgust in his voice increased her vertigo and she clasped the chair tighter.

"It should have but then I remembered her talking about how she used to role-play some of her murder scenes before sending them to her publisher. I figured I'd stumbled onto the secret of how the great Lynn Andrews created characters with such realistic dialogue and movement."

"That's plausible, I suppose. Go on."

"The shadows strayed from the window. Even from the sidewalk several yards away, I could hear Andrea yelling, her words too muffled to be intelligible. Then the taller shadow came back into view, holding something thin and rectangular—"

"Like a book? Or a briefcase?"

"More like a laptop. Andrea's silhouette also returned, trying to wrench it away. Then the visitor pulled out what looked like a knife—"

"And *that* didn't propel you into action?"

"I suppose it should have, but remember, I thought I was watching a staged murder, the inspiration for an amazing book. Still...the way Andrea retreated, using her hands to shield herself, made me...realize...it was no role-play." She shuddered but pressed on, determined to clear her name.

"I raced to the front door and jiggled the handle. It was locked. Inside, Andrea shrieked and then moaned in agony. I fiddled with my keys, jammed the right one into the lock, and flung the door open. The room, oh my God, the room was in shambles, a coffee table overturned, papers from the desk strewn in all directions. The moaning had stopped, and the silence was deafening. I ran into the kitchen, no Andrea. My head was about to explode, and I wasn't sure where to search next. The bedroom? The basement? Then I heard some mewing from the next room. I realized Denver, Aspen and Vail would be wherever Andrea was. So, I ran into the dining room and found...this."

Through tear-blurred vision, she saw Hack studying her rather than reaching out to lend comfort. His coldness chilled her. She'd laid herself bare, recounting one of the worst moments of her life, and yet, he looked skeptical. If he didn't believe her, who would?

I can't allow the police to find me at a crime scene, Grace realized, once coherence eclipsed anguish. A former mental patient, in hiding, desperate for something in Andrea's possession. She knew how guilty it made her look, how Eliot and the media would churn public opinion for maximum effect. Her survival instinct was strong, and it advised her to get as far away as possible. But how, without being noticed?

"You mentioned the kitchen door earlier as the killer's escape route. I never opened it when I housesat. Where does it lead?"

He cocked his head and hesitated before answering. "There's an alley that separates Andrea's house from her neighbors. It connects with a path that runs behind this block and leads to the next cross street...why do you ask?"

Her taxi waited nearby. It was time. She just had to be sure he wouldn't implicate her once she left. She patted his phone, resting in her pocket. If Hack were anything like her kids, that cell was his lifeline. He wouldn't cut the umbilical cord without a struggle.

"You'll need to deal with the police alone. Meet me over at 25 Bailey Court in Maywood. If you give anyone that address, or mention one word about seeing me here, I'll drag you down with me. My having your cell phone is proof we know each other. When you show up, we can sit down and compare notes, piece together who might have done this."

Grace realized she needed to remove any evidence of her presence before leaving the scene of the crime. There were too many fingerprints to erase, easily explained by her pet-sitting gig. But the key? Grace pulled her hood over her wig to escape identification, dashed to the front door, and snatched her spare from the lock. She returned to the dining room and stole a final look at the body, the first person to encourage her talent when no one else would. Then, ignoring Hack's protests, she escaped out the back door, cursing writing and Eliot and friendship and everything that had led her to the numbness and emptiness that now enveloped her.

.   .   .

Grace's retreat left Hack weak-kneed and reeling in a vortex of suspicion and despair. Outrage was the only thing keeping him from collapsing into a bawling wreck. Watching a role-play? That was her story? Does an innocent person abandon the remains of her supposed friend moments after her murder?

Grace's threats ricocheted in his head like a wayward bullet. There was no time to mourn; he needed to stay focused, erase any incriminating evidence of his visit. The cats mewed by Andrea's lifeless body; rigor mortis would soon set in. The right thing was to stay with her until the authorities arrived. But which authorities? The police? An ambulance? The coroner? And when they arrived and asked what he was doing there...questioned his whereabouts that day...what then?

If he mentioned Grace's name, she'd finger him for the murder. Somehow, she'd found out about the SleepStay and his gambling debts, both of which would have caused a giant argument between him and his sister. What if the police concluded that quarrel led him to commit a crime of passion to ensure her silence? To then forge one of Andrea's checks and cash it to cover his debts? The bank's tellers and video cameras were sure to remember him and the withdrawal now sitting in his wallet.

Medical examiners often estimated time of death within a two-hour range, at least according to television dramas. Who was to say he hadn't killed Andrea during his first visit, before he'd gone to the bank and then returned to "accidently" discover her body? Considering his past altercations with the law, and his recent break-in at the Houlahans— further testament to his desperation for cash—did he want to open himself up to that level of scrutiny?

Hack hunted for Andrea's cell phone and found it on an end table in the living room. He punched in a familiar number and waited.

"Gwendolyn Hackford."

"Gwennie, it's Joe—"

"Oh Joe, did Andrea tell you? Sorry it took longer than expected, but I handled everything like you—"

"Gwennie, that's great, thank you but..." He wavered, biting his quivering lip. "Wait ten minutes and then call Andrea's house—not her cell—three or four times, letting the phone ring. Then call the police. Tell them you're worried no one's answering. Ask them to check on her."

"What the hell are you talking about, Joe?"

His throat burned with reflux from the coffee and cake he'd consumed earlier that day. To say anything more would leave digital evidence of him visiting the house and finding the body. "Please do as I ask. I'll fill you in later."

There was a pause at the other end of the line. "Joe, does this have anything to do with what we did—"

"I doubt that played into it, but I can't be positive."

"Should I go over there?"

Hack squeezed his eyes tight, hating himself for involving either sister in this fiasco. "I'm not sure that would be the smartest thing. I need you to swear you won't tell anyone I called or said anything."

"Okay...I guess...Oh Joe, you're making me very nervous."

"I've got to go, Gwen. We'll talk later." Hack disconnected the call and wiped away a few rogue tears with the back of his hand. Then he turned off the GPS tracking on Andrea's phone, powered down, and stuck it in his pocket. No reason to make it easier for the cops by leaving his sister's phone and its secrets behind.

Hack ran through the house, searching in vain for the laptop Grace had implied was the target of the break-in. In the basement, he noticed a door jimmied open and figured that's how the culprit entered. Unless Grace had done that to cover her tracks.

He abandoned the search and switched course, using a paper towel to wipe his fingerprints from any surface he remembered touching. Then he stood over his sister's corpse one last time, beseeching God to watch over her in heaven. Only when the house phone began ringing did he pull his jacket tight, ensure the kitchen door locked behind him, and enter the alley, careful to keep his pace slow and inconspicuous. Then he swung left, headed to his car as if nothing were wrong, and drove from the scene, praying he'd made it out unnoticed.

Chapter Twenty-Six

Once he'd put a few miles between himself and the crime scene, Hack pulled into the deserted parking lot of a shuttered restaurant and turned off the ignition. Only then did he unleash the wails he'd suppressed since discovering his sister's body. First his parents' death and now this. He'd never felt so empty and alone.

At his anxiety's core was an overwhelming sense of guilt, like a lump of coal wedged in the pit of his stomach. What role had his actions played in his sister's murder? Was he responsible for her death?

Hack remembered Eliot's warnings about Grace when he'd barged in that day: *Reality distorted when unmedicated...a long history of delusions and mental hospitalizations... may appear sane for long stretches of time...a dozen doctors and asylums who'd confirm she becomes violent when sensing betrayal or frustration.* Yet, despite that laundry list of concerns, he and his sister had still hacked into her computer and shanghaied her beloved manuscript. How could their exploits have *not* triggered some intense reaction?

He played out possible scenarios: By the time Gwennie unblocked Grace's computer, the nutcase had become so impatient, she'd rushed to Andrea's house, demanding a copy of her book. When Andrea refused, Grace stabbed her in a fit of exasperation and stashed the laptop somewhere. Alternative Number Two: Grace somehow uncovered their Bitcoin extortion scheme, became outraged by Andrea's betrayal, and attacked his sister.

Then Hack carried his visualization one step further. Say she did stab Andrea. Why was she simply standing there, frozen in place? True, her eyes had been red—a sign of teary remorse. But wouldn't some of Andrea's blood have squirted out, at least staining her attacker's clothes? Wouldn't a guilty Grace have pushed past him and run out the door rather than staring at the body, trying to make sense of it all? And what killer shares the address of her hideaway? He'd checked—it was the same address Zev had handed him at Cork & Beans.

Not to mention, Andrea had discounted Eliot's every word. Her instincts about people were usually spot-on, and she'd attested to Grace's sanity.

Which left Scenario Number Three: the murder was a warning from Boris and Ving. They'd made good on their threat and visited Andrea to extract the funds he owed them. In fact, Boris resembled the body shape Grace had described. Perhaps his sister had put up a struggle—that would be just like her—and they'd lost their temper and killed her to keep her quiet.

Three possibilities, all leading to one basic truth: he dragged her into this mess. Andrea's murder was on his head. And he had no intention of letting her attack go unanswered.

When his parents died, there had been no one to blame. He had chalked it up to bad luck and equipment failure. No means to achieve catharsis or closure. But Andrea's murder was different. This was a mystery to solve, a death to avenge. He may have found his mission in life: extracting justice on his sister's behalf.

Distracted and distraught, Hack got back on the highway but hadn't realized how much he depended on his phone until he found himself on unfamiliar roads without one. He struggled to locate Maywood without consulting Andrea's GPS app, lest the police were tracking her phone. A gas station attendant on Route 17 sold him a map and some tissue to dry his eyes.

The stars were already visible when Hack found the house on Bailey. He zipped his parka as he walked toward Grace's door, but it was more than the night air causing him to shudder. He was accustomed to solving any puzzle he encountered, but this one seemed way out of his depth.

Grace must have been standing watch because she creaked open the door as he reached for the bell. "Take it slow," she warned. "I don't want the dogs' barking to alert the neighbors." Paranoia or reasonable caution?

Either way, she seemed a lot calmer than earlier in the day, which was promising.

"This is my friend, Tom Druthers. Tom, this is Andrea's brother, Hack."

Hack nodded to the heavyset man sitting on the couch, holding each of two Doberman Pinchers by the collar. Mr. *Shlumpy* himself, as per Zev's dead-on description.

"Don't pay too much mind to these two," said Druthers, as if sensing Hack's apprehension. "If you let them sniff you, they won't bother you for the rest of the evening, except to be pet."

Hack relaxed a tad when each dog licked his palms, until Grace's interrogation sent his blood pressure soaring again.

"Did the police ask a lot of questions? What did you say? Did they suspect you?"

"I didn't wait around." He noticed the look of surprise on her face.

"Why not? I assumed—"

Druthers cut her short, gesturing for them both to sit down. "Grace told me her version of what happened this afternoon. I think we're all a little shaken up. Why don't you tell me your side of the story?"

Grace took her place next to Druthers. Hack parked himself in a recliner, unsure of where to begin. Perhaps go on the offensive, since she'd run from the scene. Off the table: any mention of their extortion scheme.

"My sister and I had dinner plans. I called to check in and she cut it short, claiming she'd heard an intruder in the house. I raced over, found the door open and Grace here, standing over Andrea's dead body. Despite her wig, I recognized her as the woman I'd seen at the house a few weeks before, the same woman on the covers of all the newspapers. She claimed to have come over to get a copy of her manuscript, and then she ran off. It seems very strange. Wouldn't she already have a copy of her own book?"

Grace stuck out her chin and glared. "Someone hijacked my laptop and held it up for ransom. I needed to get Andrea's copy to download onto a new computer and write the last few chapters. With everyone looking for me, I couldn't risk being discovered there. It's a matter of life and death."

"Apparently." Hack's voice crackled with bitterness.

Grace lunged forward but Druthers interceded, putting his arm around her and pulling her close. "It's okay, Gracie. Calm down. No one is accusing you of anything."

He was." She pointed at Hack with a wavering hand. "Back at the house. But there's no way... just no way. I loved her. She was one of my only friends. I won't rest until I find out who did this."

"Well, that makes two of us," said Hack. "I have five brothers and sisters and she was my favorite. She had balls of steel."

He remembered Eliot's frenzied visit to the house, and the way Andrea stood up to him. Hack had never questioned his sister about the contents of the novel she and Grace were writing. Could it have played a part in the attack?

"Since you brought up your manuscript, this is the second time in a week I've heard about it. What's so important that you'd pay a ransom to get it back? Or that someone might have stolen Andrea's computer to take a peek?"

Brow furrowed, Grace leaned forward, Druthers still rubbing her back. "I guess it's only fair to share the whole story. You're part of this now." As she detailed everything leading up to her decision to author *Salvaging Hope*, she interrupted herself mid-sentence. "Oh my God, Eliot did this." Her entire body vibrated with fear. "Somehow, he found out about the book. He must have hired someone to hack into my computer and destroy my copy, and then killed Andrea to get hers. Anything to avoid exposing his plot. Don't you see? It had to be him."

Her conclusion sounded outlandish to Hack since he knew Eliot had nothing to do with Grace's computer encryption. And while Andrea had vouched for her sanity, he doubted she'd ever heard the convoluted tale Grace had spent the last hour recounting.

"Why do you insist he wants to kill you? Because he said too often that he loved and supported you, even when you didn't love yourself? In fact, according to your own account, he's been nothing but civil and attentive, in public and in private."

Her face turned red. "Ditch the cynicism, please. It's the *way* he said he loved me. It always seemed...empty. Practiced. Contrived. And the truth is...we...we haven't slept together since the night we conceived my son. It's not something I planned to share, but it may help you understand. I looked old, frumpy. In and out of hospitals. He may have been cordial, but he patronized me, undermined me at every turn with my sons. Cheated on me with his secretary..."

She collapsed back into Druthers' arms and he cradled her until the tears subsided.

"When I took the pills, they desensitized me, I didn't want to rock the boat, throw my boys' existence into disarray. But now, everything is much clearer. I can see through his lies, and he can't stand the thought of me sharing that truth with others. He needs to discredit anything I might say or write. Why else would he be out there lying, telling the media I'm a danger to myself?"

Because unmedicated, you may be a danger to yourself and everyone else.

Then Hack recalled how unhinged Eliot became when he learned of her entry into the literary world. Eliot might not have hacked Grace's computer, but had something more fueled his tirade than concern over her health?

"Well, I guess it's possible. I'm sorry I didn't mention this earlier, but with all the craziness, I forgot. Eliot stopped by Andrea's house a few days ago, frantic to find you. He tracked down her address through your cell phone, but he seemed more distraught than homicidal. Andrea mentioned you were both working on a book, but she wouldn't divulge more. For what it's worth, she said she didn't trust him. Neither did I."

Grace's mouth fell open as she absorbed the news, then buried her head into Druthers' chest, quaking with fear. Druthers tightened his embrace.

"About her computer… tell me what happened," Hack needed to find out if either of them suspected Andrea's culpability in the extortion, and he wanted to make sure Gwennie had lifted the encryption, so they both wouldn't perseverate on Eliot as the murderer to the exclusion of other suspects.

Druthers scowled. "Some losers hacked it. We paid ransom money in Bitcoin like they asked, but they scammed us. They never removed the encryption."

To the teen's relief, Druthers seemed sincere, not accusatory. He saw an opportunity to sway their viewpoint. "One of my friends got hacked once. It took hours to decrypt but eventually, they regained access to their files. You should check again."

Grace broke from Druthers' embrace and together, they walked over to the laptop, sitting on a small table by the window. She pressed the power button, crossed her arms and waited while the machine rebooted. Windows' melodic chimes filled the air.

"It's back. How can that be?" She crossed her arms, deliberated, and then answered her own question. "I guess he didn't need it anymore, now that he's stolen Andrea's copy."

"And left you to finish yours? Doubtful." Hack leaned back against the recliner, satisfied he'd veered suspicion away from the hijacker. "Now that you've got access to your computer again, could you please check the news to see if there's any mention of Andrea's murder?"

A minute later, Grace let out a shriek, similar to what he'd heard right before he discovered her with Andrea's body. He leapt to his feet and ran over to join them at the monitor. "What is it? Did someone finger us as being there?"

On the screen, the news headline read, "Billionaire at Death's Door" with the subhead, "Heiress Daughter Absent in Time of Crisis." Underneath was a photo of a man flanked by two boys leaving Barrington's hospital room. The caption identified the trio as Eliot Rendell and his sons.

Grace's eyes clouded in confusion, her expression slack. "If he's in Florida…then who killed Andrea?"

Hack's ringtone chimed from across the room; it was either his family calling about Andrea, or his knuckleheaded loan sharks looking for their money. "I hate to interrupt, but could I have my cell back? It might be important."

Grace staggered to the coat closet and retrieved his vibrating phone. He recognized the Caller ID and swallowed, dreading the sound of heartbreak in his sister Maaryam's voice. Three deaths in less than a year. It was almost too much for his family to bear.

"Hello…?"

"Joe, we're all at my place. There's been…just please come. We'll talk then."

"I'll be there as soon as I can." He disconnected the call, fending off alternating waves of guilt and grief.

He wasn't sure of Grace's innocence, but he doubted her involvement in the murder more now than a few hours prior. "It's my family. I gotta go, find out what they know, what the police are asking. But I'll be back. We've got to work together to figure this thing out."

Chapter Twenty-Seven

Grace bolted the door behind Hack, then returned to her computer and Eliot's newspaper interview. By his account, his "beloved" father-in-law had woken from his coma for a brief time, aphasic and therefore unable to communicate. The stroke had left most of Barrington's body paralyzed, the frustration over which, doctors speculated, caused him to suffer a heart attack. Surgeons performed a quintuple bypass, but the billionaire had yet to regain consciousness post-anesthesia, and his condition remained critical.

"My sons and I will remain by his side in hopes of a full recovery. If his missing daughter were only here with us, it would make all the difference. Grace, we miss you terribly. If you aren't being held against your will, please fly down and support your father now, before it's too late."

She dismissed his "heartfelt" plea, wondering instead how much he knew about her book. If Eliot wasn't the hacker, and Andrea had stuck to the basics when he confronted her, he remained ignorant of the full plot. He might suspect the contents and try to discredit her but without specifics, he wouldn't get much traction. She still had a shot.

Grace noticed the newspaper had included a photo of her as a toddler, sitting on her father's lap. A sidebar reiterated the sizeable reward for any clues to her whereabouts.

She didn't recognize the picture; it predated the visions. Barrington wouldn't allow anyone to photograph them together after that. How embarrassing that fate had saddled a Pierrepoint with such an imperfect child. Grace clicked away from the story, astonished at the media's dexterity—sensationalizing her family's tragedy and tugging at her guilt, all while reminding the public of her disappearance. Quite the trifecta.

Rain nudged Grace, hankering for attention. "What am I going to do, Rainie? Sick father, dead friend, homicidal husband—the obvious suspect—now with a perfect alibi. Everything's closing in. You're a smart doggie, give me some advice." If Rain had any suggestions, she kept them to herself, choosing instead to snout-butt Grace's arm a second time. Grace scratched under the Dobie's ears, grateful for the distraction.

Druthers emerged from the kitchen with two mugs and sat beside her. "I'm not sure what to say, Gracie. If you need to visit your dad, I'll take some time off work and drive you. It might be unwise to fly, even with the wig."

"That's sweet of you but no." She left one hand under Rain's ear and lifted the cup to her lips with the other. "I have no intention of heading down to Florida. It may sound awful, but I feel no love for that man, only resentment for how he's treated me."

A soothing aroma drifted up from the mug. Chai, the perfect sedative. As appreciative for the drink as she was for Druthers' constant support, Grace took a few sips, allowing the warm milk, spices and honey to comfort her. It's not Barrington's failing health that concerns me, she realized as relaxation seeped in. It's Eliot. And the way he's using the media to manipulate readers, turn public opinion against me...couldn't two play at that game?

"There is one thing you can do for me...if you're up for it."

"Anything you need."

"Once the tabloids get wind of Andrea's murder, they'll implicate me somehow. Even if people didn't notice me enter the house today, they've seen me there in the past. Neighbors might link the two events together, start raving about the paranoid schizophrenic in their midst. Leap on any opportunity to grab that reward, along with a minute or two in the spotlight. I want to get out ahead of it."

Druthers shuffled his feet. "How do you propose we do that?"

"As a forensic toxicologist, do you ever work with reporters? Fill them in on the grisly details behind victims' deaths?"

"All the time."

"Are there any you're certain could keep a secret?"

"One was my college roommate at Buffalo. I'd trust him with my life."

Rain looked up, disconcerted that the petting had stopped. Grace gave her a kiss and told her to lie down. "Once the news about Andrea becomes public, I want to give an exclusive interview. Not here, though, but in some hotel room far away...Pennsylvania. Even Ohio. Somewhere to throw people off the track."

"And say what?"

"I want to assure anyone who's following the story that I'm alive, well and completely sane. Express concern for my father's condition and sorrow for my friend Andrea, whose cats I recently pet-sat. It'll make me look less heartless and neutralize Eliot's media attack. No kidnapping, no need to drag me home for my own good. It would take the bounty off my head."

Druthers stroked Rain, who'd pushed her head onto his lap after Grace's rebuff. "But Gracie, what possible excuse would convince readers you can't be with your boys at your father's deathbed, or at a close friend's gravesite? How are you going to justify those decisions to an audience who's already brainwashed about your mental state?"

Druthers' words were a pinprick popping her bubble. Grace scrambled for a credible response. He had a point; her "me-time" excuse wouldn't suffice during a period of such misfortune. And now that the newspapers had practically canonized her husband for his bedside vigil, who would second-guess his concern regarding his paranoid wife? Especially once word got out that said wife had been co-writing a book with late celeb author Lynn Andrews. How long before someone accused her of murdering her collaborator so she wouldn't have to share any of the praise or a penny of the profits? Then, an even darker concern emerged.

"Tom...you believe me, don't you? Or do you fear I'm as crazy as the papers say?"

"I'm Team Grace all the way. But remember, I know you. I've heard your side. The public only knows what Eliot has told them. He's got the edge here."

She sat up tall and straightened her shoulders. "That's the key then. If this is about cultivating public opinion, it's about time they heard an opposing point of view."

Chapter Twenty-Eight

It was after 10:00 when Hack arrived at his Pakistani sister Maaryam's home in Parsippany. He made a quick phone call to tie up one loose end, and then joined his family, gathered at the dining table, red-eyed and despondent. No intrusive reporters had barred his entrance, vying for an exclusive photo or comment. Not yet, anyway.

"Come Joe, sit." Maaryam gestured to an empty seat between their brothers, Billy and Chuck.

He glanced over at Gwennie as he slipped off his coat and handed it to Chuck's wife, Sammie. Gwen's eyes were as dark as her skin, and shared the same foreboding he'd been battling himself, that their illegal acts had somehow contributed to their sister's demise.

"Looks serious." His tone meshed concern with irreverence. "To what do I owe the honor of his invitation? Did I screw up again somehow?"

Maaryam assumed the role of matriarch. "Nothing like that. It's Andrea...there's been an accident."

Chuck cleared his throat. "There's no easy way to tell you this. Andrea's dead. Stabbed with her own kitchen knife. When she didn't pick up her phone, Gwennie called the police and asked them to check on her. That's when they found the body. The police suspect it was a robbery."

"Oh my God." Hack bowed his head and squeezed his eyes tight, pretending to suck back tears. Not that he didn't want to cry. He was just inured to the shock by this point.

"Thing is, they didn't take much. Even left money in her purse." Billy, who worked as a guard at the Metropark prison, assumed he understood the complexities of the criminal mind. "More likely, it was a personal attack. A jealous author. Or some avid reader, angry that Lynn Andrews hadn't responded to a fan letter. Sort of like in that Eminem song, *Stan*."

They were discussing various possibilities when the doorbell chimed, followed by a series of insistent knocks.

"Cue the reporters. Hold on, everyone, I'll get rid of them." Hack hastened to the foyer and peered through the keyhole. Outside was Zev, accompanied by an unfamiliar but alluring girl with wavy, auburn hair and electric blue eyes. What the…?

He opened the door a few inches, addressing his guests in a whisper so his family wouldn't hear. "Thanks for coming, Zev. Who is your friend?"

"This is Katie, Kenzie's sister. She showed up today as a big surprise but when Kenzie saw her, she took off out the back door. We were trying to figure out why, when I got your call. I couldn't just abandon her there."

Hack noticed how Katie had Kenzie's eyes, but that's where the resemblance ended. The makeup, the pink parka, the way a lock of her bangs fell over her left eye, Veronica Lake-style…

Katie shrugged. "I thought she'd throw herself into my arms. We haven't really talked much since…well, you know. I'm shocked she ran off like that."

You know? He did not know. And as curious as Hack might have been on any other day, solving a second mystery, even one involving a beautiful stranger, had not been his intention when he'd summoned Zev to grab an Uber and meet him. "I don't want to appear rude, but would it be okay if Zev and I spoke in private? We can all get better acquainted later."

Hack noticed a news van pull up across the street. Word was out. Life was about to get a lot more complicated.

"No problem," said Katie. "Except, if you don't want us to turn into icicles, I suggest you invite us in."

There it was, the O'Malley sarcasm both sisters shared. Hack opened the door wide enough for them to slip through without revealing his identity to the van's reporters. "My whole family is in the other room, so please don't mention the SleepStay or being my tenant. We're just good friends, okay?"

Zev cracked a smile. "Hey, that's what I've been telling everyone all along. Hack and me, we're only good friends."

"Who's out there, Joe?" Maaryam called from the other room.

"A few schoolmates. We were planning to go out tonight, but when you called, I told them to catch up with me here."

He ushered Zev and Katie into the living room and helped them off with their coats.

"I hope my coming here hasn't created any difficulties for you." Katie's perfume scented the air with lilac.

"It's fine, it's just, um, kind of a difficult night. The police found my sister murdered in her home this afternoon."

Katie gasped. "Your sister was Lynn Andrews? How awful. We heard something about that on the car radio."

Great, just great. Bad news traveled fast. "Somebody stabbed her and ransacked the house. That's all we know so far."

Zev lowered his eyes. "*Ha'makom yenahem etkhem betokh she'ar avelei Tziyonvi'Yerushalayim.* In short, may God console you and the other mourners." Then he looked up and scratched at his cheek. "Weren't you supposed to go there for dinner? Did you see—?"

Hack pulled Zev away from Katie mid-sentence, inviting her to make herself comfortable. "I can't get into any of that now," he whispered. "Please don't mention our little Bitcoin adventure to anyone, especially the police if they stop by, asking questions. We don't want to steer attention away from the real culprits involved."

"Got it. No problem. I'll tell Kenzie too, if I ever see her again. But since you brought it up, could Grace be mixed up in any of this?"

"Not sure. Everything's a jumble right now. Let's talk at home later." Hack reached into his pants pocket, pulling out a roll of bills he slipped into Zev's hand. "This is why I called you, to ask you to run an errand for me. I didn't have time to pay off my debt after you left the coffee house, and the clock's still running. Remember your actor friend, Schmuel Lavendar and his pals? He knows what these guys look like. Think you could get this money to them so they could pay off Boris and Ving? They hang out at Bennie's Bar in Garfield."

Zev jerked his head back. "You trust me with all this dough, bro?"

"Yeah, I do. I know where you live."

"Can't argue with that. One last question. What makes you sure these 'private bankers' aren't behind your sister's death?"

"Nothing. Anything's possible. But if they're involved, I'd like to make sure no one else gets hurt. And if they're not, the last thing I need is another shakedown. I've got enough targets on my back. So, can you handle this?"

"I'll take care of it as soon as we get back. Though my friends are more familiar with Baruch's than Bennie's, I'm sure they'll be able to figure things out."

He hugged Zev. "Thanks. You've become a real friend. That's something I need right now."

Friends. Hack realized he'd been so preoccupied with extricating himself from any potential culpability, he hadn't taken time to process the loss of his closest ally. Andrea had been his rock growing up. Problems with school bullies, pubescent questions about girls—all discussed over a homemade dinner, followed by a late-night movie fest. Without Andrea's constant prattling about her intricate crime plots, he would have never conceived of his break-in scheme to pay off his debts. She'd been his go-to sibling and his best friend, but he could go to her no longer.

Katie walked over to the two teens and placed her hand on Hack's shoulder, a sign of solidarity. A shiver ran from her fingertips down to his toes. That frisson of chemistry was a welcome respite from his maudlin thoughts.

Gwennie wandered from the kitchen and took a double take at Hack's diverse group huddle. "I hate to interrupt, Joe, but do you have a second?"

"Why don't you both head into the kitchen and grab a snack," Hack urged his friends. "I'll join you in a minute."

Once they were out of earshot, Gwennie bombarded him with a slew of whispered questions: "What the hell was up with that phone call? Were you there? Involved somehow? And what are we going to tell the authorities in case anything incriminating comes up?"

"I promise, it won't come up. And even if it does, you and I played no role in what happened to Andrea. I spent time with Grace today, the woman we were after, the one who paid the ransom. We both saw the body, though she arrived at the scene before I did. We plan to figure this out together."

"You sure she's not responsible? Coughing up thousands of dollars to pay someone off doesn't sit well with a whole lot of folks. Including psychotics on the run. What if she suspected Andrea was behind the whole thing?"

"Grace says she didn't go there to confront Andrea about the money. She wanted a copy of some manuscript from Andrea's computer. Which unfortunately was missing from the crime scene."

"So she *says*. What's your take?"

"All I'm sure of is that if it takes the rest of my life, I'll find and destroy whoever did this to our sister."

"And that's supposed to put me at ease? That now you're turning into a *Death Wish*-style vigilante, out to avenge the caper of the missing Mac?"

Hack forced a smile. "Something like that." He understood Gwennie's concern. Andrea's laptop could harbor evidence of their Bitcoin hack, and neither of them knew the computer's whereabouts. If that evidence tracked back to Gwennie, she could lose her job, and that was minor compared to being thrown in jail for extortion. "Look, I'm aware of what's at stake—for both of us. Could you please trust me for once?"

Gwennie shrugged. "What choice do I have?" They walked back to the kitchen, where the whole family was reminiscing about Andrea. The two visitors had positioned themselves atop the island, facing the Hackfords and joining in the tribute.

Maaryam attempted to sway the mourners' focus by discussing logistics. "We can't bury her body for some time. According to the police, the medical examiner must complete a full forensic examination. But that doesn't mean we shouldn't plan a memorial service and invite her fellow meeting planners, authors and fans. Or handle some practical matters, like deciding who gets custody of the cats."

"One thing we should agree on is not to engage with the press," said Chuck. "No interviews, no off-the-cuff remarks. We only talk to the police and even then, all we mention is Andrea. We don't need them snooping around anywhere else, not after the issues our little brother has had with the law recently." He turned his gaze to Hack and his friends. "That's all behind you, right?"

Hack gave his brother a silent thumbs up.

"And we can trust your friends to go along with the plan?"

Katie and Zev nodded.

"Then it's decided." He surveyed the table. "We're all one big, collective 'No comment. Speak to our lawyer.'"

Hack exchanged one last knowing look with Gwennie. They were out of the hot seat. At least for now.

Chapter Twenty-Nine

Grace couldn't concentrate. She tried writing, reading, cooking, cleaning, playing tug-of-war with the dogs—anything to take her mind off the day's agenda. To counteract Eliot's negative media attack, Druthers had scheduled an appointment with a psychiatrist with whom he'd collaborated in the past. Her theory was that if a new doctor examined her and gave her a clean bill of health, it would bolster her story. Druthers had worked with several psychiatrists in his career; they helped him investigate overdose deaths by explaining the diagnoses behind the drugs prescribed.

Druthers insisted Dr. Aadish Kumar was one of the best, and a nice guy to boot. Nice enough to make a discreet house call to determine the extent of Grace's mental instability.

Guilt tapped on Grace's shoulder, accusing her of cheating on Dr. Leighmann. Understandable. Other than the doctors she'd met during her brief stays at various mental facilities over the years, Emma Leighmann had remained her primary therapist and psychopharmacologist. Even doctors treating Grace from afar had operated under Leighmann's guidance and supervision.

There was a level of comfort in being treated by someone who understood everything she'd been through since childhood. In fact, the prospect of recapping four decades to someone new caused Grace to break out in hives. What if Dr. Kumar agreed with Leighmann's original diagnosis? Would Druthers send her packing? To make so many positive emotional strides—only to have them dismissed by a doctor she'd just met—could send her right back to Grasmere.

Druthers was due home with Dr. Kumar at two. When the doorbell rang at 1:30, it startled her so, she almost hid in the basement. The dogs' barks reminded her she was well-protected against foul play. Sweet as they were, Druthers claimed Thunder and Rain wouldn't tolerate anyone who lifted a hand against a loved one. The attacker's arm would end up across the room, a bloody stump left in its place.

She recognized the face on the other side of the peephole and inched open the door. Two wagging stubs greeted Hack as he walked past them toward the couch. "I would have called, but I didn't want to leave any trace of communication between us. We need to talk."

She followed and sat alongside him, apprehensive of what news he might bring. "Okay, but I've got someone coming in about thirty minutes."

"That shouldn't be a problem. I wanted us to get our stories straight so if a detective asks us anything, we don't contradict each other."

Grace flinched. "Why would they even think we've met?"

"Neighbors might have noticed me on the stoop the day I stopped by while you were housesitting, or on the afternoon we found her lying there. We've both left fingerprints scattered throughout the house."

Grace threw her head against the couch and stared up at the ceiling. *When was this ever going to end? When would life return to normal?*

Hack prodded her again after a few minutes of silence. "Any thoughts?"

"Only the truth. I've been writing a novel with Andrea's help. She asked me to watch her cats while she was away, which worked out well since my family was traveling and I didn't need to be home. You stopped by to see her, and when she returned, I relayed the message."

Hack tilted his head. "And when they ask why you came out of hiding on the day of the murder?"

"Someone hijacked my computer, and I needed her copy of my manuscript."

Hack stood and started pacing. "That's the part you have to leave out. It's safer to say you wanted some advice on your story and she was the only one you trusted to not turn you in for the reward money."

Grace pursed her lips. "Why? Why wouldn't I tell the police the truth?"

"Because they'll spin it against you. Let's play out a possible scenario, shall we? The papers all report you're a paranoid schizophrenic. Your computer is...what did you call it...hacked. Right?"

His hostile tone made her bristle. She wasn't on trial for murder. Not yet, anyway.

"Who's the only person who knows you are writing the story, other than your husband, who's down in Florida, watching over your dying dad? Andrea. She reads about you in the paper and she wonders, "What happened to Ruth Allen? This Grace person has lied to me all this time. Can I trust her to share the credit or the royalties for the book we're writing together?"

"She wouldn't do that—"

His face turned crimson. "Why not, Grace? Do you have any idea what she was thinking? Or how betrayed she might have felt?" His accusations hit her with the force of an out-of-control train. She struggled to keep up.

"Picture this: she considers hacking into your computer, holding the book up for ransom and getting her cut upfront." He gestured with a flourish so dramatic, the dogs raised their heads and pricked up their ears. "She knows a ton of nefarious people she uses as resources; they'd all be willing to help. And then, paranoid as you are, you figure the whole thing out. You storm in, flinging allegations. The argument becomes heated. You stab her and steal the laptop. Neighbors see a woman exiting the scene at the same time the crime allegedly occurred. She looks different but she'd disguise herself, they figure, since she's in hiding and can't risk being seen." Hack stopped to catch his breath.

Grace heard more than just Hack's words. He was far too impassioned by his theory for it to be mere speculation. A lifetime of reading had taught her that only the guilty peddled stories with such desperation. She used the reprieve to delve further.

"What if that's what happened? What do you care if they haul my sorry ass to prison?"

His eyes narrowed, as if the question had caught him off guard. "Well...well...someone might have seen me with you," he spluttered. "Assumed I was in on it. Otherwise, why wouldn't I have called in the murder and detained you at the scene until the police arrived?"

Grace crinkled her nose. "Is that why they call you Hack? Did you help Andrea hack into my computer? Your sister made no secret that thanks to Clara Cardone, she'd earned over a million dollars in book sales. It was a great source of pride for her. So, *she* wasn't desperate for a share of my royalties. But you, you had racked up a slew of debts, from what she told me. Five thousand dollars in ransom money from an untraceable source must have sounded like a perfect solution. Am I that far off the mark?"

Hack hung his head in resignation. "It wasn't her idea, I egged her into it. You're rich. I didn't think you'd miss the money."

Now it was Grace's turn to explode. "What was so vital that you'd take a woman you believed was unstable, and not only exploit her supposed wealth, but provoke her further? Who does something like that?"

"I owed some bad people a lot of money," he said, his eyes downcast. "They were threatening not only me but my family. I was out of options."

"So, the upshot is, hijacking my computer was your last-ditch effort to save your own hide?"

"I could have gone to the police and told them about seeing you pet-sitting at Andrea's house, collected the reward. But I didn't. I kept your secret. That must count for something. Won't you please keep mine?"

She opened her mouth to answer when the dogs leapt to their feet and charged the door. She grabbed their collars and held them back as Druthers entered along with a thirty-something, dark-skinned man, dressed in a beige, gold and green-patterned sportscoat over a dark brown turtleneck and jeans. "Gracie, this is Dr. Kumar, the psychiatrist I told you about."

"Call me Aadish, please." He held out his arm.

Grace released the dogs, freeing up her hand to shake his. "A pleasure." Thunder and Rain engaged in their requisite sniffing session and after deeming Kumar acceptable, retired to the other side of the room. "This is my friend, Hack. We were discussing how much we both missed his sister."

"I heard about that." Kumar's expression turned grim. "I'm so sorry. Tom filled me in on everything, about finding the body and all. He said you'd be okay with that and my lips are sealed. I wish there were something I could do."

"There is," said Druthers. "Examine Gracie here and give us your honest, no-holds-barred evaluation of her mental faculties. That's the best place to start."

"That's why I'm here." Kumar looked around the room. "Is there somewhere private where we can speak?"

"There's nothing I can't say around my two good friends." Grace's words teemed with conviction.

"You realize that if anyone else is present, it negates doctor/patient confidentiality? Not that I'd repeat anything without your permission, but is that okay with you, Grace?"

"We're all in this together. They might as well be sure they're justified in sheltering me and protecting my secrets."

"Fair enough," said Kumar. "Let's get comfortable and we'll begin."

Chapter Thirty

Grace took her favorite seat on the couch. Dr. Kumar positioned himself on the loveseat opposite and Druthers took the recliner perpendicular to both. Hack sat cross-legged on the floor with his back against the wall.

"Grace, if any question makes you uneasy, please tell me and we'll skip ahead to something less provocative. Agreed?"

Grace smiled. "I'm an open book, Doc. Ask away."

"At what age did you realize you saw the world differently than other people?" The resonance of his voice—slow, deep and almost melodic—set her at ease.

"I was six when the visions began. My parents were so alarmed, they sent me off to Grasmere. Are you familiar with it?"

"By reputation only. Pretty heavy duty for a little girl. What were the visions of?"

"The doctors spent so much time trying to convince me I was imagining things; I must have blocked them out. I see little glimpses whenever the nightmares hit."

"Nightmares?"

Grace squirmed. With those dreams absent the last few months, was she tempting fate by mentioning them?

"I used to have them several times a week. This giant fog chasing me and my mother. We dart and dodge and try to escape. I find a perfect hiding spot and call out for her to join me, but she loses her way. I'm too scared to run into the open and pull her to safety. I keep screaming so she can locate me...she's so close, I can see the terror in her eyes...and just steps from safety, the fog catches up and swallows her. It's all my fault. For not being brave enough, fast enough, loud enough."

Grace began to tremble. Druthers hopped onto the couch and held her close, as if a tight enough embrace could force the demons away.

"You strong enough to continue?" asked the doctor.

"Sorry. It's been a long time since I described my nightmares to anyone."

Dr. Kumar jotted something down on his pad. "What happens next?"

"I have no idea. I've woken up screaming by then."

"You mentioned snippets of your visions woven into the scene. What are those like?"

Grace squeezed her eyes shut, summoning every memory to the forefront. "Just something dragging along the floor. That's all I ever see. I'm sorry."

"Don't be. It's common. Has anyone ever hypnotized you to sort this out?"

"My therapist has suggested it many times. She says if we get to the organic cause, we'll diffuse the visions and they'll go away. I've always refused. To be honest, I'm a little terrified of confronting it again. I mean, look at the consequences. A year in a sanitorium."

Kumar looked up, arching his brows. "You were there an entire year?"

Grace nodded. "Is that so unusual?"

"It's somewhere in the gray area between sadism and malpractice. Who was your admitting psychiatrist? Do you remember?"

"I don't. Emma Leighmann was a resident and we became close. My father hired her after my stay was over and she's been my doctor ever since, acting as both therapist and psychiatrist."

Kumar scribbled down another few sentences. "That's unusual. Most doctors either counsel or prescribe, not both. The hypnosis she suggested might unearth some of your repressed memories. But we can discuss that later. Tell me what happened when you came home."

"My mom was as loving as ever, but my father was the opposite. He refused to have any more to do with me than necessary."

"That must have been very hard."

"He abandoned me, and I never understood why. Kept me quarantined, not permitted to leave the grounds of the estate. My mom would sometimes sneak me out but once she drowned, right before my sixteenth birthday, it was just me, my tutors and Dr. Leighmann. My father wouldn't let me off property unaccompanied until after my second year of college."

Dr. Kumar shook his head. "What changed after sophomore year?"

"I secretly applied and got accepted to a real college, not some correspondence course. Despite my father and Dr. Leighmann's misgivings, I insisted on going. I wanted to catch up on everything I'd missed in high school. I was over eighteen, legal and free to do as I liked. If my father had refused to pay, I would have run away."

Dr. Kumar set down his pen and clapped. "Good for you. How did all that freedom feel, once you arrived on campus?"

"Three days after orientation, I met Eliot, my husband, and that was that. Come to think of it, I've never been on my own since then, except for an occasional flight to Florida, and recently, when I've holed up at the library, or housesat for Andrea."

"What about work? Did you get a job after graduation?"

"Oh, I tried, But I didn't start working out of the house until a few years ago, and even then, only part-time. Unless I'm swamped with overtime, I run out of the office around two o'clock to do chores, chauffeur the kids around, get dinner on the table."

"But before the kids were born, what stopped you?"

"Right after we eloped, Eliot wanted me keeping house while he concentrated on getting his bachelor's. Then his master's. So, I finished my studies remotely. After that, every time I decided to find work, I managed to get pregnant instead. Dr. Leighmann wouldn't let me use the pill. She insisted it would mess up my hormones and interfere with all my other medications. So, my sons became my job."

Another concerned look. "Which meds are you on?"

"Were on. Past tense. The cocktail was always changing. The last combination included Klonopin, Abilify, some other stuff."

"Well, that's what caused your nightmares right there. Clonazepam, or the brand name Klonopin, is famous for causing side effects like nightmares. And when you combine Clonazepam with Aripiprazole, that's the Abilify, you can increase the chances of dizziness, drowsiness and confusion. Have you experienced trouble concentrating since you've discontinued your meds?"

Grace shook her head. "The exact opposite. The pills never left me dizzy though, just lethargic. Since I've weaned myself off, I'm no longer walking through life like a zombie."

Dr. Kumar sighed. "I don't like to contradict other doctors, especially without seeing a patient's charts and history. And it's true that some anticonvulsants and mood stabilizers can interfere with the effectiveness of birth control pills and vice versa. But to my knowledge, that's not true with either of the drugs you're on. Not to mention, there are non-pharmaceutical forms of birth control available, like condoms."

Grace let out an ironic laugh. "Information two children too late. We used condoms for a few years until my husband graduated from college and decided he was no longer a fan. Anyway, it's a moot point; we haven't had intercourse since I conceived Xander, my youngest. It's like Eliot performed his reproductive duty twice and then clocked out."

"And this lack of physical intimacy—that's his choice, not yours? You would prefer to be sexually active?"

Grace looked at the floor so no one would see her blush. "Yes, Dr. Kumar. I'd like to have sex again before I die."

"This has been very informative. Let me ask you a few yes-or-no questions. Ready?

"Shoot."

"You ever encounter periods of disorganized thinking?"

"No. I'm a CPA. You can't do that kind of work if you can't concentrate. My pills may have left me flat and unmotivated, but never imprecise. I've realized that Eliot instigated much of the confusion in my life, playing tricks to make me doubt my own perceptions."

Kumar paused. "Tricks?"

"It's a long story. And I have proof that they're not a figment of my imagination. We can discuss it another day."

"Okay, you said you were unmotivated. Has that stopped since quitting your meds?"

"I can't wait to get out of bed now." She shot a smile at Druthers.

"Grace, you're doing good. Any periods where it seems like you're walking in slow motion?"

"Nope."

"Unexplained changes in your sleep patterns?"

"Other than sleeping in Maywood instead of Glen Valley? No." Now it was Druthers' turn to smile.

"Any lack of interest in hygiene?"

"Hell, no. I can't get through the day if I haven't showered and washed my hair."

Dr. Kumar turned to Druthers. "Tom, have you seen any extreme moodiness or violent behavior?"

"Moodiness? That's a laugh. The woman misses her kids, lost one of her best friends and fears for her life, but she still stays cheery, cleans the house, makes dinner, takes care of the dogs. All of her own volition, not at my request. Violent behavior? Never."

Grace's face grew warm. She'd experienced aggressive inclinations in the past but usually kept them under wraps. She recalled the broken dish at her father's house. Her feelings of hatred toward Eliot when she'd tired of his constant "handling." There had to be a difference between having a short temper and being homicidal.

"Does she ever talk gibberish?"

"Never."

Hack piped in from across the room. "I can second that. I've always found her very hospitable and forgiving."

Subtle.

"One last question, Grace. Is there any history of mental illness in your family?"

"My father's a dick. Does that count?"

Grace launched into an extended rant, recounting the litany of past offenses waged by her father—the nasty nicknames, the frequent expressions of disgust anytime she dared disappoint him. Even how he used to feign having a heart attack to play upon her fears and then mock her when she ran for help. She ended by admitting to one violent act, the dish she'd thrown during their recent disagreement. "Am I crazy, Dr. Kumar?"

"About your father being a dick? Not at all. He sounds like a first-class asshole. But tell me more about what Tom mentioned, about you fearing for your life?"

Grace filled him in on the reasons behind writing her book.

"Would you mind if I read a chapter or two?"

Grace rebooted her laptop, brought up her manuscript, and handed it to Kumar. "Have at it. But you'll be the only person other than Andrea, and whoever stole her computer, to read any part of it, so please be gentle. In the meantime, who's up for coffee?"

Grace wandered into the kitchen and plugged in the Keurig. The afternoon had been an emotional roller coaster, but for whatever reason, she felt refreshed, confident. There hadn't been one moment when she'd second-guessed herself. It was an exhilarating realization, almost like a reprieve from a death sentence. Or so she imagined.

She reemerged with a tray carrying four cups of coffee, along with the cow-shaped ceramic sugar bowl and matching creamer she'd ordered using Druthers' Amazon account. A few inexpensive frills to bring a little gentility into his home.

Dr. Kumar had already set aside the laptop and was rubbing his forehead.

She sat next to Druthers and grasped his hand. "What's the verdict, Doc? Am I a fruitcake or a plain old slice of white bread?"

"There's nothing bland about you, Grace. You're charming, intelligent, and for the record, a terrific writer. I'd like a signed copy of *Salvaging Hope* when it hits the bookstores."

Her face heated with pride.

"But I do think you have some problems, ones that fall outside my area of expertise. I can't speak to your husband's interest in murdering you for your inheritance. But in my humble opinion, there's nothing paranoid about you speculating that some person or persons are intent on keeping you docile and self-doubting."

Druthers eyes shone bright. "Would you be willing to put that in writing, Aadish?"

"Gladly. And there's one other thing I'd like to do to help you, if you'll trust me. Do you trust me, Grace?"

"Implicitly." And she meant it too.

"Though you've been resistant to it in the past, I'd like to come back tomorrow mid-morning and hypnotize you. What we discover may point us to which path to follow next."

"What about it, Gracie?" Druthers squeezed her palm. "It's your call."

"I'm in." In less than two hours, Aadish Kumar had given her the greatest gift ever, validation. If tomorrow's session freed her from the torments of her past, and pushed her toward a more hopeful future, she'd be a fool to turn down the ride.

Chapter Thirty-One

The following morning, Grace kept herself preoccupied by dishing out the dogs' kibble and preparing waffles for Druthers and herself. Though she'd refused hypnosis in the past, today she hummed as she anticipated her upcoming session.

"Someone's happier than a mosquito on the first day of summer." Druthers gave her a peck on the cheek before pouring them each some coffee.

"Insomnia hit. Instead of counting sheep, I read more about self-publishing and wrote two additional chapters of my book." She poured a ladleful of batter onto the waffle iron.

"That's great. How long until it's done?" He pulled the milk out of the fridge.

"I'm close to the end. Then I have to proofread it and fix any errors. I found a formatting program online. And a company that sells premade book covers. All I need to do is add my title, author name and a blurb on the back. I figure it doesn't have to look perfect, just legible and available for purchase."

Druthers stirred three sugar cubes into his coffee. "And then you'll be safe. Able to go back to your family."

The bleakness of his statement hit her hard. Once she published her book and gifted copies to reviewers, local newspapers, libraries and the police, there wouldn't be any further excuse to avoid her family. She could travel down south to visit her dying father. Go back to cooking and cleaning for Eliot and the boys, at least until they graduated, and she'd decide what to do about her marriage. Resume her position at Davidoff, Weiss & Greenburg, if they'd even have her back after all the negative publicity. Her demanding, dull, empty, former life awaited, miles from Druthers' warmth, humor and protective embrace. Far from Thunder and Rain's constant companionship. The realization tarnished the sheen of her cheery mood and dampened her appetite for the waffles she piled onto their plates.

She topped each portion with a generous dousing of maple syrup and a dollop of fresh whipped cream. "I may not be living here, but there's nothing to say we can't remain friends." She set their plates down on the table, fearing he might respond, "I don't want to be friends. I want more." A statement warranting a reply she had yet to consider, much less prepare.

"What time is Aadish due back?"

"In about an hour." She was grateful for his alternative response.

"You still up for this? It could be…"

"Traumatic? I expect nothing less. By dissecting my nightmares and tracing their origins, I might finally be free of them. If my visions turn out to be the product of a diseased mind, I won't resent my appointments with Dr. Leighmann. I'll trust her judgment and continue the weekly sessions, if not the cocktail of drugs she prescribes. But if it's something else…I need to understand what precipitated everything I've gone through since."

"Should I be here? I can take the morning off if it would help."

She reached out her hand, placed it over his forearm and gave it a pat.

"That would be perfect. If you're a witness, it won't be just my word against Leighmann's about anything we uncover."

Grace started loading the dishwasher. The bell rang, and Druthers left to answer. She heard Hack's harangue from two rooms over. It intensified as he approached the kitchen, with Druthers urging him to slow down so they could decipher his babble.

"The police were at my sister Maaryam's house yesterday and again this morning. A neighbor came forward, claiming she saw three people on the path near the house. All leaving at different times. She failed to ID them because they were wearing hoods. She also couldn't tell which house they exited. You should bury that wig and coat in case the detectives discover your connection to Andrea and stop by to question you."

"Three people, eh? Not two, but three," repeated Druthers. "I guess that should convince you that Grace is innocent."

"And vice versa," said Hack.

Grace started tapping her foot. Any mention of Andrea and the murder brought on a mini panic attack. "Thanks for the heads up. You okay otherwise?"

"I'm fine."

Druthers' cell rang and he excused himself, leaving the two of them to continue their debriefing. Thunder pressed against Hack's legs and the teen crouched down to scratch the sweet spot behind the dog's ear. "What's on tap this morning? Is the doctor returning to hypnotize you?"

"That's right. You're welcome to hang around, if you like. After he leaves, depending on what comes out, we can strategize our next step to track down Andrea's murderer." She added detergent and turned on the machine's light cycle. "You already eat breakfast?"

"About an hour ago."

"Okay, well if you're still hungry, help yourself to some fruit or whatever. I'm going back to my desk to work on my novel until Dr. Kumar arrives."

■　　■　　■

Grace wasn't sure what to expect. She'd often seen hypnosis fictionalized on film, but she doubted their "You're sleepy now…sleepy…sleepy" portrayals with the evil doctor swinging his pocket watch or asking her to concentrate on the monotonous tick-tock, tick-tock of the metronome. When Dr. Kumar did start the session, it was in the living room, lights dimmed, with Grace laying on the couch, and Druthers and Hack watching from somewhere nearby. Though out of view, their presence reassured her. She closed her eyes and tried to follow the doctor's instructions to release tension from each body part, from her toes to her scalp, drifting deeper and deeper into relaxation. Upon his command, she descended an imaginary staircase to a place of complete peace and serenity.

"It's not working."

"You're not tired?"

"Too jumpy to doze off, I guess."

They made a few more attempts. Nothing. Each time, Grace's stress level swelled until she feared she might burst.

As a last resort, Dr. Kumar pulled a bottle of pills from his briefcase and handed two to Grace.

"They're Midazolam. They're fast-acting and their effects don't last long, but they'll relax you enough for us to begin."

Druthers handed her a glass of water, she swallowed, then resumed her supine position. After about five minutes, her arms and legs transformed into blocks of cement.

"Grace, I want you to travel back to when you were a little girl. It's the day when everything changed. Do you remember?"

"Yes." Her words took on a childlike quality.

"Where are you?"

"I am in the house. Upstairs in my room."

"What time of year is it?"

"It's winter. Near Christmas. I'm excited because Santa will come soon."

"What time is it?"

"It's dark. Past bedtime. But it's too hot in my room. I don't feel good."

"What do you do?"

"I get up to tell Olivia, but my door is locked."

"Who is Olivia?"

"She takes care of me when my mommy is busy. Or away."

"And she locks you in your room?"

"They do that sometimes, so I don't come downstairs and disturb my daddy's meetings."

"He has meetings late at night?"

"Sometimes. There are always pretty women coming in and out."

"Do you call for Olivia?"

She shook her head. "Daddy doesn't like me making noise after bedtime. I am so hot, I feel sick. I want to open the window to make it colder."

"That's a good idea. What happens next?"

"Before I reach the window, I hear yelling from downstairs. It scares me so I hide under the covers. Where I'll be safe. A few minutes later, my doorknob jiggles. That makes me even scareder. It's ghosts. Or monsters. I stay very quiet, so they'll go away."

"It's okay, Grace. You're safe here. Did you stay under the covers for the rest of the night?"

"No. That's making me even hotter. I want to throw up. If the ghost is outside the door, I can still open the window. He can't be in both places at the same time. I walk over and try to press up the bottom half."

"Is it heavy?"

"I can't tell. It won't open. Then I remember Olivia locks my window, so I won't fall out by accident. There's a little chair by my desk and I drag it over and climb up so I can open the latch. The moon is so bright, it's lighting up parts of the whole backyard. I look down to see where I left my bike. And..."

Grace shivered.

"What is it, Gracie? What do you see?"

"It's a man. He is dragging something behind him. I can't see who it is because he's dressed in a black coat and hood. He's moving slow so I figure it's heavy, the thing he's dragging. Then I see another man. He's wearing a hat like the ones our gardeners wear. They talk, and the new man takes half and they start again.

"They are almost under my window when I figure out the thing they're tugging is a body. A woman's body. She's wearing a skirt that's hiked up around her waist. She's close enough now that I can see her face. I bang on the window. 'Stop doing that! Leave her alone!' Both men look up, but they can't hear me..."

"Who is it, Grace? Who's dragging the body? And whose body is it?"

Despite the engulfing swelter, she forced herself to continue. "I unlock the window and push the bottom pane up as high as I can. 'Daddy? Daddy?' I scream. 'What are you doing? What's wrong with Olivia? Where are you taking her?'

"He shushes me and whispers something to the other man. Then my father runs away. The other man takes both legs and keeps dragging. A few minutes later, I hear footsteps on the stairs, then the key in the lock. My father comes in and turns on the light. I'm standing by the door, waiting for him."

"'Gracie, are you all right?' he asks. 'Are you having a nightmare?'"

"'Why isn't Olivia walking, Daddy? Why are you pulling her? Is she sick?'"

"'No one is pulling anyone, honey. You're seeing things.' I run back over to the window and look outside. The man and the body are gone.

"'I know what I saw, Daddy. Let me speak to Olivia. Bring her upstairs right now!' I stamp my foot.

"My daddy walks toward me, grabs my hand and pulls me back to bed. He hands me a glass with some orange liquid he's brought from downstairs. It looks like the same thing I see him drink every night. 'This will make you all better,' he says. 'I promise you can see Olivia first thing in the morning.'

"I take the glass and sniff. It smells awful and I set it on the nightstand. 'I don't want this,' I tell him.

"Ouch!" Grace twisted her head toward the back of the couch. "He slaps me across the face so hard I fall back against the bed. I start screaming. 'Drink this,' he says again, pushing the glass back into my hands. 'Drink it and never speak of this night again. If you mention one word of what you imagined you saw tonight, I'll kill your mother and tell everyone you did it. You'll spend the rest of your life in jail.'"

Grace's eyes shot open and she sprang upright, unable to control her shuddering. "I remember it all now. Barrington killed her! He killed her, and I saw him hiding the evidence, and I blocked it out to keep my mother alive. He made me drink every drop of that damn scotch and the next morning, he committed me to Grasmere."

Kumar signaled for Druthers to turn up the lights and then handed Grace a bottle of water. She pushed it away, her terror replaced by a level of fury she'd never allowed herself to experience before.

"Close to forty years! That's how long that tyrant cost me. Forty years of second-guessing my every thought, convinced I was delusional. Four decades of bullying and cruelty, destroying my confidence, keeping me from normal interactions…" She squeezed her fists so tightly, her nails sunk into her palm, drawing droplets of blood. She looked Kumar in the eye. "Do you think Dr. Leighmann knew? Do psychiatrists ever treat patients for diseases they don't actually have?"

"It's impossible to be sure." He placed the water on the coffee table. "The drugs she prescribed to reduce your agitation may have prolonged the nightmares. If she mistook those nightmares as recurring visions, she might have further upped the dosage, thus perpetuating a vicious cycle. If your father kept reporting paranoid tendencies to your therapist, it's possible she took his word over yours. You may have presented as paranoid even though your fears were legitimate."

"There's one way to tell," said Hack. "Let's figure out a way to break into her office, look around, check out her files. And we should also try to verify Grace's story, so it's more than her word against her father's."

"But how?" Grace tried to coax her flicker of hope into a blaze of clarity and potential retribution. "She works out of her house. And it's not like my father would spill his guts to purge his conscience, even if he weren't comatose. And how is any of this going to bring us closer to uncovering Andrea's murderer?"

"The second we can prove you're not some violent, paranoid schizophrenic, we've reduced the likelihood the police will implicate you in the attack," Hack said. "No one will suggest you're some scorned author who killed Andrea out of fear she might release your book under her name alone. That would leave them free to pursue other theories and suspects, and free you to come out of hiding.

Grace looked at Druthers. A silent message passed between them.

Dr. Kumar nodded. "He's right. I can't condone any break-ins, but my written appraisal of your mental state, backed by proof of your therapist's failure to find any evidence corroborating your father's allegations, would be helpful in reversing your diagnosis. And if you can uncover proof of this attack against your nurse, I'd say you're home free. But you're missing one important piece of the puzzle."

Grace's face tightened "What's that?"

"You are racing to write a book because you fear your husband will murder you for your inheritance. That fear is responsible for a huge amount of stress in your life. Wouldn't you agree?"

"What's your point?"

"It's less a point than a question. Do you have any idea what's written in your father's will? Does Eliot? If you find out you're both cut out, it might ease a lot of your anxiety."

Grace's jaw hung open. Why had she never considered that before?

"Let's add that to our plan," said Hack. "We'll look into Leighmann, Barrington and his lawyer. I have a crack team of helpers at the ready and an active imagination. Let me make a few phone calls and then I'll explain how we're going to pull this whole thing off."

Chapter Thirty-Two

Hack went into the next room to make his calls, but soon realized he had spoken before thinking things through. Kenzie, the one member of his "crack team" resourceful enough to unravel any mystery, had responded to his request with a flat, "Yeah, sure, whatever," and then hung up before he could explain the details. So, he called Zev to ask what might have left Kenzie so out of sorts.

"Hack, you've been too preoccupied to notice, but ever since Katie's surprise visit, she's been moping around, not even laughing at my jokes. She wouldn't come back to the house that night until I assured her the coast was clear and I wouldn't ask her any questions. The only intel I gathered was that she never wants to see any of her family again, including her sister."

"A stud muffin like you, surely you got Katie's number?"

"Yes, I did. And stop calling me Shirley."

Hack shook his head, ignoring Zev's cliched humor. "We have to figure out how to fix Kenzie's problems with her sister, so I can enlist her help to solve Grace's issues and find Andrea's killer. Oh, and your help too. I'll need all the brainpower at my disposal."

There was a moment of silence.

"Well, thanks for your ringing endorsement. I'm so excited to be a mere drop in your ocean of brainpower. And here I was, about to suggest a tsunami of helpful suggestions but..."

"Oh brother, you're so damn sensitive. Okay, Zev, fine. You are the Pacific Ocean of brainpower, okay?"

"I prefer the Dead Sea. Please let me be the Dead Sea of brainpower?"

"You're going to be the Dead See-You-Later if you don't describe this big idea of yours."

"Fine. You ever hear of an Escape Room?"

"Yeah, a locked room where you need to solve a bunch of puzzles to escape. You've been to one?"

"No need. We Jews are quite familiar with the concept, having escaped or been expelled from Rome, Alexandria, Spain, France, Hungary, Portugal, Russia, Germany…shall I go on?

"No need, I get the point." Hack rolled his eyes. "Why do you bring it up?"

"There's one down on Franklin Avenue called Narrow Escape. We should go as a group, ask Kenzie to join us. Something to get her out of her doldrums. Meanwhile, I'll text you Katie's number so you can invite her to round out our team. Have her hide and then surprise her sister. I noticed you staring at her the other night. This could be a great excuse to schmooze."

"I see where you're going with this, Zev. I was wrong about the Dead Sea though. You're a virtual aquifer of aptitude, a canal of cleverness, an inlet of intelligence—"

"Now you're being silly. But you'll meet me there at 6:00?"

"You got it, you fjord of fabulousness."

Once Zev's text arrived, Hack reviewed Narrow Escape's website on his cell phone before making his calls. The first was to Katie, reasoning that if Kenzie didn't agree to his plan, he'd still get a date out of it, one with a girl he'd been crushing on every free second since they'd met. Katie sounded surprised to hear from him, perhaps because she'd never given him her number. But when he described a reunion with her sister, she gushed with gratitude and agreed to meet him later that afternoon. Her flirtatious giggle gave him hope something more might develop between them.

The second call was rougher. After the shelter's receptionist spent ten minutes tracking Kenzie down, she came to the phone annoyed by the interruption.

"I appreciate the invite Hack, but it's been a lousy morning," she said after he suggested the outing. "We're having some funding issues and a few of the earlier grants I applied for fell through. I wouldn't be good company."

"Kenz, I'm sorry you're having a hard time. Would $15,000 help?"

He detected her attitude shift from five towns over. "Hell, yeah. Keep talking."

"Zev's meeting me over at Narrow Escape later today. They're part of some big nationwide tournament. Every group is being timed. The month's three fastest teams move into the regionals against other winners in the area. It all leads up to some big finale in the summer with $15,000 as the grand prize. We'd have a shot, considering those razor-sharp detection skills of yours."

"Not to mention my competitive streak. That sounds amazing, Hack, thanks."

"Glad you're up for it. Meet Zev back at the house around five; you can drive over together. He's got the address. See you then."

Hack called to reserve the room, trying to ignore his guilt over thrusting Kenzie into an awkward spot when she was already having a bad day. He focused on the greater good: two sisters working out their problems, while helping him solve his. And who knows? If all went well, some prize money for Kenz.

He arrived at the escape room later that afternoon, delighted to find Katie waiting, decked out in a white, button-down shirt, purple skinny jeans, and a bright, silver belt. Hack reminded himself this wasn't a date, but an integral part of a larger mission. He hadn't counted on so many choices of rooms, each showcasing a different set of puzzles. He asked the operator to place them in whatever room had lots of nooks and crannies, so they could jump out and surprise a member of his group who'd be arriving later.

A stocky man with a mustache named Fritz led Hack and Katie to a room called "Boardroom Scuffle," where a team of C-suite execs must avert a corporate overthrow by angry stockholders before time ran out. The furnishings included a long, mahogany table and chairs, surrounded by various desks and file cabinets, no doubt brimming with clues. Hack decided it was perfect for their needs.

Fritz handed him a key. "If anyone gets claustrophobic or wants out, use this. There is also a panic button behind the desk, but please, press it only if you lose the key or if someone's having a heart attack or some other emergency. Got it?"

"Got it. One thing, though. We're expecting two others. He's thin, bearded and sarcastic; she's got a buzz cut and a gold barbell septum piercing. You can't miss them. Please don't tell them we're already inside the room, or that there's a way out. Hack slipped Fritz a crumpled ten-dollar bill. "We understand each other?"

The man's nose twitched as if his mustache were trying to distance itself from his chin. "Not a problem. I hope you have a wonderful adventure." Then he left Hack and Katie to their own devices.

"It's nice to see you again." Hack prayed she wouldn't notice he was blushing. "I hope you are okay with us trapping Kenzie like this. I'm not sure she would have come otherwise."

"I'm fine with it. If she's going to treat me as *persona non grata*, I'd like to understand why." Katie plopped down on one of the boardroom chairs.

Hack surveyed the room's decor. "When we hear them coming, you can hide under the desk and let them get settled before springing out. Sound good?"

Her lips upturned in a broad smile that highlighted her dimples and set Hack's heart aflutter. "Whatever you say. You were brilliant, dreaming up a way for us to speak without giving her the option of running off. Thank you."

For a moment, Hack considered giving Zev the credit, but what fun would that be? Instead, he shrugged and threw her an "aw shucks" look. "You planning on staying in town long?" He forced himself to concentrate on the conversation and not the errant lock of hair that bobbled seductively as she nodded yes.

"I'll be working in Manhattan; the Chandler Hotel hired me as a sales and marketing associate. The job starts in a few weeks, which means I've got to find a decent apartment, then go home and pack. I thought commuting from Bergen County would give the O'Malley sisters a chance to grow close again. If this reunion doesn't work, I might have to rethink my plans."

Now Hack had another motivation to make sure his scheme succeeded. If Katie stayed in town, who knew what might happen between them?

Footsteps echoed in the hall and Hack gestured toward the desk with his head. Katie scampered over and hid in the kneehole. He remained seated at the boardroom table, desperate to figure out what to do with his hands, how to appear normal until Kenzie was well inside, with the door sealed behind her.

"Hack, OMG, this place is dope," gushed Kenzie as soon as she and Zev walked in. "I was looking at some of these rooms—spaceships to save from crashing, a hospital under zombie siege, terrorist bombs to defuse. Enough intrigue to fill a month of afternoons."

"Glad you approve. Take a seat. Zev, make sure the door is closed, k?"

"What am I, the office flunky? Who nominated you boss? I demand we elect a chairman of this corporation."

"Just do it."

"Fine. It's locked. But for the record, this type of harassment is why unions form."

Get serious, Zev," said Kenzie as he sat beside her. "When does the timer start? Where are the rules? I have every intention of win—"

"Kenzie?" Katie's murmur silenced all further discussion. She stood at the head of the table, with wide eyes and a quivering lower lip.

Kenzie's face tightened. She pushed back on her chair and without a word, stomped across the room and pulled at the doorknob, but it wouldn't turn.

"Hack, I'm not sure what you imagined you'd accomplish with this ambush. I want out of this room, now."

Zev stood up. "Kenz, it wasn't Hack's idea, it was mine. I don't know what happened between you and your sister, but the thing is, neither does she. Maybe you should talk about it, give her a chance to explain herself. As my people say, *a shlekhter sholem iz veser vi a guter krig.* A bad peace is better than a good war."

Kenzie's eyes were shooting laser beams at everyone in the room, everyone but Katie, whom she refused to acknowledge. "Thank you, King Solomon, but I'll settle this on my own terms. Now open up."

"We can't get out until the hour's up," Hack lied. "I'm sorry, but since we're all stuck here, why don't we do something useful. Like clear the air between you two."

Kenzie glared at Hack and then turned toward the door, willing it to open. Katie positioned herself a few feet behind and addressed the back of her sister's head.

"I don't know what I did, Kenz, but I'm prepared to do whatever it takes to make it right. Why can't you give me a chance?"

"I don't know what I did," Kenzie mocked.

Katie's voice choked with frustration. "Well, are you going to share, or just commune with the wall?"

"You don't want to hear about it, trust me." The venom with which she spat out the words made Hack suspect his friend was teetering on the verge.

"Have a little faith. Try me."

Kenzie spun around, claws drawn, a tiger ready to pounce. "The first week, it was just talking, some meds. Hour-long cold showers, as if that would change anything. By Monday of the second week, the therapists bound me naked to a chair and forced me to watch videos of women while they zapped me with a cattle prod. They wanted me to associate intense pain with the faces of those girls, so I'd no longer find them attractive. Hours of torturing a sixteen-year-old. I begged them to understand I was born this way; it wasn't a choice. But they refused to listen." Each of her words was a dagger seeking a target to wound in self-defense.

"I had to get out before the third week. I'd heard rumors...girls being locked in rooms with boys...videotaped...expected to have sex and experience the supposed joys of life as a straight person. If the boys hesitated, the doctors took over, and made sure the 'therapy' was 'administered correctly.' I wasn't about to stick around and get raped..." She broke down, unable to communicate the rest of her ordeal.

"I didn't know. How could I have known?" Katie tried to touch Kenzie's shoulder, but the older girl pushed her away. Hack and Zev sat open-jawed, watching and listening.

Kenzie regained enough composure to continue. "A little research, perhaps? The gay and lesbian message boards on the Net? I escaped by climbing a fence rimmed with barbed wire." She yanked up the sleeve of her sweater and revealed her battle scars. "I hitchhiked from Central

Pennsylvania to a New Jersey shelter for LGBTQI teens, the same place I work now. That card I sent you after I turned eighteen? It was my way of gloating to the whole family that you and your homophobia could never lay another finger on me. I'd won, and I needed you all to realize that. But I swore it would be the last time I acknowledged any of you existed."

Hack's pressure points pulsated with anger over how a state like Pennsylvania, so proud of its Liberty Bell, sanctioned treatment that represented the exact opposite. He wondered how many others were out there like Kenzie, looking to escape brutal caregivers with a moralistic agenda.

"I can understand why you hated Mom and Dad for that. It's awful…unthinkable… unforgivable. But why me? Why are you taking this out on me?" Katie sounded like she was pleading for her life.

"Because, you were the one who urged me to come out to Mom and Dad 'Trust them,' you said, 'They'll love you no matter what.' Well, that was a fucking lie. They shut me out, couldn't look me straight in the eye. And then when they planned to send me away, you never warned me. As close as we were, you stayed silent. Their ignorance was almost understandable, given their age and upbringing, but you? I vowed I would never forgive you."

"You're assuming I knew. But I didn't!" Katie's face turned purple. "One morning you were there, that afternoon, I got back from school and the place was empty. When Mom and Dad came home, they said they'd sent you to a hospital for help. "Help with what?" I asked but they shook their heads like I was a simpleton and refused to discuss it again.

"So, you forgot about me. Pretended I didn't exist."

"Forgot about you? You believe that? Once we heard you escaped, I didn't have a clue where to look. I published your picture on the Internet and stuck 'Missing' posters on utility poles in three neighboring towns, all offering a cash reward for any information that helped me locate you."

"Uh huh. I bet."

"You're calling me a liar?' Katie wrenched her phone from her pants pocket and scrolled for a minute while the room remained dumbstruck.

Then she walked to Kenzie's side and thrust the cell in her sister's face. "Read these if you don't believe me."

Kenzie deigned to turn her head toward the screen.

"No matter how much I posted, no one would help me. It was like you'd vanished. And then we got that card, postmarked from New Jersey. I was so relieved you were okay, that now I had a clue to your whereabouts. I took every penny I'd saved and hired a frigging private detective. You wanna see those emails too?"

Katie pulled the phone back, scrolled again and flashed the screen under her sister's nose. Kenzie grabbed the cell and looked for herself. "The day he told me where you were living, I couldn't stop dreaming of the moment I'd get to hug you again. So, when I showed up on your stoop, too excited to stand still, and you ran out the back door? Do you have any idea how devastating that was?"

Both sisters remained silent for a moment, with Kenzie still eyeballing Katie's email correspondence before murmuring, "I...I...I never knew."

"Well, welcome to the club."

Both sisters stared at each other, tears welling in their eyes. The victims of a conspiracy both were helpless to prevent. Chins quavering, they fell into each other's arms, where they remained for several minutes. Then Kenzie walked over and embraced both Hack and Zev. "I'm sorry for how mean I was, the horrible things I said. You meant well and I treated you like crap. How can I make it up to you? How can I thank you for giving me back my sister?"

"Well, now that you mention it," said Hack, "we didn't solve this escape room's puzzle, but I have a real-life mystery that needs your expertise. And that means you too, Katie and Zev. Grace Rendell feels as powerless fighting her situation as you did, battling your parents. Can you lend me a hand investigating her past, so we can help her get out of this mess?"

"I'm in," answered Kenzie and Katie in unison before collapsing into half-tears, half-laughter.

"I'll make it unanimous. This all reminds me of another saying my people share, something to remember the next time you assume you know someone else's intentions: *Keyner veys nit vemen der shukh kvetsht, nor der vos geyt in im.*"

Hack cocked his head. "Which means?"

"No one knows whose shoe pinches except the person who walks in it."

Chapter Thirty-Three

Before returning to his office, Dr. Kumar promised to send Grace a written assessment of her mental state by the end of the day. "If ten psychiatrists examined you, I believe they'd all agree you're competent and sane," he said. "Promise to contact me if there's anything else you need." She shook his hand, sorry to see him go, but even more sorry for all the years she'd wasted seeing a therapist who hadn't looked past her father's lies to diagnose her true mental condition.

The next morning, Grace calmed her nerves with chamomile tea while rereading Kumar's assessment and awaiting Hack and his team's arrival. Druthers left, flanked by his brace of Dobies eager for their morning walk. Grace sent up silent thanks for this empathetic, supportive man, whose quiet life her presence had thrown into chaos. In his absence, she busied herself with washing the breakfast dishes, brewing another cup of tea— anything to diminish the stress of what revelations the morning might bring.

Hack showed up before his companions, planting himself on the sofa and scrolling through his emails. Druthers returned ten minutes later, his expression grave. A curled newspaper peeked out from his jacket pocket. "There's been a development. You may want to sit down."

Impatient, she grabbed at the tabloid, almost gagging as she read the headline, "Billionaire Given Last Rites." She scanned the article: second stroke, feeding tube, pneumonia. Girlfriend, son-in-law, and grandsons still by his side. Like Atlas, the weight of the world pressed down on her shoulders. *Time's up. Even if it takes all night. I must finish 'Salvaging Hope' and send it to the online self-publishing outlets by tomorrow.*

Then she noticed the sidebar. A picture of Dr. Emma Leighmann, psychiatrist to Pierrepoint's heiress daughter, warning the public to do all possible to secure her safe return. "I don't like to break patient confidentiality," she told reporters, "but Grace Pierrepoint Rendell has lost touch with reality. I've learned she's writing a novel fueled by paranoid delusion. It bears no semblance to reality. In her present distraught state, she's even more of a danger to herself and others than we originally feared. Please contact the police with any information immediately."

"I'm going to be sick." Grace threw down the paper and locked herself in the bathroom. For the next five minutes, she retched the remains of her breakfast into the toilet bowl. Weak and woozy, she staggered back into the living room and plunked herself down on the couch beside Druthers, her cheeks wet with tears.

"Eliot must have told her what Andrea said about me writing a book. And now look. She's discredited the novel before it's even been published. No one will read it. Nothing can save me."

"You're looking at it all wrong," said Hack. "I read the whole article while you were off, worshipping the porcelain gods. Dying billionaire? Missing heiress dishing out the secrets behind all that money and power, thinly disguised as fiction? Grace, it reads like Page Six of the New York Post. Sensationalism at its finest. You couldn't ask for better publicity."

Grace looked up in surprise. "You think?"

"Sounds like you've got a bestseller on your hands." Druthers moved to her side and brushed his lips against her cheek.

Hack clapped his hands to get their attention. "You're both missing something. Leighmann is trying to get out in front of the story, diffuse it. In fact, if she's aware of the book, she may know Grace was co-writing it with Andrea. We're lucky she didn't tie her to the murder."

"Not yet, anyway." Druthers displayed an uncharacteristic scowl. "This might be the first in a series of sincere pleas for Grace's return. Remember, unlike Eliot, there's no upside for Leighmann to keep Grace quiet. She has no agenda to conceal. If she's bought into Barrington's appraisal of his daughter's mental state since day one, with Grace's meds perpetuating her symptoms, her concern is legitimate. The real question is, how much does Leighmann know about the book? Gracie, could Andrea have grown suspicious about the content? Contacted her, concerned about your mental state?"

"Unlikely. She knew me as Ruth Allen. I never gave her my real name. She wouldn't have heard it until the papers started splashing my picture around."

"Was your therapist quoted in those early articles?" asked Hack.

"I'm not sure. Does it matter?"

"It would have given my sister the ability to contact her. But from our conversations together, it never sounded like Andrea questioned your sanity." Hack scratched his head. "It's more likely that whoever stole the computer may have seen or heard you in the house and worried you could identify him, so when your name appeared in the papers, he emailed her the manuscript, hoping Leighmann would see it as further proof of your worsening delusions. With you locked up in some asylum, there'd be less chance of anyone giving credence to your testimony or trusting your identification in a line-up."

"Kind of farfetched, isn't it, Hack?" asked Druthers.

"It's one possibility. You got a better one?"

A rapping at the front door, followed by an eruption of barking, cut short Druthers' answer. He let the dogs out into the yard as Grace greeted the newest additions to their team: a tall African-American girl with an Afro who introduced herself as Hack's sister Gwennie; a teen in khakis with a buzzcut named Kenzie; and a lanky, olive-skinned man with sweet, dark eyes who asked her to call him Zev.

Hack frowned. "Katie's not coming?"

"Sorry we're not good enough for you, lover boy," said Kenzie. "She's out looking for an apartment."

Hack ignored the jab and the heat burning his cheeks. He shepherded them into the living room to join Grace and Druthers. The older man balked upon seeing Zev. "Haven't we met?" He ruminated for a second. "The Bitcoin place...aren't you the guy—"

Hack lunged between the two men. "All water under the bridge. We don't have time to waste on finger-pointing." Druthers threw Zev a nasty look but remained silent as Hack recapped Grace's situation, including the results of her hypnosis session.

Kenzie's eyes grew so wide, Grace feared they might pop out of her head. "That's some story. But it raises two questions: First, did Barrington actually kill Olivia, or was it a hallucination? We need independent verification for an event that happened...how many years ago, Grace?"

"Almost forty."

"Second, who killed Andrea? Assuming it was to get at the manuscript in her computer—"

Zev cut her short. "I doubt there's another reason. My friend Schmuel says Hack's loan shark buddies swear they had nothing to do with any murder."

Kenzie twisted her mouth. "Oh, well that settles it, then. No one is as credible as a career criminal denying involvement in a publicized celebrity murder. Now, as I was saying, the third question is, what part was the killer trying to keep secret? Grace's memory of her nurse disappearing? Or the suggestion that Eliot plans to kill her for her inheritance? Something too self-incriminating to pull off after publication."

"I didn't remember about Olivia until yesterday, though," said Grace. "There's nothing about her in the book, though I did implicate Hope's father in a Ponzi scandal."

"Remember, any copy the killer has of the manuscript is incomplete. If it includes credible evidence of Barrington's financial crimes, said killer might fear the final chapters document something even worse," said Kenzie. "I'm no lawyer but I'm betting when Barrington dies, the courts might use Grace's allegations to freeze his assets until the whole thing gets sorted out. Anyone expecting an inheritance might have a motive to keep allusions to your father's illicit past out of a novel."

"Which begs one final question," Zev said. "Who else besides you, Eliot and the kids stand to benefit from your father's will, Grace? Ex-wives, girlfriends, former employees?"

Grace racked her brain. "My mother's dead and he never remarried, so there are no ex-wives. He's been with his current girlfriend Caprice for several months now. When I was down there last, she confided that he'd threatened her and the dogs. It made me wonder if she'd triggered the stroke somehow, so I suppose she's a possibility. Though knowing my father, I doubt he would leave money to her or any of his ex-girlfriends. His relationships don't tend to end amicably. From what I've seen, he tires of them and then bombards them with criticism until they can't stand it any longer. The pulling-wings-off-flies approach to breaking things off."

Druthers leaned forward. "How about people he worked with, Gracie?"

"No, not one. Of that, I'm certain. People worked *for* him, not *with* him, and I'm sure he was as miserly with his wages as he was with his compliments. I remember when he'd sit at the dinner table and complain about Christmas bonuses. Like it was unfathomable that his employees might expect a penny more than the pittance they'd already earned."

"The real question may not be who killed Olivia or Andrea, but how Barrington has avoided being murdered this long." Zev's comment met with uneasy chuckles.

"Here's how I think we should tackle this," said Hack. "Gwennie, any way you can hack into Dr. Leighmann's computer, see if you can access the files for Grace Pierrepoint or Grace Rendell? That should tell us if she's ever mentioned anything about seeing her father that night with Olivia. For all we know, Leighmann uncovered the truth and has been blackmailing Barrington for decades. Or she tried to pressure Grace into hypnosis, so Grace would divulge something juicy, something Barrington would pay millions to keep secret."

"Grace's father doesn't sound like a man who would tolerate being blackmailed," said Zev. Like the Yiddish say: *A leyb hot nit moyre far keyn flig.* A lion isn't scared of a fly. If he's that powerful and has already murdered once, he would have swatted her long ago."

"This theory is baseless," Grace said. "I've known Emma Leighmann for most of my life. She wouldn't do anything that wasn't for my benefit. It's like Tom said, she trusted my father when he called me paranoid, and my medication left me too docile to wage a counterargument. Any time I grew rebellious enough to object, they just chalked it up to my illness. But if Eliot told Dr. Leighmann about my book, embellishing its contents, she might have reason to urge the public to turn me in for my own good."

Hack wrinkled his nose. "I appreciate your faith in your therapist, but double-checking can't hurt, and can only help. Right?"

Grace was mulling over Hack's point when Gwennie clapped to get everyone's attention. "There's one way to settle this: let me hack in and rummage around. You got a computer I can use? Something I can download some software onto?"

"I have a laptop. It's now protected by some anti-virus software." Grace threw Hack a dirty look. "I hope that won't impede your search."

Gwennie coughed and avoided Grace's gaze. "Virus protection won't affect outbound searches. It's good you...got some."

Grace walked across the room to retrieve her computer and handed it to Gwen.

"Great. I'll also need the name and email address of whomever you want me to hack, a quiet place to work, and a credit card to buy a few pieces of software. It shouldn't run you too much."

Grace wrote out her therapist's email address and Druthers pulled a Visa card from his pants pocket. "My bedroom is at the top of the stairs to the left. No one will bother you there. Buy whatever you need. Nothing's more important than keeping my girl safe."

Hack commandeered the remaining group's attention once Gwennie departed. "Grace, your next step should be to call your father's attorney and find out what's in the will. If he's left his billions to his alma mater and you relay that information to the world somehow, I bet you'll feel less threatened."

"I'm finishing this book no matter what. I plan to add a few chapters about Hope's father duping his daughter into a lifetime of battling a trumped-up mental illness."

"Do whatever you gotta do. But please call him now so we'll know what we're dealing with."

Grace went into Druthers' office and searched the Internet on his desktop computer for the phone number of her father's estate attorney. He had so many lawyers, but she remembered this one because when she'd met him years before, he'd equated his last name with Barrington's eventual demise, quoting Shakespeare and "the winter of our discontent." A pleasant if doddering man, face and arms covered in age spots, his gait supported by a cane. After a bit of digging she found it: Charles Snowden, Esq.

She punched the number into her burner and tensed as she waited for Snowden's receptionist to pick up. Her mind flooded with self-recrimination: why hadn't she made this call months ago? Why hadn't she checked on Barrington's condition over the past few days? She had a list of excuses: respect for her father's privacy concerning his final wishes; doubt in her right to question anything instead of swallowing dictums whole; and the need to keep a low profile. But none of her justifications silenced the damning voice of contrition, accusing her of disloyalty and neglect.

"Charles Snowden's office."

"Good morning. I'd like to speak with Mr. Snowden please."

"May I ask who's calling?"

"This is Grace Pierrepoint Rendell. Is he available?"

"Well, Gracie, hello. You're lucky you caught me. The office is closed; I'm just here scavenging for a few papers. You're quite the star these days, aren't you?" Was his comment snide or friendly? He spoke in an avuncular manner, so perhaps no offense meant.

"Hello, Mr. Snowden. I'm taking a needed break from life. I've kept up with my father's condition though, and to be prudent, I need to understand what we're looking at regarding the contents of his will. Should he take a turn for the worse, I want to be prepared."

"I appreciate your concern, my dear. But even if my duty of confidentiality allowed me to give out that information, I'd never do it over the phone."

"Sure." She rubbed the back of her neck with her spare hand. She hadn't counted on there being an issue, but with all the paparazzi out there, snooping for a scoop, it made sense.

"Is there anything at all you can tell me? Like, are there multiple beneficiaries? Anything?"

"I can't tell you anything about his bequests, but I will share something funny...well, not as funny as coincidental...I met with your father hours before he had his stroke. He insisted I come over to the house and remind him of the contents of his will. Like he had a lapse of memory and needed reconfirmation."

Grace blinked. That *did* seem peculiar. "Then you must be familiar with its contents."

"I am, indeed, dear lady. And while I can't give you any details, I can share a prediction for the future. Like a soothsayer. You won't have any financial worries when your father passes. Does that put your mind at ease?"

"No. Quite the opposite, in fact." Grace shuddered. It was as bad as she'd feared. Once Barrington was gone, Eliot would be one murder away from becoming an instant billionaire. "He made no changes the last time you met with him?" Perhaps Caprice had exploited his failing mental faculties to wheedle a few dollars to compensate for nursemaid duties? Grace needed to be sure.

Snowden launched into a coughing fit on the other end of the line and then apologized for the interruption. "Moving back and forth between the heat and the air-conditioning, I'm not sure how I've lasted in Florida this long. When I lived in New Jersey—"

"Mr. Snowden, I don't mean to cut you short, but I have to hang up in a minute. Just tell me, did he make any changes that day?"

"Only one, Grace. Remember, you had left Quiet Pines a few months prior. He'd once hoped you'd be competent enough to manage the Pierrepoint estate. But, after that altercation in November—it must have been a doozy—he made one revision to his will."

"Did he add on beneficiaries? It's important I know."

"Grace, I wish I could say more. Trust me, anything your father decided was for your own good. It was nice catching up. I'm praying for your father."

"Wait, I need to be sure—" It was pointless to continue. The line had gone dead.

Chapter Thirty-Four

Grace stared at her phone in disbelief. One simple question, that's all she'd wanted Snowden to answer. She walked into the next room to report to the others.

"He wouldn't discuss my inheritance, except to hint it was sizeable. No mention of other beneficiaries. Only that he changed something in the will on the day of his stroke, prompted by my "bad behavior" last November. My father intends to scold and control me from the grave." She collapsed on the couch next to Druthers, his reassuring arm squeezing her tight as they all waited for Gwennie to complete her hacking assignment.

About an hour later, Gwen returned downstairs, carrying the laptop and bearing bad news. "I got in, but Dr. Leighmann doesn't appear to store anything of import on her server. She must handwrite all her notes or type them out old school and then store them in a filing cabinet. Physical break-ins are outside of my wheelhouse; I only handle digital spying."

"There was nothing?" Hack sounded incredulous.

"She must delete her emails as soon as she answers them, and then removes evidence of the answers. I got nothing except a bunch of vacation photos."

"Let's look at those," suggested Zev. "Perhaps they will entertain us, provide some small reward for our efforts."

"Help yourself. I'm getting a soda…if that's okay with you, Tom."

"Anything you want. That goes for all of you."

Gwennie set the laptop on the coffee table. Zev and Kenzie squeezed in next to Grace and Druthers on the couch. Zev leaned forward and started scrolling through photos of Leighmann on some tropical beach, accompanied by two very pale white people in the distance, a man and a woman.

"Looks like someone's been hitting the SPF100," said Zev. "It's so strong, it removes the color from your skin." The next photo showed a close-up of Leighmann with a slim-hipped younger woman, her arm around the doctor's shoulder.

"Wait...stop...her face looks familiar." Grace stared at the slight figure filling part of the laptop screen. She looked to be in her forties, sporting shoulder-length, wavy brown hair and a turquoise swimsuit adorned with pink roses. She squeezed her eyes shut, trying to place the face. Where was it, where was it...?

She ran through a list of places she frequented. Was she someone Grace had encountered at high school on Parents' Night? A client at her CPA firm? A fellow shopper at the Grocery Garage? Another patient... "Oh wait, I remember now. I saw her outside Dr. Leighmann's office awhile back. She'd hogged two visitors' spots and Eliot told her off. Doesn't it seem odd that a therapist would travel with a patient?"

"Maybe she's not a patient. Could she be a lover? Or a relative?" asked Kenzie.

Zev tsked. "Whoever she is, she's got terrible fashion sense. Let me blow up the photo a little. I might recognize her too." After a minute, a smile spread across his face. "She's local. I've seen her at a club where I hang out occasionally."

Hack rolled his eyes "Should I ask what kind of club?"

"It's a little dive in Union City called The Fringe. Somewhere Kenzie and I would be more likely to frequent than the rest of you. And yes, I remember her." Zev moved onto the next photo, another close-up of the woman but this time with her friend. "And that's the guy I usually see her with."

Grace's gasp caused Zev to pull his hand from the keyboard as if he had burnt his fingertips. "What? What's wrong now?"

She glared at the photo, her mouth agape, unable to speak. The woman in the floral one-piece had her lips pressed against the cheek of a man with black hair, green eyes and gold-rimmed glasses.

Hack stared too, then pulled out his smartphone and scrolled for a bit. "Here's what she's upset about." He held up the results of his research next to the laptop's screen. It was a tabloid shot of a distraught man with two sons answering reporters' questions after leaving his father-in-law's hospital bed. The man in both photos was Eliot.

"I don't understand," Grace muttered. "When was this photo taken?"

Zev clicked back to the details view of the pictures folder. "The week before Christmas last year."

"December…He said he was going to Dallas to some advertising conference. Left me alone with the boys. I commented it was an unusual week for a meeting, so close to the holidays, but he said it was some exclusive motivational reward for top salespersons."

"Looks like he's pretty motivated."

Kenzie punched Zev in the shoulder. "Be a little sensitive, Z. The woman just outed her husband as a cheat."

"Dr. Leighmann kept urging me to visit my dad that week. Guess she didn't want me stopping by the office while she wasn't there."

Grace put her elbows to her knees, her head in her palms, as if doubled over with pain. "All those late nights… blamed it on work…years without sex…" Druthers rubbed her back, but it was of little comfort as she scanned through twenty-five years of marriage, noting each time he'd disappeared for a stretch of a few days. Sometimes blaming a meeting, other times offering no explanation. Since overhearing the bathroom gossip at Eliot's office party, she'd assumed he'd spent those absences giving his secretary Sheryl a little extra "dictation." But that's all it was, an assumption. Without physical proof, hope lingered. Now there was no question that her entire life had been one giant lie.

"I can't believe this." Grace sprang upright as wrath triumphed over confusion. "My therapist knew my husband was cheating on me with another patient. Not only didn't she tell me, she joined them on vacation. What the hell is going on?"

Gwennie nursed her soda from the kitchen doorway. "Want me to track her down, run a background check?"

"You can do that? From a picture?" Grace was incredulous.

"It's easy. I can copy the photo into some facial recognition software. The program will try to match it against similar pictures on webpages and social media sites. It shouldn't take more than a few minutes to figure out her identity."

Gwennie took the laptop into the kitchen for some quiet. Even waiting for a minute was interminable. Grace tapped her foot against the hardwood floor, unsure of which issue irritated her most: that this woman was part of Eliot's life, or that Dr. Leighmann was aware of his cheating, condoned it, and kept it from her. The identity of her husband's lover was superfluous. Her intrusion into Grace's world was not.

Druthers called the dogs back in just as a scowling Gwennie returned to the living room and set the laptop on the coffee table. "No dice. Whoever this gal is, she doesn't plaster her face across the Internet."

Grace tapped faster. "Are there any other pictures or documents in Dr. Leighmann's drive? Anything to give us a clue?"

"I'm sorry, that's all I found. Perhaps she keeps most of her personal stuff on a separate computer under a different email address and password. I don't have access."

"I have an idea." Zev pointed at Hack. "You up for an adventure tonight?"

"You want to break into her therapist's office?"

"Nah, something much less illegal and far more fun. We go to The Fringe. Hang out, make some discreet inquiries. See if we can put a name to the face."

"And you need me because…?"

"Prime piece of manhood like me? They'll mob me as usual when they find out I'm available and then I won't get anything accomplished."

Kenzie lifted a single eyebrow.

"Sounds like a plan," said Hack. "Gwennie, I'm sure you have to head back to work, but would you run one other search after you get home tonight?"

"You're the boss. What do you need?"

"Search online for any mention of an employee disappearing from the Pierrepoint household dating back 39 years. Her name was Olivia…something. Grace?"

"No idea, sorry."

"Okay, just Olivia. Grace, do you remember the names of any other employees who worked for your father around the time Olivia disappeared?"

Grace pressed her eyelids tight, trying to recreate the staff roster from the estate where she'd grown up in Short Hills. "There was a butler…middle-aged English guy…his name was…Malcolm. His wife, Winnie, was a maid. The cook was…mmm…French. But from France, not from Haiti or French Polynesia. My father always used to make that point of distinction to his guests. The chef's name was…Auguste something…he used to tell me it was like the book…Babar. That's it. Auguste Babar."

"Well, that's a start. Gwennie, if you can, try to track down Auguste Babar. If we're lucky, he's still somewhere in New Jersey." Hack turned to Grace. "The rest of us have nowhere to go until tonight. Is there anything else we can help with?"

"I am about to finish the final chapters of my book. There's nothing that says once I'm done, I can't send you each a copy. I need proofreaders to point out the typos, grammar mistakes, anywhere that something doesn't work. But you've got to promise to delete the manuscript from your hard drives and phones after you send your edits to me. There's one too many copies out there already."

Chapter Thirty-Five

Two hours later, Grace finished the first draft of her novel. Normally, she would have reveled in her newfound sense of pride and accomplishment. But tempering her joy was anxiety over getting her manuscript edited and published before her father exhaled his final breath. The tome was 320 pages long, totaling around 80,000 words, which she'd read was the perfect length for a mystery. She sent eighty pages each to her helpers: Druthers, Kenzie, Hack and Zev. They read the book on their smartphones and emailed her back their notes and corrections. Druthers ran out and picked up a few pizzas. By the time Hack and Zev put on their jackets and left for The Fringe, Grace was already incorporating everyone's final notes into a master copy.

.   .   .

Zev grinned as they drove southeast to Union City. "This is a bi-club, Hack. Ready for your initiation into alternate sexual realms?"

"I'm not worried. I've never been much of a homophobe and anyway, I'm not there to pick anyone up."

"They're a nice group—an older crowd, so there's less hooking up, more thoughtful conversations. Sort of the difference between a coffee house and a singles bar in Straightland."

"Straightland, huh? Where do *you* fall on the sexual map, Zev?"

"Middletown. By way of Brooklyn. Thought you'd have figured that one out by now."

Hack stifled a laugh. "The two of them are straight. I'm assuming, anyway. Why meet at a bisexual club?"

"Well, if I were a Straightland resident, and didn't want any of my boring, close-minded, vanilla friends to stumble upon my secret lover…"

"Point taken. Though a straight person can still be interesting and open-minded. You know that, right?"

"Whatever you need to tell yourself, Hack."

The two drove in silence through some of Jersey's less glamorous neighborhoods.

"You one hundred percent sure Grace is who and what she says, Hack? That she didn't kill your sister to get the only other existing copy of the book and not share the profits?"

Hack glanced at Zev before turning his attention back to the road.

"Not at first, but I am now. She's been through hell and back. Why would a future billionaire kill my sister to save a few measly royalty dollars? In fact, if she didn't fear for her life, why write the book to begin with? If you had watched her under hypnosis, you'd be convinced too."

Zev tilted his head from side to side, unconvinced. "Might be a set-up. Those pills you told me the doctor gave her, Midazolam? They can cause hallucinations, so who knows if what she said she remembered was the truth. What if she's feigning her paranoia altogether? Sharing royalties is one thing, but what if she's trying to get her husband locked away so she doesn't have to share a much bigger bankroll—her inheritance? Blame him for what she's trying to pull off herself. Maybe we're the patsies in a much larger scheme."

"You always this skeptical, bro?" Hack pulled into the parking lot behind a six-story, brick office building. "This is the address you gave me. You sure it's right?"

"To answer your second question first, yes, this is it. You missed the tiny neon sign out front. It's subtle and nondescript. As for your allegation, there's an old Hungarian expression, lest you accuse me of only quoting the Jews: 'He who trusts is happy; the doubter is wise.' Hmm, that's pretty good. Must have been Hungarian Jews." Zev stepped from the car and zipped his jacket against the wind.

"Since we're quote-swapping, Zev, my mother used to quote Ralph Waldo Emerson, who wrote: 'Trust instinct to the end, even though you can give no reason.' My instincts have always been pretty good, so I plan to follow them." He locked the car and the two walked toward the club's entrance. "Got your fake ID ready?"

"Always, dude, always."

A bouncer guarding the front door asked for a ten-dollar cover and then admitted them to a dimly lit, open space with an oversized bar bordered by a smattering of already-occupied stools. There were no tables or chairs, but Hack noted a platform against the back wall where a band was setting up.

"This is not at all what I expected. Don't you "hip" people ever sit?"

"Nah Hack, we do it in the middle of the floor while spectators form a circle and cheer us on." Zev shook his head. "Seriously, bro. They must have cleared out the tables and chairs tonight for dancing. It's after ten. Dinnertime is over, remember?"

Hack scrunched his mouth to the right in dismay. He had intended to observe the action from a rear table and remain inconspicuous. This configuration forced him to walk the room and check everyone out—and vice versa. "What do you want to drink?"

"I'll have a Mai Tai with a little umbrella, please."

"Are you kidding me? I can't order that. Can't you drink a screwdriver or whiskey, like everyone else?"

"When in Rome..."

Hack shook his head in mock-disgust. "Stay here and look around. I'll be right back." He sidled up to the bar and tried in vain to wave down the bartender. While he waited for the man to finish flirting with a couple of guys a few stools away, he overheard a few snippets of the surrounding conversations.

"I pray I get the part. Then I can quit this goddamned waiter gig."

"He cheated on me; I saw him. But when I accused him, he looked at me as if I were crazy."

"After she inherited the money, we would have been home free."

Hack swiveled toward the speaker of the last comment, a wavy-haired brunette. Then he backed away from the bar with a huff, as if appalled by the bad service. Zev was still where he'd left him, being chatted up by a Freddy Mercury lookalike.

"I turn my back for one second and this is what happens?" said Hack, determined to validate their cover. The Freddie-wannabe sulked back to the bar.

"Was that necessary? And where's my embarrassingly effeminate alcoholic beverage?"

"Forget the drink. Look over at the bar. To the left of where I was standing. Is that our girl?"

Zev squinted for a better look. "Yup, that's her. Let's go make small talk."

"Hold on, Chatty Cathy. Why don't we just stand nearby and listen?"

"Spoilsport. You suck the fun out of everything."

They edged their way to the bar, with only a solitary drinker sitting between them and their target, who was commiserating with a female friend.

"The Mai Tai's any good here?" Zev's question to the bartender earned him an elbow jab from Hack.

"Twenty-six years and it could all go down the drain," said Target, slurring her words. She gestured for the bartender to pour her another bourbon.

"Why aren't you down there with him, Gab?" asked her friend.

The band started tuning their instruments and Hack strained to hear.

"My mother's her therapist and she says...*unintelligible*...So, he's down there alone with the kids." Someone's margarita order drowned the rest of the sentence. "...at death's door." She downed half the bourbon in two gulps.

"Well, it's not too far a leap. Florida *is* heaven's waiting room."

Hack's heart beat faster than the drummer warming up his sticks. The longer "Gab" sipped, the easier her anger-tainted words escaped liquor-loosened lips.

"We've got this plan. Rock solid. But...there have been some issues. Truly sucky issues. If my golden goose turns into a dead duck...*unintelligible*...more than half my life for nothing." She drained the last of her drink and slammed the glass down on the bar. "I gotta get home. Thanks for listening."

"You don't look like you're up for driving. You need a ride?"

Gab fumbled with her smartphone. "Uber. See you later." Hack and Zev watched as she stumbled outside.

"Still doubt Grace's story?" Hack whispered into his friend's ear.

"No, your intuition remains supreme. Let's go back to the car and figure out our next step."

Chapter Thirty-Six

Hack and Zev returned from The Fringe after midnight, stunning Grace with their report. "Her mother? I didn't even know Dr. Leighmann was married."

"There's no evidence she ever was." Gwennie had returned to the house after dinner to share the results of her Internet search. "While I was checking out Mr. Babar, I ran a background check on Dr. Emma Leighmann. Age sixty-five. Only living relative, that I could find anyway, was one daughter, Gabrianna, age forty-two. I'm assuming that's the woman in the picture which means Leighmann was twenty-three when she gave birth, probably still in med school.

"Fast forward a few years," Gwennie continued, "when Barrington offered her the job as Grace's primary psychiatrist. Guess there's not much you won't agree to when you're a single parent trying to cover both tuition and childcare—even overlook a lack of symptoms to please your boss. The daughter's current address is the same as hers, 47 Pemberton Way."

"That's also Dr. Leighmann's office address." Grace forced herself to focus through her haze of confusion. "She lives upstairs. I guess that's why her car was in the driveway. Eliot made such a big deal of reprimanding her about how she parked that day. Maybe it was a signal to preempt any overt signs of affection because I was in the car, watching."

"So, if they've been a couple for twenty-six years, they started going out when she was sixteen. That's a year before you got married, right Gracie?" asked Druthers.

Grace reeled between sorrow over a life built on lies, and excitement over piecing together the puzzle that would finally reveal the truth. This revelation added weight on both sides. "Right around the time Eliot and I met at Trinity. It seemed like kismet. Barrington fought me tooth and nail over that relationship. Now I'm wondering if it was all a calculated ruse, so I'd marry him out of spite. After that, whenever I made noises about pursuing my career, I'd end up pregnant. Raising two boys a year apart kept me too busy to work. It's like everyone wanted to make sure I was never on my own, free to abandon my meds, remember what he'd done to Olivia, and blab about it to the police."

Kenzie munched on a piece of pizza left over from lunch. "That would also mean that Leighmann was in on everything from the start."

"Not necessarily," said Zev. "Barrington could have expressed concern about Grace being off on her own because of her tenuous mental state. Leighmann may have pressed her daughter's *friend* Eliot, who was also entering Trinity, to watch over her. And to everyone's surprise, they fell in love. Hey, don't look at me like that. It's a possibility."

"Though foisting Eliot onto Grace would have been an excellent ploy to get into her benefactor's good graces. He did set her up in a practice, after all," Kenzie said.

"Aside from that, what else did you find out, Gwennie?" asked Hack. "Any newspaper accounts of a missing person at the Pierrepoint estate? Any trace of Auguste Babar?"

"Not a word in the papers but that's no surprise. Easy for someone as rich as Barrington to buy off a publisher. As for Babar, he's alive, kicking and living down in Manahawkin at the Shore's Edge. It's a retirement home and assisted living center. I'm not sure if he's living on the healthy side or being treated for Alzheimer's, but at least I found him. Fun fact: a quick peek at the institution's records revealed his bills, hefty ones at that, are being covered via personal check by Mr. Barrington Pierrepoint himself. Until recently, anyway."

"And the plot thickens. Great work, sis. Good to have a professional hacker in the family."

Zev rubbed his hands together, an evil genius formulating his master plan. "What do you say, Hack? Up for another excursion, my little goy boy? A trip down to the shore to question Mr. Babar, and discover why Barrington is being so generous? And afterward, maybe you can still treat me to the Mai Tai you reneged on tonight."

"I wouldn't count on it, Yidkid, but you're welcome to come. You too, Kenzie. If the three of us work together, we might help jog Babar's memory about Nurse Olivia. You know what they say. An elephant never forgets."

.   .   .

Shore's Edge was a misnomer. The modern yet institutional compound lay at least ten miles inland from any opportunity for residents to dip their toes in the tide's foam. The twenty-something nurse on duty blinked twice when three contemporaries requested a visit with Auguste Babar.

"You're the first young people to ever come see him. Usually, it's an older man." She lowered her voice. "And not a very nice one at that. His visits always leave Mr. Babar a bit shaken. You'll treat him right, won't you? He's such a gentle old soul." Reassured by their nods, she resumed her previous decibel level. "Please wait in our visiting area." She pointed to an adjacent room, adorned with unforgiving, traditional-style furniture, upholstered in bright gold, red and black arabesques.

They were the only ones who'd shown up for visiting hour. Hack watched Kenzie fidget against the couch's stiff cushion, guessing that she was not yet comfortable with her new role as sleuth. He, on the other hand, relished the thrill of the chase as they drew closer to resolving Grace's past and by extension, unmasking Andrea's killer.

Zev grabbed a newspaper from a side table and glanced through the pages while they waited. After a minute, he broke their collective silence. "Hack, wasn't Snowden the name of Barrington's estate lawyer?"

"Yeah. Why?"

"Because he won't be reading the contents of the old man's will any time soon. Someone will read his." Zev folded the paper and tossed it to Hack. Kenzie cursed as she read the headline over Hack's shoulder: "Dying Billionaire's Lawyer Found Dead from Apparent Suicide." Littered throughout the article were phrases like *gunshot to the head* and *note left behind*.

Before they could discuss the lawyer's unexpected demise, the nurse appeared at the doorway, wheeling in an ancient man with ghostlike skin, wearing thick glasses and dressed in pajamas and a robe. Hack tore out the page with the article and stuffed it into his pocket.

"Who are these people? What do they want?" he asked the nurse with a raspy, French accent.

"Some well-wishers, Mr. Babar. Isn't it nice to have a little surprise?" she shouted. Then, she addressed Hack and his crew in a normal volume as she locked the wheelchair's brakes. "His hearing isn't what it once was, and he wasn't expecting visitors, so he hadn't dressed. I'll be at the reception area if you need anything."

Babar watched the nurse depart and then narrowed his eyes and waited for an explanation.

"Sir, let me introduce myself. I'm Joe Hackford."

"I'm sorry, I can't hear you. What did you say?"

Hack looked around to make sure no one else was within earshot and then raised his voice.

"I said I'm Joe Hackford. These are my friends, Kenzie and Zev. We need information to help someone from your past. You might have worked for her father a long time ago. Her name is Grace Pierrepoint."

Hack wouldn't have believed the man could grow paler than he already was, if he hadn't seen it for himself.

Babar looked down at his lap. "I'm sorry. I know nothing about that." His body started to tremble.

"But that's not true, is it, Mr. Babar?" yelled Zev.

"I swear, I never said a word. Tell Mr. Barrington it wasn't me. Please, I beg you."

Hack started to apologize for Zev's accusatory tone when Kenzie squeezed his shoulder and pushed him aside. She crouched down so she was right in Babar's face and wouldn't need to scream. "That's not the story we got. He's telling everyone you killed Olivia and begged him and the gardener to drag her away."

Zev repositioned himself between Babar and the door, so no nurses or passersby would witness the elderly man's collapse into quiet sobs. "That's not so. Not so..."

"He's a powerful man with a lot of influential friends," Kenzie continued. "He's threatening to cut you off and then you'll be out on the street until they cart you away to prison. This is your chance to tell your side of the story, set the record straight. We want to believe you, but maybe Barrington's police and judge friends won't."

Babar stopped sobbing and tried to compose himself. Kenzie pulled a tissue from a box on the side table and blotted away his tears. "It's okay. We're here and we're listening." She pulled out her phone and opened the recording app. "We'll make sure everyone else listens too."

The elderly man sighed, solemn but resigned. "It was late at night. Mrs. Pierrepoint was out of town. I heard yelling from the library. The door was ajar, so I peeked in."

He grew still and Kenzie's eyes opened wider. "Go on."

"Mr. Pierrepoint and the nurse. I figured it was a lover's quarrel, rumors had been flying among the staff for weeks. She claimed she was pregnant, and that because she was Catholic, she had no choice but to keep the baby. He wasn't happy about it."

"And?" asked Zev.

"I...I saw him walk behind her to the mantle and pick up a cast iron candlestick holder. He brought it down hard onto the back of her head. I saw her collapse, and that's when I ran back to the servant's wing. Later, I heard his little girl crying out across the courtyard for her daddy, so I looked out my window. She watched from her bedroom as her father and the gardener removed the body. The next day, they deported the gardener and sent the child to a mental hospital."

"A woman disappears, and no one asked questions?" Zev looked flabbergasted.

"I don't know if anyone else saw what I saw, or if Barrington was aware of my observations. But he told the whole staff Olivia had run off in the middle of the night to elope with her boyfriend. We were never to mention her again. If we remained loyal, he'd make sure we remained employed by the estate for the rest of our lives and he'd take care of us until the day we died. If we disobeyed..." His words drifted off.

"What would happen then?" Kenzie asked.

"It never came up. I had seen what he was capable of, so I never asked. Minded my business, kept up my side of the bargain, and he's kept his. Why would he pick now to accuse me?"

Kenzie turned off her recorder and stroked the old man's arm. "You make a convincing argument. Would you be willing to repeat it to the authorities? Or the press?"

"I'll do what I have to. I might be loyal, but I'm not going to prison for something I didn't do."

Kenzie patted the old man on the shoulder. "Thank you, Mr. Babar. We're leaving now but we promise, we'll stay in touch. Don't worry. I'm sure everything will be okay."

Babar grasped Kenzie's arm as she rose to leave. "That little girl, Gracie. Is she well? It never seemed right, what he did to her, making her believe she was crazy."

Hack shook Babar's hand goodbye. "Gracie will be fine. And a big part of that is thanks to you."

Chapter Thirty-Seven

"Suicide?" Grace opened her eyes wide with disbelief. She handed the article to Druthers. The usual suspects gathered around the dining table for their afternoon debriefing. Hack started with Snowden's death, the last revelation Grace had expected from the trio's fact-finding mission, and it was not sitting well.

"He must have done it right after I called. But when we spoke, he didn't sound depressed. What if someone—an individual with a personal stake in Barrington's will, someone who didn't want him to reveal its contents or any recent changes—forced him to write that note and then threatened him with something so dire, killing himself was preferable?"

"That's quite the speculation," said Zev. "You can't evaluate someone's mental state by their level of cheerfulness during a phone call. You should know that better than anyone."

"Then why didn't he tell me the contents of the entire will when I called, Zev? You think he cared that much about his reputation that he wanted to protect it while suffering from a depression major enough to take his own life? Oh please."

"Okay, you two, enough," said Hack. "Let's lay out the rest of what we learned today, aside from Snowden's death."

With Thunder on one side and Druthers on the other, Grace leaned back in her chair and listened to Hack, Zev and Kenzie recount their visit to the nursing home.

"Babar confirmed everything you described from your hypnosis session, Grace," Hack said as he brought the story to a close. "Kenzie recorded the whole thing. He's willing to go public, to both the police and the press."

Druthers slipped his hand into Grace's. "You must feel so relieved. We all knew you were telling the truth. Now the world will know too."

Relief was the last thing on Grace's mind. Wrath oozed from every pore. Barrington better slip from his coma into a peaceful death because if he came to, she planned to make him spend the rest of his days looking at the world through the bars of a jail cell.

"Problem is, we still don't have any idea who killed Andrea," said Zev. "Eliot was at Barrington's bedside. So, who's left? A hired assassin? Some *nishtgutnik*? Or the dutiful lawyer, carrying out his boss's final directive, and then killing himself out of guilt. Where do we go from here?"

"One way to find out," said Hack. "Grace, it's past office hours now, but tomorrow morning, why don't you call Dr. Leighmann? Use the burner so the police can't track the call. Tell her you've decided to switch therapists, and you'd like your records transferred to Dr. Kumar. Let's see what happens. If she's innocent, she'll say she's sorry to see you go and we'll get to see the files."

Grace turned cold as artic winter. "If she or her daughter are caught up in all of this, won't that put Dr. Kumar in danger?"

"I wouldn't worry about Aadish," said Druthers. "When we saw him out to his car after the hypnosis session, he said he was flying to New Delhi for a conference. He'll be accessible only by phone and Internet. The worst the killer might do is transmit a virus to his computer."

"If my guess is right, things will never progress that far," said Hack. "Are you up for this?"

"I am, but she's going to object, demand answers. I'll need help figuring out the script." Grace shivered but she wasn't sure if it was from fear or excitement. It didn't matter. By this time tomorrow, she might have the answers she needed to move forward with her life and leave the past behind.

Chapter Thirty-Eight

Phoning Dr. Leighmann was one of the hardest things Grace ever had to do. Here was the one person she'd trusted since childhood. Their sessions represented sanctuary from Barrington's cruelty and Eliot's constant hovering. Now she was one step away from calling the medical board and having the therapist's license revoked for malpractice and conflict of interest. Deep down, Grace knew she had every right to request a transfer of her medical records to any psychiatrist of her choosing. So why the hesitation? Was it the pent-up vitriol she feared might seep into the conversation?

She sequestered herself in her bedroom. Even Druthers' presence might have worsened her nervousness. This had to be an Oscar-worthy performance. She sent up a prayer to the god of divas to help her carry it off and then punched in the number.

Leighmann answered on the second ring.

"Dr. Leighmann, it's Grace Rendell."

Silence followed. Grace put a hand over the receiver to mute the chattering of her teeth.

"Grace, do you have any idea what you've put your family through? Eliot? The boys? Not to mention me. Do you have any concept of how much we've worried? What was so important that you'd disappear like that, especially with your father hanging on by a thread?"

Grace launched into the speech she'd rehearsed with Hack and Druthers for the past half hour.

"Dr. Leighmann, I appreciate your concern, but I am an adult woman, free to come and go as I choose without reprimands from you or anyone else. I need a change, the viewpoint of a different therapist. I'd like my records transferred to Dr. Aadish Kumar. His office is at...do you have a pen handy to take this down?"

Leighmann adjusted her tone from accusatory to maternal. "Grace, have you been taking your pills?"

"Again, thank you for your concern, but I am the most clear-minded I have ever been. Now, do you have that pen ready?"

There was hesitation on the other end of the line. Grace looked at her phone to make sure they hadn't been disconnected.

"Grace, you are correct. You are an adult, and you have every right to consult any doctor you choose. But I would like to schedule one last session for closure. Discuss this crazy book idea I've heard about. I don't want you to embarrass yourself or your family."

It was time to deliver her final shot. Her one poison arrow hidden in her quiver of revenge. Grace savored the thrill of victory, as she prepared to tell Dr. Leighmann how, after a long night of last-minute rewrites, they followed Hack's hunch and called the nation's largest publisher, offering them first crack at the book the media had hyped so persistently on her behalf. Her only demand: an immediate distribution of the press release she'd penned to those same media outlets, titled, *Missing Heiress Grace Pierrepoint to Release Bombshell Novel*, with the subhead, *Therapist and Family's Worst Fears Realized*. Included were a few choice tidbits indicting her lead character's husband and therapist, snippets she imagined would make the evening news.

The publisher had agreed, and offered her a six-figure advance, but the money was superfluous. For forty years, everyone she'd ever trusted had kept her off-kilter, silencing her using any means possible. Well, guess who wasn't keeping quiet any longer? It was the sweetness of knowing she'd finally be heard that burned like a flame on the tip of her tongue.

The delay must have signaled to Leighmann that something was afoot, that she no longer held the upper hand in the relationship. Just as Grace opened her mouth, Leighmann fired her own parting shot: "Grace, be here at 3:00 p.m. and come alone, if you ever want to see your sons alive again." *Click.*

Chapter Thirty-Nine

Walking in circles, Grace called each of her son's cell numbers, willing them to pick up, but there was no response. She even swallowed her pride and called Eliot, but the results remained unchanged. No answer. Her phone call to Dr. Leighmann had been a tactical misstep. Her family was now in danger. And out of reach.

She ran back to a tableau of expectant faces, which turned solemn as they listened to her frantic account. "She's got my kids. She says she'll hurt them if I don't show up at three o'clock!"

Druthers rushed to her side. "Grace, don't panic. We'll figure this out together." But she could barely hear his words through the whoosh of air being sucked from the room. She fell to the ground, desperate for oxygen as the walls closed in, crushing her. Then everything went black.

She was lying on the couch with her head on Druthers' lap when she came to. Disoriented and weak, she struggled to focus. "How long was I out?"

He glanced at his watch. "Less than thirty minutes, but you gave us quite a scare."

She looked up at his bald head and wrinkled, XXL striped shirt, glad for his calm during her cyclone of chaos. "Tom, what should I do? If I show up there, what assurance do I have that she won't kill us all?"

"There's no guarantee. But while you were out, the group started cooking up a plan. You up for hearing it?"

．　　　．　　　．

Grace's Uber pulled up outside Dr. Leighmann's office at 2:57 p.m. Her knees wobbled but by sheer will, she exited the Chevy. Her jacket unzipped, she nervously fingered the center button of her blouse. It was go time. She'd spent hours evaluating the risks, but if she didn't follow through now, what kind of hell awaited her? A future guaranteed behind the sterile walls of whichever asylum they chose to commit her. Forever patronized, doubted, ignored. Death by institutional suffocation.

Out of options, she propelled herself toward the front door and hesitated. Did one ring the bell when answering an ultimatum? She turned the knob and found it unlocked.

Dr. Leighmann, the therapist she'd trusted and confided in since childhood, waited in the foyer, a gun aimed at Grace's chest and a satisfied expression dancing on her lips. The daughter Grace had seen in the photos, cavorting with Eliot, stood by her side. "How nice that you could make our appointment, Grace. Please allow Gabrianna to take your purse and help you off with your jacket."

Gabrianna removed Grace's coat, searched her pocketbook and then threw both to the floor. She ordered her guest to spread her legs apart and then ran her hands across every inch and crevice, as if she were more mannequin than human. Grace's resentment replaced her sense of trepidation. She remained silent, forcing herself to swallow her indignation whole.

"She's clean. No gun, no wire."

"Now that you've felt up both sides of the family, any preference?" Grace oozed with sarcasm.

Both Leighmann and her daughter blinked with surprise. "Let's go into the office, shall we?" said the therapist.

Grace followed Gabrianna's lead, Leighmann following behind. She pictured the gun cocked and pointed at her head. Inside, rather than Xander and Damian, she saw Eliot standing by the window, red-faced and stammering.

"I'm sorry, Grace. I-I didn't want it to come to this." Dr. Leighmann placed the gun into his trembling hands, then assumed her usual spot behind her desk. The surface was clear, except for a pile of eggrolls on a silver platter.

"I've missed you too, Eliot." Her tone was flat, mechanical. Just like the twenty-five years of their imaginary marriage. "Where are the boys?"

"With my parents in Arizona. I'd never allow any harm to come to them. You know that, right?"

"You spent our entire marriage keeping me drugged and off-balance, planning to murder me after my father died, and *now* you're looking for brownie points? That's a laugh. Tell me Eliot, did you ever love me? Or were you simply doing a favor for your girlfriend's mother, so one day you two could bury me and collect a big payday?"

Eliot remained silent, but his eyes watered. Gabrianna took a spot beside him and grasped the hand without the gun, a soundless show of solidarity.

Behind them, on the bookshelf, Grace noted a flash of turquoise with a "Morocco" decal sticking out. Andrea's computer.

Leighmann shook her head. "No one ever planned to bury you, you paranoid moron. If you had kept to the plan, you would have had a nice, easy time of it once Barrington passed. A healthy allowance every month, doled out by the estate executor, namely me, as per your father's revised final instructions."

"We made sure of it when we visited him in February," Eliot said. "Something you never got around to doing."

"You were there? You caused his stroke?"

"We didn't intentionally instigate anything. We had no way of knowing how vulnerable your father would be to some…intense questioning," said Gabrianna. "Barrington made the three of us a promise 26 years ago. Keep you quiet about his little indiscretion, or failing that, destroy your credibility, and he'd make us rich beyond our wildest dreams. We had to make sure he still planned to hold up his end of the bargain. It was a good thing we flew down and insisted his lawyer read us the will."

"You call murdering my nurse a small indiscretion?"

Leighmann ignored Grace's allegation. "A few alterations were needed. But even still, you would have enjoyed the merry life of a divorcee. If you hadn't started asking questions, writing novels, making a general nuisance of yourself. Now you'll get nothing but a hole in the ground."

"Like Andrea? And Snowden?"

Leighmann shrugged. "Sacrifices in the name of a greater good. But if it makes you feel any better, your author friend stayed loyal to you until the end. And Snowden only shot himself when Gabrianna threatened to murder your sons."

The thought of her friends dying on her account fueled Grace's determination not to succumb to her fear. "You think killing me won't raise questions? That you'll get away with it, when you're a beneficiary of the will?"

Leighmann bristled. "First off, he didn't leave me a penny. I'm executing the will and Eliot will be monitoring. Though I expect he and my daughter won't be watching too closely from their bungalow on Bora Bora. And secondly, I'm not planning to shoot you. You came here for one last session, to gain closure before being treated under Dr. Kumar's loving care. I arranged for a special farewell surprise, one final meal together. Chinese for a change. You reached for an eggroll, famished, neither of us realizing it contained peanuts. When your throat started constricting, you rifled through your purse but oh no, the EpiPen was missing. By the time I rushed to the phone to call for help, it was too late."

"Sounds like you've got it all worked out. Except what makes you believe I'd eat an eggroll?"

"Easy. Because if you don't, your sons along with your in-laws, will die in a tragic gas leak explosion. One phone call sets it all in motion."

Eliot stiffened and pointed the gun away from Grace and toward Leighmann. "You never said anything about this, Emma. Quick and painless—those were your words. And that the boys would remain untouched."

"Don't be stupid, Eliot. This late in the game, do you think I would leave anything to chance? You're one allergic reaction away from the billions you've spent nearly thirty years dreaming about. Don't throw it all away now."

"She's right, El," said Gabrianna. "For years, you've been complaining that you wanted your life back. Once she eats the eggroll, we're free and clear. Your sons will be fine. We'll see them as often as you like. And think of it, no more secret phone calls. No more holidays apart. No more hiding in the shadows."

Eliot pointed the weapon back at Grace, but his face lacked conviction. Gabrianna must have sensed his indecision because she grabbed the gun from Eliot's tremulous hand and aimed it at Grace's head. "Bon appétit," she said with a chuckle.

Grace reached for the eggroll and then retracted her hand.

"One last question. Who catered the meal? I'd like to give credit when I leave my review."

Leighmann gave her a quizzical look. "What the hell are you blathering about?"

Grace took a deep breath, knowing that if anything went wrong—if the mic and camera had stopped working, if her posse weren't hiding outside—she'd be dead within seconds. "My publisher suggested this video would make a great supplement to my upcoming book release. Some of my friends stopped by earlier today and set up wireless speakers in the garden. I've broadcasted everything you just said to the reporters waiting outside. They're assembled for the joint press conference "we" called for 4:00 p.m. to elaborate on the gaslighting accusations contained in the book. But you know reporters. They're always early."

The smug smile fell from Gabrianna's face and she looked to her mother. "What now? What should we do?"

Leighmann went ghost pale but regrouped. "She's bluffing, Gabbie. Hold the gun straight, you're wobbling."

Gabrianna tried to steady her aim when a mob of reporters rushed in, led by Hack. "We heard your cue. The door was open. Hope you don't mind." The flash of the cameras and the bright stream of light from the video recorders blinded Grace. Her survival instinct revived, Gabrianna wrapped an arm around her neck and pressed the hard barrel of a gun against the back of her skull.

"Keep your distance. We'll be leaving now. Anyone who gets in our way will get Grace's brains splattered all over their nice, clean outfits."

Grace considered overtaking her captor, but the gun was a powerful deterrent. They edged toward the door, the reporters parting like the Red Sea, while still filming the scene. Grace's knees gave way, but Gabrianna's sturdy grip, now around her chest, kept her upright, propelling her forward. The throng became a colorful blur through water-filled eyes. "Boys, I'm sorry, I love you," she cried into the lenses as they passed.

"Watch out," screamed Leighmann.

Grace heard a *crack* and an "*oomph.*" Gabrianna released the pressure from her chest, but the weight of her unconscious body sent them both hurtling to the floor. Struggling to push her off, she saw Eliot behind them, Andrea's computer in his hands.

The police rushed in and apprehended Dr. Leighmann and Eliot, then lifted Gabrianna's unresponsive body onto a gurney. Druthers and Zev helped a shaky Grace to her feet and then the three hugged like long-lost friends.

The reporters went wild, the room crackling with the sound of questions flying and shutters clicking. "Do you love your wife, Eliot? Is the affair over? Did Gabrianna kill Lynn Andrews, or was it Dr. Leighmann? Grace, do you plan on writing a sequel?"

Hack walked to the front of the room and cleared his throat, willing the cacophony to subside. "Ladies and gentlemen of the press, please allow my client to catch her breath. Then we'll answer all your questions, right in time for the six o'clock news."

"Come on, buddy, we're live. You gotta give us something, anything," yelled an impatient reporter as the room buzzed with chatter.

Zev jumped up and joined Hack, hands outstretched like an evangelist ministering to his flock. The crowd hushed, pens poised, cameras filming. "My people have a saying for times like these: *A mitsve, fun a khazer a hor oystsuraysn.* It's a mitzvah to pull a hair from a pig."

"What the hell does that mean, kid?"

Zev shrugged and offered a sheepish grin. "To be honest, I haven't got the foggiest idea."

Chapter Forty

Three Years Later

Grace couldn't decide which she enjoyed more—the moment when she learned she'd been nominated for Best Adapted Screenplay, or the surprise party her friends threw a week later at Il Segreto to celebrate. So many well-wishers, cheering and applauding as she entered—it seemed like all of Bergen County had jammed into one small venue. Now she understood why Druthers had suggested an Italian dinner, followed by a request that she wear his favorite red dress.

They pressed through the horde toward the bar, Grace shaking hands and high-fiving both friends and strangers in her quest to get a drink of anything to take the edge off. Crowds still left her awkward and claustrophobic. Like the flocks of soundbite-hungry reporters and cameramen waiting outside the courthouse the day she testified against Dr. Leighmann, Gabrianna and Eliot, and again when the judge sentenced Leighmann and her daughter to life for murder, and Eliot, their accomplice, to seven years behind bars. The paparazzi at her father's funeral last year had practically barred her entrance to the church. Even now, when the multitudes were admiring rather than sensation-seeking, they still left her uneasy.

"Who organized this?" she asked Druthers after she'd downed half a flute of champagne. "I need to thank them."

"Believe it or not, it was Caprice. She's so grateful for what you've done for her, she called and suggested it. She left the guest list to me, though from the looks of things, too many people invited too many plus-ones. Sorry about that."

"Don't be. It's amazing. I'm a very lucky woman."

She scanned the swarm for her father's former mistress and found her by the kitchen, giving instructions to the waiters. She caught her eye and smiled. The younger woman winked and started pushing her way through the crowd.

Such a cut above Barrington's former floozies. While everyone else had forgotten about him as he withered away in his hospital bed, she still visited every day, maintained his home, paid the bills, cared for his dogs. She was the one who, at the investigators' request, pulled the security videos that revealed Leighmann and Eliot pressuring Barrington to verify the contents of his will, and requesting their adjustments. In court, doctors testified that the stress of that visit had brought on the stroke that felled the devious patriarch.

As far as Grace was concerned, Caprice had earned the beach house she'd gifted her from the proceeds of her father's liquidated estate.

"Are you enjoying yourself?" Caprice asked after making her way through the throng. "You can't imagine how hard it was to keep this a secret!"

Grace knew all about secrets. Their power. Their toxicity. How Barrington and Eliot's secrets had destroyed her world. How Kenzie and Zev, now waving from the bar, had revealed their confidences to close-minded families, only to be forced to flee their homes so they could live peaceful, authentic lives.

Not to mention Hack, whom she noticed nuzzling with his girlfriend Katie in the corner. On his nineteenth birthday, after one beer too many, he'd confessed his darkest secret—the tremendous guilt he harbored over Andrea's death—and how, to redeem himself, he'd given up his string of petty crimes and instead, had dedicated his free time to Kenzie's shelter for marginalized teens. The story had touched Grace. On that day, she committed every penny of the royalties from *Salvaging Hope* to help fund the Rainbow Railroad and the Gay Grid. She had all the money she'd ever need from her inheritance, and it seemed only right to use the book proceeds to help others like her, whom society had robbed of their voice and their dignity.

Despite their somewhat confrontational introduction, Hack had become one of Grace's closest friends and confidants. Without his suggestions, she would have never conceived of the idea to sew a mini camera, disguised as a button, on her shirt, and then call a press conference to broadcast the video and expose Leighmann's homicidal plot to the world. He'd been the one to urge her to try her hand at writing the screenplay for her bestselling novel, and the one who'd given her Andrea's entire library as encouragement. "She did it. Why can't you?" he'd insisted.

Hack had also befriended both of her sons, still shaken by the entire incident. They needed a strong male influence in their lives and gravitated more toward Hack than Druthers, probably because he was closer in age and understood what it was like to lose a father. She wished they were at the party to share this happy moment, not off in Arizona for the weekend with their grandparents.

Hack's family sold the house and he'd rented a local apartment with Zev. When not volunteering alongside Kenzie, he spent his days at college, pursuing a degree in fundraising with an eye to opening the Andrea Lin Memorial Shelter for the Homeless. "It's sad that it took the death of my sister to help me find meaning in life," he'd mentioned once, before admitting how much he missed the excitement of a detective's life. Grace offered to buy him a complete collection of Sherlock Holmes novels. He said he'd already read them, but books would never quench his newfound taste for danger. The legal kind.

"Think we'll have this big a turnout at our wedding?" Druthers shouted over the din, pulling Grace out of her private thoughts.

"Oh, God, I hope not," she yelled back, fighting off chills. "I'd be a wreck by the end of the night. Maybe we should elope instead."

"Any place in particular? Paris? Beijing? Vanuatu? You've spent too many years being hidden away from the world. I want you to go anywhere and everywhere your heart desires."

She hugged him and kissed him hard on the lips. "You darling man, I can't wait to be your wife. Let's talk more after I get back."

Grace pushed her way to the rear of the restaurant and entered the ladies' room. Both stalls were occupied by two women deep in conversation, so she reapplied her lipstick while she waited. She didn't recognize either of the voices, so she figured they were strangers who'd come along for a fun evening out.

"She looked nice, but did you see that guy she was with? Fat, bald, creased shirt. All that money, couldn't she have done better?"

"I've heard that he's one of those hangers-on. She must be too busy writing to find someone decent." The women giggled.

Not this time, thought Grace. She walked over and banged on the doors. "Thanks for your concern, ladies, but here's a secret for you. Never talk dirt when you're not sure who's listening."

The bathroom went silent. She waited until both ladies flushed and exited their stalls, glaring at them as they washed their hands. What a pity she hadn't had the guts to call out jerks like this years ago. She'd spent a lifetime buying into negativity without ever checking the tag. What a steep price she had paid.

The women squirmed and avoided her gaze, waiting for her to step aside and let them pass. Grace lingered for a minute, savoring their discomfort. Then, channeling Andrea's bluntness, she delivered one final piece of advice: "Ladies, I'm afraid you've wandered into the wrong party. This one celebrates the lifelong battle for self-acceptance we fight daily, despite our wrinkles, mental scars and extra pounds—all the imperfections that make us human. If you're willing to admit you share that battle, help yourself to another glass of champagne. Otherwise, please don't let the door hit your asses on the way out."

The End

About THE AUTHOR

The award-winning author and/or editor of eight books, including *Expired Listings: Revenge Begins at Home* and *Murder Worth the Weight*, D.M. Barr is a vice president of Sisters in Crime-New York, Mystery Writers of America, and is the president of Hudson Valley Scribes. She lives happily in New York's Hudson Valley, where she reads, plays competitive trivia, stops strangers on the street to pet their dogs, and concocts tales of sex, suspense. and satire. Her husband and two adult children are very afraid.

NOTE FROM THE AUTHOR

Word-of-mouth is crucial for any author to succeed. If you enjoyed *Saving Grace*, please leave a review online—anywhere you are able. Even if it's just a sentence or two. It would make all the difference and would be very much appreciated.

Thanks!
D.M.

·

www.ingramcontent.com/pod-product-compliance
Lightning Source LLC
Chambersburg PA
CBHW070442120726
47910CB00003B/898